REVOLT

Tracy Lawson

REVOLT

BOOK FOUR OF THE RESISTANCE SERIES

© 2017 by Tracy Lawson

Cover design by EbookLaunch.com
Back cover image by Ashley M. Hofmaster

First Print 2017

978-1-948543-37-8

DysCovered Publishing
TracyLawsonBooks.com

For Keri, Reagan, Madison, Alex, Jules, and Ainsley

To Carolyn

We know how this ends, right?

:)

REVOLT

Tracy Lam

Chapter 1

Tommy Bailey's likeness, gun in hand, stood frozen on the huge television screen, staring down at Careen Catecher's crumpled, lifeless body. In reality, it was Careen who held the gun, nostrils flaring as she drew rapid, panicky breaths. Tommy, hands raised in surrender, wanted to kick himself for underestimating the complexity of her emotional state. When he'd rescued her from ongoing torture and abuse at the Office of Civilian Safety and Defense, he'd assumed she'd be glad to see him.

Witnessing that convincing video of her own murder had freaked her out. Her eyes flicked to her wrist, where the LED light on the personal identification and GPS tracking device she wore flashed in time with her racing heartbeat. When the OCSD's new security mandate went into effect, everyone under the age of eighteen would be fitted with a Link.

"If Atari can fool people with enhanced video, the Link won't be reliable or honest. False evidence like that can be created and used against anyone." Tears filled her eyes, and she bit her lower lip to stop it from trembling. "The OCSD said the Link is to protect children. I believed it was true! It would be such a good thing to know nothing bad could ever happen to the defenseless. Tommy, what are we going to do? How can we stop him from ruining the integrity of the Link?"

Sabotaging the Link was top priority for the Resistance. Careen had been one of the rebel group's most passionate and visible members, but now she didn't seem to remember whose side she was on. He pulled an exaggerated look of surprise. "We? You said *we*."

She blinked, confused. "What?"

"You just said 'what are *we* going to do?' You still think of us as a team, don't you? Come on. Admit it."

"Even if I did say that—which I didn't—do you seriously want to argue semantics?"

He folded his arms on his chest. "No time like the present. Hit me with your best semantics."

"Don't try to distract me. They've pitted us as adversaries so you can prove your loyalty to the OCSD." She tilted her head toward their doppelgangers on the screen. "That's your task, isn't it?"

"I don't have to prove anything to the OCSD. I'm Resistance, and so are you. You may not trust Atari or his videos, but we can trust each other. My enemy's enemy is my friend, right?"

"How do I know if you're my enemy's enemy? You and Atari are probably besties."

"Hardly! I can't stand the guy. *You're* my best friend."

She bit her lip as she glanced up at their images again, and he recognized her resolve wavering. As if to prove him wrong, she raised the gun a few inches. "If it comes down to you or me, Tommy, I swear to God I'll shoot you."

Her words hung in the air for a split second before he lunged at her and grabbed both her wrists in one hand, pointing the gun up and away until she was standing on tiptoe.

"Come on, Careen, just let go."

"No!" She thrashed and twisted in his grip.

He drove her backward and pinned her against the door, which shook and rattled in its frame as she tried to throw him off. He deflected the knee she aimed at his groin and clamped one hand around her throat. The blazing fury in her eyes began to fade, and she gasped for air.

He felt her losing strength and slammed her hand against the wall. As soon as the gun clattered to the floor, he released her and picked it up. Careen slid down the door and huddled there, coughing, arms covering her face. Her whole body trembled, and Tommy realized with a pang that she was waiting for him to fire the kill shot.

He removed the magazine from the gun with a flick of his thumb and ejected the chambered round. "You keep this part, and I'll keep the bullets. Deal?" She didn't respond, so he laid the empty gun beside her and pocketed the magazine. "I'm sorry if I hurt you."

Her hand shook as she picked it up. "How do you expect me to trust you now?"

"You don't build trust with a loaded gun. Besides, if you kill me you'll be alone here with Atari. Is that really what you want?"

She gulped. "No."

"Okay, good. I know this is confusing. The Resistance—meaning me, Kevin, Pete, and Atari—rescued you from OCSD custody. We're at a Resistance safe house. The OCSD has no idea where you are. The quadrant marshals aren't coming to get you, and there's absolutely no chance that I'm going to execute you, no matter what you saw on that video. Do you understand?"

She pressed her lips together and nodded.

"The Link is never going to work anyway. Atari will see to that." He held out a hand, and she let him help her to her feet. He opened the door, and she marched back down the long hallway to his room, where she gathered the comforter and one of the pillows into her arms and disappeared into the bathroom. He heard the lock click.

Tommy moved a club chair across the room so it blocked the bathroom door and settled himself there to discourage her from nocturnal roaming. "Good night, Careen."

She didn't respond. He took a deep breath and forced himself to breathe slowly to calm his jangled nerves. This should have been a night of celebration. The Resistance was on a roll, using guerilla-style tactics to assault the credibility of the OCSD and its director, Madalyn Davies. Atari, the Resistance operative who had infiltrated the OCSD, was truly the one in control of the Link. Careen was back where she was supposed to be, even if she didn't recognize it yet. Helping her transition from captive back to freedom fighter was going to be harder than he'd anticipated. How could she believe he'd kill her? He'd intended to tell her that he was in love with her. He reached into his back pocket and brought out the bracelet with the lock and key charm that had belonged to his mother. He'd given it to Careen the day she'd been accused of Stratford's murder, when he'd vowed to protect her and make everything all right. The promise had proved impossible to keep. He'd been carrying it with him ever since the Resistance had evacuated the diner in BG-098 last month. If he offered it to her now, he was pretty sure she'd throw it back in his face.

It was his fault that she'd found his gun. He hadn't hidden it well, just dumped it in the bottom desk drawer upon his arrival at the safe house, hoping his mom's favorite saying, 'out of sight, out of mind,' would prove true. Shutting the gun away, however, had not banished his memory of how he'd used it to kill a quadrant marshal. Self-defense or no, it was the most horrible moment of his life, and it ran on a constant loop in his brain like one of Atari's videos, except it was one hundred percent true.

After a time, Careen must've thought he'd fallen asleep. He chafed at his helplessness as he listened to her sobbing on the other side of the door.

1:45 AM
Quadrant DC-001

Kevin McGraw fought to keep from smiling as he watched OCSD Director Madalyn Davies storm around her office.

"Security and the quadrant marshal patrols have all reported in. They've searched the entire PeopleCam building and the surrounding area. There's no trace of Careen." A vein stood out on her forehead. "She didn't show up on the surveillance tapes. No one saw anything. Where could she have gone?" She sighed dramatically and sagged against the back of one of the wing chairs that faced her desk. The light on her Link pulsed.

Kevin's sober expression masked his elation. When Madalyn had appointed him Assistant Director of the OCSD a few weeks ago, she'd had no idea that he, a longtime employee of the government agency, had recently pledged his allegiance to the Resistance. His all-access security clearance and proximity to Madalyn had proved useful—like tonight, when he'd orchestrated Careen's escape from OCSD custody. He was still wearing the tiny earpiece that connected him to the Resistance's leader, Mitch Carraway, who had been listening in all evening.

A tense silence stretched on until Kevin decided he should say something to fill the void, but then she started up again.

"If the Link software hadn't crashed, it would have taken only moments to locate Careen. Now, we're wasting time and resources while a dangerous criminal roams free. Atari was smug and disrespectful when he should have been apologizing. He'd better figure out what's wrong with the Link and fix it. Fast."

"I'm sure Atari comprehends the gravity of the situation."

"Are you?"

"Umm, yeah."

She sniffed dismissively. "Too bad your opinion means absolutely nothing."

"If you say so." Kevin made sure his tone was deferential. "Madam Director, what are you going to tell the PeopleCam reporters about Careen?"

"Why would we say anything?"

"You're going to have to eventually. Two of them are camped out in the lobby clamoring for the name of the person who was arrested after the high-speed car chase. They know something's up."

Her eyes narrowed. "It was your idea to bring Careen's mother to PeopleCam and broadcast a live reunion between them. What if you tell them Jessica Catecher was arrested for her part in a terrorist attack on the Link's spokesperson?"

Kevin was prepared with a response. "That's a bit of a stretch." *Even for you.* "Jessica Catecher wasn't on any suspected terrorist watch list. We vetted her before we brought her here. There was no evidence that she was involved in the Resistance and no reason to believe she would try to help her daughter escape. Besides, I don't think this situation qualifies as terrorism."

"It most certainly does. I must interrogate her right away. She may be able to tell us where to find Careen. Call my driver."

Kevin glanced at his watch. "You can't go to a correctional facility in the middle of the night. We kept Mrs. Catecher's name off the prison's intake list to avoid awkward questions."

"Fine. Then you go tomorrow."

"Of course."

She shook her head as if to refocus her thoughts. "Where are we on the search for Trina Jacobs? Tom Bailey? The rest of the Resistance?"

"No trace of any of them."

"Send a message to Chief Garrick and tell him I want him in my office first thing tomorrow morning. He's been slacking. His investigation is a joke."

He nodded.

"I just know the Resistance is behind Careen's disappearance." She gasped. "Trina Jacobs could be in the capital right now! We must find her and stop her before she kills someone else."

Kevin kept his expression neutral while he imagined Trina's reaction. The driven, young research doctor was his closest friend, and though she had a quick temper, she was definitely not a murderer. Madalyn was the one who had killed Lowell Stratford, the former OCSD director—albeit accidentally—and then framed Trina and Careen for the crime. Garrick was slacking on the Trina Jacobs investigation so he could devote his energy toward building an ironclad case against Stratford's real killer.

He continued, his expression benign. "Now, about the—"

"Oh, gads—what next?"

"Umm ... you announced that the Linking begins next week. Nationwide."

"I did say that, didn't I?"

"Yes, you did."

"Well, obviously I had to. Careen's escape—I mean, disappearance—is all the more reason why. I mean ... oh, honestly! What will it matter if we begin Linking a tiny bit early?"

Kevin enjoyed watching Madalyn's composure unravel before his eyes, and raised his voice a notch to fuel her panic. "Nothing is ready! The software has bugs and the sensors haven't been installed anywhere but the capital quadrant. According to the latest status report from the factories manufacturing the Links, there won't be nearly enough ready to meet demand by next week."

She began to pace while he scrolled through documents on his tablet, and he spoke as though he were thinking aloud. "You think everything can happen just because you want it to, but the rollout wasn't supposed to begin until after the first of the year."

"Get the production manager on the phone."

"At this hour?"

"Do it."

Kevin dialed. "Mr. Stemmons?... So sorry to wake you, sir. This is Kevin McGraw, Assistant Director of the OCSD.... Yes, really. I'm calling with regard to the Cerberean Link production schedule. We need all of them finished and at their destination by the middle of next week. Yes, I'll hold while you pull up the information.... I see.... How long? Oh. Well, can you ship what you have, and we'll make do until the rest arrive? I suppose we can start a waiting list or something." He raised his eyebrows, and Madalyn mouthed *are-you-kidding-me?* He cleared his throat. "Director Davies asks— no, insists—that you keep production running twenty-four-seven until... Yes, I understand that will incur additional costs. Please send me all your production and delivery schedules to"—he recited his electronic mail address—"at your earliest convenience. Yes, thank you. Good night."

Chapter 2

Pete Sheridan, half of PeopleCam's studio news team, sat at the news desk and flipped through the pages he'd been given for the morning broadcast. There was no mention of Careen Catecher at all. Madalyn would have insisted on distorting the facts if word of her escape had been allowed out, but he'd been part of the operation, so he knew exactly what had happened. He'd helped Careen, disguised in his co-anchor Shelia Roth's winter coat, slip out the rear of the building to where Tommy Bailey and Atari had been waiting.

Sheila, bubbling over with the urge to gossip, slid into the chair beside him. "I was afraid for my life last night. I still can't believe what happened." She lowered her voice a notch so she appeared to be sharing a juicy secret—but loudly enough that everyone in the room could hear.

"Careen Catecher attacked her own mother and held her hostage. Why, it gives me chills when I realize that could have been you or me. That deranged girl is a murderer, you know."

Pete chuckled. "I don't think we were in any danger, Sheila."

"It's one thing to report the news and quite another to have a brush with death and *be* the news."

He tapped the sheaf of papers in front of him. "We're not airing anything about what happened last night."

"But ... well, my goodness! We have a duty to the public. They should know that a terrorist is on the loose."

"Oh Sheila, really. She's a college student, not a hardened criminal."

"Yes, she is, too. I won't be able to sleep until she's apprehended." She sniffed. "And to think she gave up the opportunity of a lifetime.

I don't understand her popularity, but she was well on her way to becoming a PeopleCam celebrity."

"Perhaps she didn't view her celebrity quite the way you do. Anyway, look at the bright side. You don't have to worry about her taking your job."

She ignored the jibe. "My coat with the hood is missing. Do you think she stole it?"

The floor manager counted them down. "And we're live in five ... four ... three ... "

Pete pasted a winning smile on his face. "OCSD director Madalyn Davies announced last night that Linking is set to begin this coming week. Good news, all you kids whose last names begin with A through L. You get to miss school on Friday morning to get your Link! Those with last names in the second half of the alphabet will be dismissed after lunch."

Sheila chimed in, "How wonderful! I, for one, feel better knowing the Link will protect our country's children from all the hardened criminals and terrorists running around loose out there." She delivered her trademark grin with a sidelong glance at Pete.

He read the next lead-in from the teleprompter. "And there's more good news. The food shortages are nearly over! Just ten percent of quadrants are still reporting delays in Essential Services deliveries."

When their segment was over, Pete hurried out of the studio and locked himself in one of the editing bays. For years, he'd reported the news, no questions asked, but he'd had a change of heart a few months ago. The QM had murdered his son, Ben, for refusing to take the government-mandated CSD antidote, and Pete had been directed to report that Ben had died because he had made the choice not to take CSD, and had succumbed to the airborne poison. His son had been maligned as an ingrate and held up as an example of what not to do, and Pete had been too devastated by the loss and cowed by the OCSD to tell the truth. When an old friend had approached him and asked him to help spread the Resistance's message, he'd viewed it as a chance to avenge his son. He made sure bootleg videos made it on the air at the state-controlled television station and forwarded any information that could help the Resistance's cause. Just recently, he'd discovered that Careen was being held captive in one of the luxury suites in the PeopleCam building.

For too long, he had been a purveyor of propaganda, delivering stories that pandered to people's fears. Even when he lied outright, the people accepted what he said because they had to. They had no perspective. PeopleCam and PeopleNet were their only sources for news. No information was allowed in from other parts of the world, and when incoming reports from PeopleCam's affiliate stations contained information deemed harmful or unflattering to the government, they were squelched before they were aired. He'd begun to archive those stories. It was his mission to preserve the evidence of things the OCSD didn't want people to know and expose the truth about America's supposedly perfect, secure existence under the OCSD's thumb.

9:22 AM
Quadrant BG-098

Mitch Carraway sipped coffee at his diner's counter while he watched the morning PeopleCam broadcast. *So they say they want to begin the Linking next week? We'll see about that.*

He was poised to step up the Resistance's campaign against Madalyn Davies, rather than waiting to let her implode on her own. It was more important than ever for his operatives to stay in touch, but Atari seemed to consider it beneath him to keep Mitch in the loop. He dialed his satellite phone and rubbed his tired eyes. As soon as he heard Atari's voice on the line, he demanded, "Well? Was the extraction successful? Kevin managed to feed me information while he was right under Madalyn's nose, but he only knew part of what happened. I've been up all night waiting to hear from you."

"I'm busy, all right? We saved the girl and foiled the villain. Sort of. Madalyn totally freaked out when Careen went AWOL and the Link couldn't track her down, and now I'm dealing with a massive amount of fallout. If we'd left Careen where she was, Madalyn wouldn't be hell-bent on starting the Linking. We could have had more time."

"I relied on Kevin's assessment when he insisted we extract her. Pulling her out had the potential to involve the OCSD in another scandal."

"Instead, we can chalk it up as a fail. All it did was make my life harder."

"Oh, poor you. Quit complaining and learn to deal with the unexpected."

Atari's retort was angry. "Linking Madalyn was never supposed to happen, but when it happened, I embraced it, man. I ran with it. That. Changed. Everything. I can bring her down single-handedly, without you, the Resistance, and your penny-ante plan."

"I'm calling the shots, and I want you to swear to me that you're *not* going to activate the Link."

"You're not the least bit curious about what would happen?"

"No."

"And you don't care that it's the best way to restart the free flow of information?"

"Not at all. Now do as you're told and string her along while I mobilize our ground forces. We'll have her arrested before the damn thing ever becomes a threat."

"Whatever you say, *mon capitan*! Don't get your knickers in a twist. I'll be ready to take over when you lose control of the situation." Atari hung up.

10:03 AM

Fuming about Atari's insubordination, Mitch slung his backpack over his shoulder and trudged out to the bunker hidden in the woods. For the first time in his life, he lived alone, and it had been quiet with his daughter away. Though Jaycee's departure with Tom and Lara Bailey had felt more like a defection, he supposed it was as good a time as any to let her have a little freedom. In the unlikely event that their guerilla tactics failed to remove Madalyn from the OCSD director's position, there was no telling how many more Restrictions would be clamped down on them in the future. The Link would be just the beginning.

It had been several years since he'd first sought out attorney Tom Bailey, and then Atari, the young computer expert, and recruited them to help further his goals for the Resistance. Until recently, he'd been the only one calling the shots, and now he felt like he was clashing with them as much as their mutual enemy.

Had he given Atari too much autonomy? He would have liked to ask Tom's opinion, but their relationship was so strained lately that he'd rather die than admit his operative was out of control. Madalyn had to be neutralized before she could tempt Atari into testing his invention.

Tom had disappointed him too. After all his talk about preserving people's liberties and fighting against government overreach, he'd taken off for the capital on his own last month and parlayed with Madalyn. When that hadn't worked, he'd finagled a meeting with the president and the chief QM to ingratiate himself with higher-ups in the current government, probably hoping to be included in the new world order after Madalyn fell from power.

Just three members of the Resistance, who'd escaped their captors at the OCSD and fled to Resistance headquarters after Lowell Stratford's death, remained nearby, hiding in an underground bunker on his land. David Honerlaw, Grace Hughes, and Trina Jacobs were all motivated by the desire get their lives back. If the plan to oust Madalyn worked, they'd no longer have to live in hiding.

Mitch left the dirt path and began his descent through the trees, skidding on pine needles and fallen leaves, until he arrived at the metal door concealed in an outcropping of granite that jutted up from the forest floor. He'd always thought of the rocks as a symbol of the stronghold that lay hidden beneath the surface of the earth. He punched a series of numbers on the keypad, stepped into the semidarkness, and clomped down the metal stairs to the bunker's main room.

The two women sat at the scarred wooden table. Trina was scribbling on a legal pad, and Grace was glaring, arms crossed, at her ex-husband, David, as he paced.

David and Grace's personal relationship was prickly, but Mitch had confidence in their ability to draft a plan for life after the OCSD. Professors specializing in economics and public policy, they had spent their careers collecting data to study how curtailing people's freedoms hurt the economy and weakened the individual. Soon, he hoped their theoretical work would be put to practical use.

He shared his news without preamble. "They got Careen out

last night. I just heard from Atari. She and Tommy are at the safe house with him."

Smiles broke out all around. Grace and Trina hugged each other, and David nearly slapped Mitch across the face with an exuberant attempt at a high-five.

"Here." Mitch pulled a heavy textbook from his pack and laid it on the table. Grace pounced on it.

"Our seventh edition! This one was my favorite. I'm flattered that you have a copy on hand."

"It's one of my pet subjects, and you and David wrote the book. Literally." David winked at Mitch, appreciating the joke.

"It will be nice to be able to refer to the text. I know it well, but not by heart." Grace began to leaf through the pages.

Mitch nodded at Trina. "How's it going?"

"Writing my vision of a big, dramatic showdown between Madalyn and me? It's even more fun than I thought it would be, especially since Tom said we could use the information on the chip drive he left with David. Who knew Madalyn's deepest, darkest secret was so juicy, and so—Madalyn? Here, take a look for yourself."

He sat beside her, and she pushed her notes toward him. He scanned the lines. "Think you're being a little melodramatic?"

"When Lowell Stratford hired me, he tricked me into working on his mind-control project, and then he drugged me and locked me up when I tried to blow the whistle on it. After I managed to get off the drug and risked my life to help the Resistance, Madalyn framed me for murder." She pulled the notes back with a grin. "The whole situation is melodramatic, and I want the ending to be consistent."

"How much acting experience do you have?"

"I was in a play in high school, once."

"Murder mystery?"

"Actually, it was a comedy. A farce."

He nodded. "That's fitting."

She laughed. "There won't be much acting involved. I'm just telling it like it is. I can't wait to see what Atari does to bring it all to life. Do you think it'll be convincing?"

"Oh, yeah. People believe what they want to believe, especially when you put evidence right in front of them."

"Now all we need is the perfect arena."

Trina and Mitch set up the video camera to do a test recording of her monologue that would be used later to set the final phase of their attack against Madalyn in motion. Trina had delivered only a few lines when Mitch's phone rang. He paused the camera. "It's Kevin." He answered, and after a few muttered "uh-huhs" he said, "Send it to me and I'll get on it right away."

He hung up, and Trina, who had been hovering nearby, slapped him on the arm. "I wanted to say hi!"

"No. Business only."

"But he's my best friend. Next time you talk to him, be sure to tell him I said hello."

Mitch rolled his eyes. "I have to download the information he's sending and make a call to Danni and a few others." He motioned her back in front of the camera. "Do another paragraph and then you and Grace take a look and make sure you're coming across as authentic. The segue between the recorded you and the live you has to be seamless."

Trina nodded and launched into her speech again.

Mitch spent an hour reading the documents Kevin had sent to his phone and scribbling numbers on a legal pad. Trina had viewed the video with Grace several times and made notes before Mitch disconnected his final call and turned his attention back to her.

They'd barely begun to record again when the satellite phone at his hip vibrated. He glanced down, and when he saw who was calling, he seemed reluctant to make eye contact with her.

"Come on, Mitch! You can call them back. What's so important, anyway?"

His anger flared. "None of your business. I'm going to take it outside." He hurried up the stairs, and Trina heard him hail the caller and begin to speak before the door closed behind him.

David had called Grace over to the sofa when Trina and Mitch were recording, and now they were engrossed in their notes and textbook. Trina stretched, quietly left the room, and crept after Mitch. *I know a guilty look when I see one.*

She, David, and Grace had been living in the bunker's close quarters for far longer than she would have liked, but when she'd asked about moving back down to the boardinghouse or one of the rooms over the diner, Mitch had insisted it was still too dangerous. Trina suspected it was mostly Mitch's secrets, rather than fear of the QM returning for another raid, that made him insist on living at Resistance headquarters alone.

She opened the door just enough to look out. Mitch stood about ten yards away, his back to the bunker.

"The timing couldn't be better. Thank you for your persistence." He paused to listen, and Trina strained not to miss anything. He laughed. "I always believed that lawmakers voted on bills without reading 'em. Now I know it's true. Oh, yeah. I've got my list of must-haves ready to go. Thanks, Congressman. You've done a great thing for your country."

Hands on hips, Trina watched Mitch hurry back up the hill through the evergreens. He hadn't even bothered to say goodbye. What was he up to now?

11:25 AM
Quadrant OP-439

Danni Carraway smiled wickedly at Jude Monroe as she disconnected the call and slipped her satellite phone into her back pocket. "Hey, college boy. You up for a little adventure?" She moved across his living room as fluidly as a prowling cat, leaned over the back of the sofa, and draped her arms around his shoulders. "Come with me on some Resistance business." She caught his earlobe between her teeth just long enough to jump-start his heart before she released him and cast a come-hither glance over her shoulder as she sauntered toward the bedroom. "It'll be fun."

He grinned as he set down his coffee mug and followed her down the hall. How could he resist?

At her instruction, he changed into dark clothing. She zipped her jacket, tied a bandanna around her neck, and when she finished by pulling on a cap and sunglasses, he followed suit. The sunglasses were a hindrance. With winter less than a week away, days were short in the Midwest and the sun an infrequent visitor. He pulled them down his nose so he could see as they left the building.

Out in her truck, Danni rummaged under the seat and emerged with a handgun. She checked the magazine, found it fully loaded, and stuck it in the back of her waistband.

They drove out of the university quadrant, through the surrounding city, and headed northeast on the sparsely traveled, poorly maintained inter-quadrant highway. After half an hour, they had met no other vehicles. Danni guided the truck easily from lane to lane as she navigated around the potholes, some large enough to serve as a child's wading pool. Though their speed never topped thirty-five miles per hour, she slowed to a crawl several times to avoid blowing a tire or breaking an axle on the sections of badly damaged pavement.

Some time later, she took a lonely exit ramp that spit them out onto a narrow two-lane road. Jude looked both ways. "Where are we going?"

"Meeting a friend." She glanced at the clock on the dashboard. "Won't be long now." They passed rolling, wooded hills and over-grown fields that Jude assumed had once, in another time and season, been lush with plantings of corn and soybeans. He'd no sooner re-laxed, enjoying the scenery, when a delivery truck appeared on the rise ahead.

"Do you have your phone?"

He fished it out of his pocket.

"Record this."

As soon as they were close enough to see the other driver's face, Danni yanked the steering wheel to the left and skidded into the middle of the road, blocking the oncoming lane. The man's eyes grew wide as he slammed on the brakes, and Danni pulled up her bandanna and stepped out, gun drawn, before the truck screeched to a stop.

The holdup played out like something on television. She yanked open the driver's-side door and kept the gun trained on the man as he stumbled to the ground. "Got a phone? Give it to me." He kept one hand raised while he fumbled in his pocket, drew out a phone, and tossed it onto the ground. Danni picked it up, never taking her eyes off the man. "Hands on your head. Get over there!" She prodded him to the far side of the road and down the embankment. Jude rolled down the passenger window as she ran back to him.

"You can turn off the camera now. There's a second gun in the glove box. I'll drive his truck. You follow and cover me. Got it?"

"Yeah, I guess.... " His hands shook and he fumbled to put his phone away before he opened the glove box.

"What's the matter?" She didn't actually say *chicken*, but her tone was taunting.

"I never learned how to drive."

"Oh for crap's sake, that's the easy part. You just watched me. There's no one on the road but us. I'll turn it around and point you in the right direction. You can handle it from there."

The tires squealed as she brought the truck around and put it in park, and she was gone again in a flash, running back to the delivery truck. Jude slid over into the driver's seat and glanced back once at the hapless driver standing on the side of the road before he clumsily put the truck in gear and lurched after Danni.

Though at first driving took all his concentration, he grew increasingly confident as they put miles behind them. He was almost sorry the trip was over when they turned into a rutted dirt lane that led past a boarded-up house. Danni stopped the delivery truck in front of a dilapidated barn and jumped down from the running board. He parked behind her with a sigh of satisfaction. His hands were no longer shaking.

She looked like she was having the time of her life. She flashed a wide smile and called, "Hey, grab one of the other license plates from under the floor mat and change it out with the one on the back, will you? I'll just be a minute."

He flipped up the mat, chose a plate that had originated in the neighboring MG quadrants, and set to work while she tugged open the rough, wooden barn door and parked the truck inside. She came to rummage in the toolbox, selected a padlock, and dashed back to secure the door. He climbed back in let her have the driver's side.

She pulled off the black cap and shook out her hair. "That ought to slow down the Linking in the OP quadrants, anyway."

"What about everywhere else?"

"We weren't the only ones with this assignment today. I can't tell you everything, but one of our operatives got his hands on the supply chain information and the delivery schedules from factories that manufacture the Links. After that, it was just a matter of logistics and timing."

She glanced back at the abandoned farm as the truck bounced down the dirt road. "Lucky for us, no one lives out here. It's the perfect place to hide something as large as a truck. At the same time, it's a shame. I bet this was a good farm once. Since the Travel Restrictions went into effect, people who couldn't get permission to drive had to move in closer to an urban center or risk being totally isolated."

She turned onto the main road and laughed, good humor restored. "We're going to send that video you made to PeopleCam. I've got the perfect lead-in for the story that will never air: 'In an ironic turn of events, trucks full of GPS trackers disappeared from highways all over the nation today.'"

Chapter 3

Careen opened her eyes. She didn't need the flashing light on her Link to help figure out where she was. She'd spent the night on the cold tile of Tommy's bathroom floor, huddled in the comforter and clutching the empty gun as she'd struggled to stay awake. Eventually sleep had overcome her, and when she'd awakened just now, the gun was still in her hand. It had some value as a short-range weapon, but it would be better if it had bullets.

This rescue wasn't real—it was just another of Madalyn Davies's periodic loyalty tests. Careen knew she was bereft of allies. Tommy had every reason to hate her. Any act of kindness only reinforced her belief that he was undergoing a test of his own. He was no longer her friend or lover, and she meant what she'd said to him the night before. She was determined to die fighting.

She hid the gun behind her back and opened the bathroom door with as much stealth as she could. Tommy, sprawled in a chair blocking the doorway, awoke with a start.

Knock him out. Run for the elevator.

He rubbed his eye as he sat up. "Are you all right?"

The concern in his voice was so genuine that she wavered, and the opportunity for a surprise attack passed. She kept her voice harsh. "When were you released? How did you get here?"

He reached over and turned on the desk lamp. "Good afternoon to you too."

"Everyone in the Resistance is in prison. Why did they let you out?"

"Can't we discuss this over lunch?"

She shook her head.

"Okay, fine. Why do you think I was in prison?"

"Madalyn said I was responsible for putting you there."

"To that I'd say consider the source, but she was probably your only source, right? And why do you think it was your fault?"

"Because I told them where to find you." She was going to slam the door, but he threw out a hand to block her.

"Hang on a minute, Careen. Listen. Madalyn lied. How can you be to blame for something that *never happened*?"

"Yes, it did too happen. Otherwise why would she reward me with pretty clothes and let me sleep in a beautiful room?" She read the look on his face as revulsion, dropped her gaze to the floor and tried, more gently this time, to shut the door.

"Jeez. Come on, don't lock yourself in again." He moved the chair. "Come out."

She obeyed, eyes still cast down, and kept the gun concealed behind her back.

"Are you hungry?"

She shook her head.

"Well, I'm starving. I can go to the kitchen and bring something back. Maybe you'll change your mind and eat a little."

She shrugged.

"Okay." She didn't pull away when he ran his fingers down her arm and squeezed her hand. "I'll just be a few minutes. Stay here. Everything's all right. Count on it."

Out of the corner of her eye, she watched him leave. As soon as the door shut behind him she picked up the comforter, put it back on the bed, and concealed the gun under one of the pillows. Tommy wanted to trust her, and that gave her an advantage. She was still being held against her will, but she'd learned a thing or two. She'd never be without some kind of weapon again.

2:30 PM
Quadrant DC-025

Kevin submitted to a perfunctory pat down before he was admitted to the prison, hoping the guards wouldn't sense his trepidation. If Madalyn ever found out that he was part of the Resistance, he'd be lucky if he ended up in a cell. More likely, he'd disappear and no one would ever hear from him again.

He wondered if he'd have to speak to Jezz on one of those telephones with her on one side of bulletproof glass and himself on the other. He'd only seen her one other time, from behind the glass wall at PeopleCam studios.

A guard walked Kevin down the hall to an interrogation room. "That gal's been a-hollering to talk to someone from the OCSD since she got here last night." Kevin stood, his leg jiggling nervously, until another guard brought Jessica Catecher, handcuffed and dressed in an orange prison jumpsuit, into the room. He shackled her to a cleat on the table.

Kevin dismissed the guard, and when the door had closed, he took the seat across from her. He'd meant to inquire about how she was being treated, but she didn't give him a chance.

"What happened to my daughter?"

"She hasn't been located."

"Good. Now get me out of here."

"Mrs. Catecher—"

"Call me Jezz."

"Jezz, then, that's not why I'm—"

Her chains clinked against the table as she leaned toward him. "I'll tell you everything. They sent a limo to my house to pick me up. I met with Tommy Bailey and some other guy in a suit. Didn't get his name though. Said I was at their secret headquarters and the guy in the suit was with Internal Affairs for the OCSD—like you people have an Internal Affairs department, am I right? So I called him on it, and he admitted they were Resistance, and they were going to rescue my daughter because the OCSD was holding her captive and torturing her. It would have seemed heartless to refuse to help, so what else could I do? When I saw her, she was dressed nice and didn't look like she was beat up too bad. Maybe they were exaggerating. How could I know? But I did what I agreed to do. They tricked me. You're the assistant director of the OCSD, aren't you? You must have the power to get me released."

He stammered, and her eyes narrowed. "Something tells me this whole thing was an inside job, if you know what I mean. Dollars to doughnuts, the Resistance has a spy at the OCSD. Maybe more than one. Maybe even in a top position."

Kevin blanched. "Mrs. Catecher, I don't have the authority to release you, but I'll take your request to the director." He stood and knocked on the door.

She raised her voice. "Then let me talk to the head honcho. Get Madalyn Davies in here."

Before he could reply, the guard opened the door, and he hurried out without looking back. He broke into a sweat as he strode down the long corridor. Jezz knew just enough to throw suspicion his way. If she was released, there was no telling what she'd say to the press, or anyone else who would listen. He hesitated outside the chief of security's door and mustered the resolve to knock.

Once admitted, he closed the door behind him and spoke as though he expected to be obeyed. "No more visitors for that prisoner. Keep her away from the other inmates. She's manipulative and dangerous—and a flight risk. Yeah. In fact," he gave the man a pointed look, "I wouldn't be surprised to learn that she was shot while trying to escape. Do you understand what I mean?"

They locked eyes for a moment and the chief of security nodded. Kevin, already hating himself, turned and left the room.

2:40 PM
Quadrant DC-005

Tommy stretched the kinks out of his back as he headed down the hall to the kitchen. The chair in which he'd spent the night had been a poor substitute for the bed in his room. Still, one night of discomfort seemed like a small sacrifice compared to what Careen had been through.

There was no time to cook a hot meal, so he grabbed a few yogurt cups from the fridge and put them on a tray with bottled water, energy drinks, a couple of oranges, and some granola bars. He was so focused on hurrying back to Careen that he jumped when Atari's voice rang out from Command Central.

"Hey!"

Tommy stepped into the room, where his and Careen's images still dominated the largest television screen.

"Snooping around in the video files last night, were we?" Atari spun around in his leather chair, and Tommy stifled a laugh. Atari's beaky nose was swollen to twice its normal size. The bruising around his eyes had blossomed spectacularly since the night before, when Careen had taken offense to one of his characteristically tactless comments and broken his nose with a well-placed left hook. "Stay out of my space."

"Why? You never cared about me being in here before."

"I've changed my mind. I don't want you and what's-her-name messing with my stuff." Then his demeanor changed, and he practically licked his lips as he asked, "Did you show her the other video I made too? You know, to get her in the mood?" Tommy expected his turn to punch Atari's lights out would come sooner rather than later, but for now he ignored the questions and gestured at the screen. "Switch over to PeopleCam. What have they said about the escape?"

Atari's derisive snort seemed to get caught in his broken nose, and he winced in pain before he spoke. "So far the OCSD has failed to acknowledge last night's incident. There is no nationwide man—or woman—hunt in progress. Nothing. Apparently, the little minx lost value once we drove her off the lot."

Tommy shook his head in disbelief. "What do you mean, there's nothing on the news? Careen went berserk and attacked her mother on live television. Even if the OCSD won't admit that she escaped from their custody, that meltdown was epic. They have to offer some kind of explanation."

"That live"—Atari made air quotes with his fingers—"program wasn't really live. When she didn't stick to the script, they scrapped the show. Since it never aired, the OCSD has nothing to explain." Atari pulled up a video of a man sitting at a desk. "You need a tutorial. You should watch this."

"What is it? Another sim?"

"No, it's a game I created. Wanna play?"

"Not really. Where are the dragons and monsters?"

Atari smirked. "This game is all about lying and deception. Keeps my skills sharp. It's extremely difficult to pretend like you're in total control when you're not. It's hard to behave like your sworn enemy is really your best friend. Everyone should practice telling convincing lies." He studied Tommy for a moment. "Though brute force has its place too, right, Hercules?"

"No, thanks. I don't lie. Not about anything important, anyway."

"You have to know how to lie! What else can you do when you're out of options? Besides, limiting ourselves kills our creativity and our ability to innovate. How will we ever do new things if we don't push the boundaries?"

"I guess I never thought of it that way."

"But of course, *you* don't need to lie. You're as transparent as rainwater, aren't you, hayseed?" He looked around. "Where is your princess, anyway?"

"She's exhausted. She had a bad night."

"If she's exhausted, it should've been a good night." He wiggled his eyebrows. "Was it good for you?"

"I meant ... just never mind."

Atari laughed. "See? You need to learn how to lie."

Tommy shook his head as he left the room, determined to limit Careen's access to Atari until she was less fragile. He balanced the tray in one hand as he opened the door and looked inside.

She had commandeered the bed and was burrowed under the covers so he set the tray on the desk, opened his book, and read while he breakfasted alone. When he was done eating, he glanced over his shoulder. She hadn't moved. He folded his arms on the desk and put his head down.

3:18 PM
Quadrant DC-025

Kevin's heartbeat pounded in his ears. He had the sensation of running away, even though he moved down the prison hallway at a normal pace. The double doors that stood between him and freedom seemed miles away. Sweat trickled down his cheek and left a spot on his collar. His tie threatened to strangle him, and he loosened it before he stepped into the security check area, where he was gestured through with no more than a cursory glance.

Such an easy departure heightened his feelings of guilt and panic. He was in too much of a hurry to put on his overcoat; the sweat that ran down from his armpits turned icy, and he shivered as he hurried down the walk, sucking in great gulps of the wintry air. His driver came around to open the car door, and Kevin slumped against the leather seat, covering his face with his hands. He wanted to go back to the chief of security and say he'd been kidding when he'd ordered Jezz Catecher's execution. But he couldn't. Removing Jezz from the equation was necessary, not just to preserve the Resistance, but also himself.

They were hardly out of the prison gates when he called out, "Pull over. I need to—" He opened the door before the car came to a halt and, leaning out, vomited onto the gravel shoulder of the road until there was nothing left in his stomach. He pulled the door closed with a shaking hand and rode the rest of the way to the OCSD lying on the seat.

Back in the building, he made his way to his office, where he brushed his teeth, splashed his face with cold water, and put on a fresh shirt and tie before going next door to Madalyn's suite. She was in conference with Art Severson, who, when they'd first met, had fumed about Kevin being named assistant director of the OCSD. Now he gave Kevin an icy glance. "Madam Director, you can count on me." He all but bowed himself out of the room.

Madalyn turned her attention to Kevin.

"Well?"

"Mrs. Catecher didn't know anything about the Resistance or Careen's whereabouts." He took a deep breath. "She can't help us."

"Too bad." Just like that, she moved on. "We need to deal with the Essential Services issue. When he resigned, Victor Martel promised that people would be able to opt out of receiving food deliveries beginning at the first of the year. That's only two weeks away. One of the main benefits of the Link is that it assures people's access to food through Essential Services. If someone opts out, the Link can't be expected to protect them against hunger."

"Can you override Martel's decision to make ES subscriptions optional?"

"I may have to, though it would be easier if he hadn't made that announcement so ... publicly. We can delay putting up the opt-out Web page for a month or two, and I suppose the IT department could set it up to crash if too many people try to access it." She made a dismissive noise. "Maybe I'm worrying over nothing. Honestly, how many people will walk away from a government-sponsored food plan and choose the uncertainty of having to actually find food for themselves?"

He took a deep breath and changed the subject.

"So should we go to the press about Careen?"

"No, not yet. We need to focus on the Link. If we get the program started right away, more families are likely to stay enrolled in ES."

Her phone rang. "Yes?"

Kevin watched her face fall. She listened without comment, and when she hung up, he asked, "What is it?"

"Now maybe everyone will believe me when I say we're in constant danger." She sank down in her leather desk chair. "Garrick missed our meeting. There's been another crisis! Terrorists. They're everywhere!"

"Attacks?"

"Hijackings. All over the country. They're stealing shipments of Links before they can reach the Distribution Centers."

"Has anyone been hurt?"

"No. But trucks full of Links are gone. How are we going to start Linking on Friday if the wristbands don't get delivered?"

She closed her eyes and steepled her fingers under her chin, almost as if she was praying. After a time, she spoke. "We'll create demand. People want what they can't have. So if they show up and get turned away.... Yes! We'll keep them coming back until the new shipments arrive. And while we're at it, I think it's time to redefine some of the parameters for the Link."

"How do you mean?"

"We need to Link criminals and dissidents. Think how much easier it will be for the QM to do their job. Crime rates will drop. People will love it."

"How will you get criminals and dissidents to report to the Distribution Centers?"

"We won't need to if we Link everyone who gets arrested. We'll get them all eventually."

"If the Links have been stolen, how do you expect to—"

She opened her eyes and laid both palms on her desk. "There must be a way to recover the stolen ones. I'll call Atari. You call the factories. Double the original orders!"

"Double?"

"Hmm, you're right. Maybe that won't be enough. Let me tell you what I'm thinking so we can get the PR department on a new campaign right away."

Chapter 4

"Get away from me!"

Tommy, startled awake, jumped out of his chair, heart pounding. His book hit the floor with a *smack*. His desk lamp provided the only light in the room, and he scanned the shadowy corners in search of an intruder.

"Stop it!" Careen knelt in the middle of the bed, screaming and crying as she fought off an unseen attacker. Her eyes were wide open, glassy and unseeing.

He'd experienced her bouts with night terrors before, but now the manifestation of her inner turmoil had risen to a whole new level. He stood back with hands over his ears, watching helplessly as her thrashing and screaming went on and on until the tendons stood out on her neck. It creeped him out to watch; it was as though she was possessed, and he was afraid he'd make it worse if he tried to wake or comfort her.

She extended her arms, pantomiming pointing a gun.

"Get back! Get back or I'll kill you!"

She pulled the trigger and reacted to the recoil of the imaginary gun.

Just when he was about to seek Atari's help, she stopped striking out at nothing, lay down with a shuddering sob, and within seconds was perfectly calm and still.

Tommy sank down on the desk, drained and breathless. He picked up his book and found his place, but there was no way he could focus. He got up and crossed the room to stare down at her. Sweat glistened on her brow, now smooth and untroubled. Her lips were slightly parted, her cheeks flushed, and she was breathing normally.

He wondered if he'd ever be able to sleep peacefully in the same room with her again.

He double-checked to make sure he'd collected every stray round from the desk drawer where he'd first hidden the gun and then wrapped the magazine and bullets in a T-shirt and shoved the bundle to the back of the top closet shelf.

Even with that precaution taken, he jumped every time she stirred or mumbled in her sleep. Four hours later, he was nodding over his book, struggling to stay awake, when she yawned and rolled over.

"Where's your mom?" Her tone suggested she hadn't given up on trying to catch him in a lie.

He closed his book. "Not here. But she's fine. She has her memory back. She's worried about you."

"I want to talk to her."

"Me too. I'm pretty sure she's at home in OP-439, but she hasn't had a phone in months. Neither has my dad."

She sat up and folded her arms. "So she *could* be in prison?"

"No, she couldn't. Atari gets regular communiqués from Mitch, and he's in contact with all the other members of the Resistance. If anything bad happened to anyone, we'd hear about it."

"Why are you here with Atari?"

"I can't leave right now."

"Why not?"

"Because I'm wanted for the university bombing—among other things—and also because you're here." It didn't matter that he'd omitted a large portion of the truth. He tried to change the subject. "PeopleCam didn't report anything about your escape."

"Of course not. Why would they? I told you, Madalyn already knows I'm here. It's part of the loyalty test." She hadn't changed her mind about anything since last night.

"There is no loyalty test."

She gave him a *yeah, right* look. "What about Trina? I want to talk to her."

"Last I knew she was in hiding. Like I said, we can't just send a text or call her up."

"Don't lie to me."

"I'm not! Ask Atari."

"If you want me to believe you, then let me talk to Lara. Or Trina or Eduardo. There are plenty of people in the Resistance who I can trust. Atari definitely doesn't count."

Tommy stood up. As he started across the room, she shrank away from him and slid her hand under the pillow. He froze and avoided eye contact, as though trying not to antagonize a frightened animal. He would have welcomed his mom's or Trina's advice on how to deal with her.

"Relax. I'm not going to hurt you." He reached for the rolling desk chair, drew it into the middle of the room, and sat a safe distance away. "I missed you, and I'm glad you're here."

She regarded him warily. "Don't lie. Don't try to be nice to me."

"That's a dumb thing to say. I'll be nice to you if I feel like it."

She drew her knees toward her chest and hugged her legs. The fading bruises and lack-of-sleep smudges under her brown eyes made them seem even larger in her pale, thin face. If only he could erase all the bad things that had happened to her.

"Did you sleep all right?"

"Fine."

He nodded. It was good that she didn't remember the horrors she encountered in her sleep. "I never stopped worrying about you while you were gone."

"There was no reason to worry. Madalyn protected me."

He shook his head but made an effort to keep his voice nonconfrontational. "How can you call Madalyn a protector? Don't you remember all the awful things the OCSD has done? They kidnapped my parents and David and Grace. They lied about a terrorist attack so they could use CSD to control what everyone thought and did. They accused you and Trina of a murder you didn't commit. They hunted you down, and when they finally found you, they beat you and tortured you."

She turned indignant. "Madalyn is under a lot of pressure. Everyone criticizes her, but she's doing an excellent job. It would be easier if the press would leave her alone."

"Are you kidding? The press doesn't dare criticize her."

"Besides, you're leaving out the part of the story where you and your father tried to kill me."

"How could we have done that if we were in prison?"

She paused. "No. Wait. You're trying to confuse me. You and Tom weren't caught in BG-098 with everyone else. You were caught after you tried to break into PeopleCam."

"I'd never been to the PeopleCam building before last night." He shook his head. "The way you rewrite the past, you could have come out of the pages of this book." He held it out to her. "'War is peace. Freedom is slavery. Ignorance is strength.' Or in your case, truth is lies, right?" She didn't respond, and he found it ironic that the doublespeak seemed to puzzle her. "I've been reading a lot since I got here. Atari's not nearly as good company as you." Not a hint of a smile. *Jeez. Tough room.*

She took the book as though it was something precious. "I wasn't allowed to have anything to read."

"Seriously? You said Madalyn treated you well. Didn't you tell her how much you love to read?"

She shook her head, and he pressed a little more.

"Do you want some books?"

She nodded but without much enthusiasm. He hoped a visit to the safe house's library would remind her of her former interests—even if he wasn't on that list. Yet.

11:38 AM
Monday, December 18, 2034
Quadrant DC-001

Pete read the tease for the noon PeopleCam report. "'Reliable intelligence sources claim the recent uptick in terrorist activity threatens the Link program.' That's all we're allowed to say?"

Sheila leaned closer. "If you think that's too short, why not allude to the high-speed car chase from the other night? Those two things could be related."

"That sounds like we don't know what we're talking about." He sighed. "We should be able to tell our viewers what's really happening instead of cobbling together unrelated bits of information and passing it off as news."

Sheila smiled knowingly. "Pete, loose lips sink ships. We're in the middle of a war. We can't say anything on the air that might give our enemies an advantage. It's good that what we say on the news doesn't make any sense."

"Then why say anything at all?"

Sheila giggled. "So people will keep watching, that's why, silly!" She slapped his shoulder playfully and stood. "I've got to get to Hair and Makeup for a touch-up."

Pete sighed again. The affiliate stations were sending video evidence of lingering food shortages, quadrant marshals bullying people who tried to trade for food at the now-legal marketplaces, and student protests, but any more, the occasional feel-good story from an outer quadrant was all that got through the network censors. Just a few hours ago, he'd received a file from a Resistance source that contained amateur video footage of a truck being hijacked.

Sheila probably had no idea what was going on in the rest of the country. What he had seen was making him nervous, but it also gave him heart.

1:04 PM
Quadrant DC-005

Atari's phone rang with Madalyn's special ringtone. *Every breath you take…* She'd waited longer than he'd expected to get in touch, but when he connected the call, she didn't waste time with pleasantries.

"Do you know how many quadrants haven't received their Link shipments? Thousands! Actually, tens of thousands! Trucks have been hijacked."

"That's unfortunate."

"Well, can't you do something? Locate the stolen boxes. I mean, they're full of GPS-enabled trackers, aren't they?"

Atari sighed with affected patience. "I'm afraid it's not that simple. The GPS function only works once the Link has been activated and is drawing power from its host. That is, when someone's wearing it."

"Oh. I assumed you'd be able to recover the ones that were lost. Now we won't have enough."

"Sounds like you'd better postpone." Atari smirked. *We can delay ... oh, say ... until after you're arrested.*

"Oh, we're not postponing."

"But Madam Director, delaying the implementation by a week or two has an upside. You do realize that the software associated with the Link is quite complicated. It will take some time to train all the officers who will be using it."

She seemed taken aback. "No, I didn't ... well, then you should begin training right away. Garrick can call in representatives from every quadrant—"

"We're still in the final stages of software development, and last minute changes are inevitable. Do you want to pull high-ranking marshals off their regular duties and then find they need additional training later? I know it's hard to hear this, but it could be weeks before the Link is one hundred percent ready."

"I refuse to let the Resistance take credit for crippling this important security initiative. The Linking will proceed as scheduled."

"If you're certain, then of course we'll proceed, but in the meantime, I could upload a simple simulation program. It won't actually track Links, but it would give the QM a chance to experience the visual on their scanners."

"Yes, that will do for now. Once children begin wearing the Link, it will serve as a constant reminder of their responsibility to themselves and to society, even if it's not activated or monitored yet. We must make sure parents know that the terrorists in the Resistance have targeted their children, and demand their unwavering cooperation."

6:30 PM
Quadrant DC-001

Madalyn addressed two PeopleCam reporters in the OCSD's briefing room. "Small, localized attacks mean we're in more danger than ever. We must begin Linking as soon as possible. The terrorists in the Resistance are never going to leave us alone. Soon they'll get tired of blowing up buildings, and they will come for our children."

When she'd first assumed the directorship, she'd expected to enjoy being in the limelight, but the reality was quite the opposite. Everyone knew the press existed to support the government. She should be able to give her statement, pose for a few photos, and leave without answering questions about things she would prefer not to discuss.

The man raised his digital recorder. "Where were the recent localized attacks?"

"One or two shipments of Links bound for the outer quadrants were hijacked and stolen in the last few days."

"But there haven't been any attacks against people."

"The drivers of the trucks were certainly people, and they were attacked. The attacks are, by proxy, attacks against all American children, as they were carried out to delay the implementation of the Cerberean Link program."

She pointed a finger at them. "The Cerberean Link will become part of life in our country. Participation is not optional. All children under the age of eighteen are required to report to the designated Distribution Centers and receive their Links beginning on Friday."

The other reporter raised her hand. "What happens when a child turns eighteen? My son will be an adult in six months."

Madalyn nodded. "It is possible to deactivate a Link once your child reaches the age of majority. This option will be made available once the implementation phase of the program is complete. We remain confident that the majority of young adults will recognize the Link's benefits and choose not to cancel their coverage. The OCSD will keep Americans free by making them feel safe. The Link will be good at that."

The two reporters glanced at each other and then began firing questions at her.

"Why haven't we seen Careen lately? Where's she been?"

"There are rumors that she had a meltdown."

"An off-the-record source said she's been hospitalized for exhaustion."

Madalyn's smile was tight. "No more questions." She practically ran from the podium. Kevin was waiting for her in the next room.

"I didn't know people could disconnect the Link once they turn eighteen."

Madalyn made a dismissive gesture. "Oh, that. I don't know if it can be done or not. I only said it would be a *possibility* after the implementation phase is complete. Please! The implementation phase is going to take years. By the time the cameras and scanners are all installed and operational nationwide, millions of Linked children will have grown into adults. There won't be any more unsolved crimes or dissident behavior among the people who have a Link. Just think, Kevin. No one will want to disconnect a Link once they have it. Everyone's going to love it."

Chapter 5

Another two days went by before Careen, showered and dressed in a blouse, cardigan, and pair of jeans from the stack of clothes Tommy had brought her, was ready to leave the now-familiar surroundings in Tommy's room for the promised tour of the safe house.

He passed Command Central's doorway without pausing, but she lingered in the hall while she unbuttoned one more button on her top. She suppressed a shudder as she stepped up beside Atari's leather chair.

"When will I be going back to Madalyn?"

Atari didn't look up from his keyboard. "I'm not in the habit of making things easier for her and the OCSD, so the short answer is never. The long answer is also never. Followed by an exclamation point."

She tried another approach, changing her tone to sweet and girlish and twisting a strand of hair around her finger. "Did I pass the loyalty test?"

"I have no idea what you're talking about."

"Oh. I get it. You're not allowed to tell me." She took a step closer and rested her hand on his shoulder. "Can I talk to Lara?"

"No can do." He turned his head and his gaze lingered near where she'd just unbuttoned.

At least I've got his attention. "How about Trina then?"

"Nope."

Tommy appeared at her shoulder and took her by the arm. "There you are. Come on. I promised you food and a tour, remember?" He pulled her toward the hall as Atari asked, "Time for a game first?"

"No."

"All right then. You kids have fun and stay out of trouble." Atari reached for another of the many keyboards on his desk. "See you later, Careen."

As soon as they were out of earshot, Tommy stopped and faced her. "Were you flirting with him?"

"Why, are you jealous?"

"No, but do you think that's a good idea?"

She whispered, "What's the big deal? Haven't you ever had to say or do something you didn't mean to get what you wanted?"

He hissed back, "You're too smart to resort to the dumb-girl act. You didn't get what you were after, and if you're not careful, you'll get more than you bargained for."

She shook off Tommy's grip as they crossed the elevator lobby and entered the restaurant-style kitchen, where she perched on a stool at the far end of the stainless steel counter.

He didn't speak to her while he rummaged in the refrigerator and pantry and set about making breakfast, mixing batter and spooning it onto the hot griddle. Before long, he was sprinkling powdered sugar over two plates of fluffy pancakes topped with fresh strawberries and blueberries. He set one in front of her, pulled up another stool, and dug into his own portion.

She had no appetite and busied herself by rearranging the fruit with her fork. He glanced up from his food. "I thought you liked pancakes."

"I do. I'm not hungry."

He shrugged. "Suit yourself. There's plenty of food if you'd rather have something else. Danni keeps this place well-stocked."

"Danni?" She knew the tone of her voice left no doubt about her opinion of Wes and Jaycee's cousin.

"Yeah. She stops in every now and then." He paused for a moment and scrutinized her face. When he spoke, it was with a hint of defensiveness. "She's not that bad."

"That's the same thing you said about Wes before you and he—"

"Danni saved me from getting picked up by the QM. Twice."

"That's interesting. A few weeks ago she was all too eager to put you in harm's way."

"She's no threat to you. She spread the word about the CXD civil disobedience thing you started, and now there are tons of people, mostly college students, involved. She organized the black market food dealers to keep people from starving during the shortages last month. I know she's not perfect, but I admire her commitment to the Resistance."

Careen laid down her fork and responded without enthusiasm. "That's great. Really great." *Danni probably loves that she's getting credit for fixing my mistakes.*

He shrugged, cleared their plates, and led her down the hall to the foyer. "This used to be an office building. It was empty for years before Atari and the Resistance took it over and built it out as their safe house. It's soundproofed and runs on its own generator. It's actually pretty awesome."

She trailed behind, determined to show no enthusiasm for her new prison.

"One floor up"—he led her through a fire door and into the stairwell—"there's a library and media room and more bedrooms. Everyone we know in the Resistance could end up here, and we'd still have plenty of space."

He paused in front of the double glass doors that led to the library. "If you were impressed by the books in my dad's home office, you're going to love this. It's about fifty times larger, and there's a film database too. I didn't realize there were so many books and movies that had been banned by the government. It will be cool when someday we can give everyone in the country access to what we have stored here."

He opened the door and let her go first, then gestured for her to follow him into the stacks.

She glanced around as she obeyed, and her nonchalance melted away. Floor-to-ceiling bookcases were crowded with reference books, textbooks, and novels. She inhaled the intoxicating musk of old paper. "I didn't realize you liked books so much."

"Well, yeah, I've always liked to read. It was just that I was more focused on learning to fight and shoot when we got involved in the Resistance. After you were gone, I spent most of my time with my nose in a book, because I wanted to understand the Resistance's point of view. You had a better handle on that than I did, remember? I especially love the banned stuff, because it's a total slap in the face to the OCSD. They don't control what I learn and think."

She reached the end of the row, and he followed her around the corner. "Do you recognize any of these?"

"No." She ran her fingers along the spines. "Wait!" She pulled out a battered paperback copy of *Slaughterhouse-Five*. "My dad had this one. I meant to take it to college with me, but I couldn't find it before I left. We moved a lot after he died. Things got lost along the way." She opened the book and closed her eyes, breathing in the scent of the yellowed pages. "It doesn't smell the same as my dad's copy, but that's okay." She pulled two more books off the shelf and started a pile on a reading table.

"You can take as many as you want with you. We can watch movies from the database on any monitor in the building too." He brought up the catalog on a computer at the end of the aisle.

She came to stand beside him and looked at the list. "I've never heard of any of these."

"Yeah. They were all banned when we were little. I saw a really good one the other night, and I'd watch it again if you're interested. It's about a kid who goes to wizard school. If you like it, we can watch the other seven in the series together."

"Eight movies?"

"We'll have time. Like Atari told me when I first arrived, you're going to be here a while."

She almost believed him.

1:23 PM
Quadrant DC-001

Kevin stepped into the Analysis and Integration Department's suite of offices and addressed the young man seated at the reception desk. "Is Mr. Fischer available?"

Before the assistant could pick up his phone, Jack Fischer stuck his head out of the inner office. He was tall and thin, about Kevin's age but with prematurely gray hair. A grin broke out on his tired face as he crossed the room to offer Kevin a firm handshake. "Look at you! Long time no see." He led Kevin inside, gestured toward a chair, and settled in behind a desk on which stacks of paperwork at least a foot high covered every available inch of space.

"Man, talk about a meteoric rise! You're assistant director! How does the other half live, anyway? We miss seeing you among the commoners."

Kevin dismissed the comments with a wave of his hand. "It's ..." then he couldn't help grinning too. "It's pretty freaking cool, actually."

"I bet! No more slogging away in the trenches."

"Jack, don't downplay the importance of what you do in Analysis and Integration. Your department is the last line of defense between the public and a potential attack."

"So they tell me. We're so overwhelmed with reports from the professional Watchers—and private citizens too—that sometimes I wonder if we'd recognize a real terrorist if we saw one."

"You're getting slammed, huh?"

"Yeah. Ever since the people quit taking CSD the reports of terrorist activity have tripled. People accuse their neighbors, friends —sometimes they even turn in their relatives. The Resistance and the CXD movement make the so-called law-abiding citizens nervous. Bunch of alarmists is what they are. Mostly." He rubbed his eyes. "Who can tell anymore?"

"That's one of the reasons I wanted to speak with you. I need a reality check. How many people have you investigated that turned out to be no threat to public safety?"

"About ninety-nine-point-nine percent of them pose no threat. But we can't cut back on the number of people we investigate. What if we do, and miss a real terrorist?"

"What if you change the focus of your investigations? You could eliminate a huge threat to our country."

Kevin got up, closed the office door, and took a chip drive out of his jacket pocket. "I need you to handle this one personally. Top Secret, okay?"

Fischer took the chip. "Seriously?"

Kevin nodded. "Seriously. And Jack, I'm not kidding about keeping this under your hat. The information in that file can bring down a major terrorist. But if word gets out about this investigation, it could get us both killed."

"Who? Is it someone in the public eye?"

"Yeah." Kevin met Fischer's gaze and mouthed, *Madalyn*.

Fischer's hand trembled as he held the chip drive. He ran the fingers of his other hand through his hair. "Are you out of your tree?" he whispered. "What if ... oh, hell. I can't. No way." He held the chip out to Kevin, who folded his arms.

"I used to think I couldn't either. But I need your help."

"Linking is just for the kids. Kids aren't threats. Now the teenagers, maybe ... "

"No. Linking the kids is just the beginning. I'm afraid Madalyn's not going to stop until we're all Linked. The safety features for kids were just a way to get people on board with the idea. No one can leave the country, or even their quadrant, unless they're willing to abandon their children.

"The lawmakers in our government are just as paralyzed by fear as the average American. They're afraid of doing the wrong thing, of getting blamed for some tragedy, so they blindly follow Madalyn's whims.

"The Link isn't a solution for national security. It's a giant step toward slavery and oppression. We have to make sure people understand that—when the time is right. Please. I came to you because I trust you. Read this file. If you determine that she's no threat then destroy it. But I believe you'll agree with me—that we have to destroy her."

Chapter 6

2:05 PM
Quadrant OP-439

Tom Bailey led his co-conspirator Eduardo Rodriguez into his home office and shut the door. He'd never actually spoken to Eduardo in all the years he'd been the Baileys' postal carrier, but now he recognized him as a brave and valuable ally. Eduardo had put his own safety on the line to rescue Tommy twice, and he'd been the one who'd established a line of communication between the Resistance and the White House. Eduardo glanced at his cell phone every few seconds. When it rang, he jumped and answered it. "Hello? Yes, I'll hold for the president."

Tom grinned as Eduardo put the call on speaker. President Christopher Wright came on the line.

"Good afternoon, Mr. President."

Wright cut straight to the chase. "It's clear we're going to need to work outside the usual channels to get Madalyn Davies out of power. Congress has been reluctant to challenge her. I think we'll have a better chance of success if the Resistance is able to join forces with a few key government officials, myself included."

"Agreed, sir. Our plan is in motion already, and we'd like to go over it with you and firm up some of the logistics. We're concerned about the long-term ramifications of the Link program. We need to neutralize Madalyn before she does any more damage."

The president cleared his throat before he spoke. "Madalyn and I haven't been on good terms since before I rescinded the Restriction on food sales and distribution. Back when she tried to get everyone to take the transitional CSD, she threatened to stage a terrorist attack if I didn't support her agenda. I thought the university bombing was her retribution."

Tom skirted the bombing reference. "Terrorists seek to destroy our freedoms and undermine our society. By passing laws that limit our civil liberties, we're playing right into their hands. In this particular case, however, I consider the OCSD the terrorist. Madalyn knows how to exploit people's fears. Even yours, sir." Tom paused to let that sink in. "I've been thinking. What if Senator Renald were to introduce a Joint Resolution that called for downgrading the OCSD's powers?"

"I'm afraid it would take too long to pass. If Madalyn heard about it, she'd do everything she could to halt the process. She has a great many supporters in Congress."

"There might be another way around her." Tom sat on the edge of his desk. "One of Congress's functions is to investigate and oversee the executive branch of the government. In this case, we could make a case that their powers should extend to include the OCSD. It's practically the fourth branch of the government."

"True."

"What if you call an extraordinary session of Congress during the State of the Union address?"

"I *am* supposed to recommend measures that I deem necessary and expedient. It's not usually done like that though."

"All the better. Madalyn won't see it coming, so she won't be able to rally her supporters. You could ask for an immediate vote."

"Madalyn sidestepped my plan to appoint Senator Renald to the assistant director post at the OCSD. She's always behaved as though her power eclipses mine, and, God help us, it does. We need to attack without advance warning."

"We also need to move quickly, before her Link program gets off the ground. How soon can the address take place?"

"How about New Year's Eve?"

"Perfect."

"Can you come to the capital? I'll set up a meeting with Renald and Garrick."

"We'll leave tonight."

"Do you have a safe method of travel?"

"Yes. We'll be fine."

"Then I'll look forward to seeing you both in person."

Tom ended the call, and Lara walked in, laptop in hand, just in time to witness the two men high-fiving each other.

"Why the celebration?"

Tom changed the subject. "I didn't know you still had your laptop."

Lara deflected the parry with a shrug. "The QM never found it when they searched the house, and I never mentioned it because it's my personal laptop. As I'm sure you've noticed, personal space has been at a premium lately." She eyed the cell phone in his hand. "Where did you get that?"

Eduardo spoke up. "It's mine. We just spoke to the president. He's asked us to come to the capital and meet with him and Senator Renald about making Madalyn's crimes public during the State of the Union address."

"Well then, let's go. I can be ready anytime."

Tom shook his head. "You and Jaycee should stay in OP-439. You can sleep at Eduardo's while we're gone."

"Oh, I see. Are you going to tell Mitch you're going, or are you shutting everyone else out as well?"

Eduardo glanced at his watch and excused himself. "I need to find Jaycee."

As soon as they were alone, Tom took on an authoritative tone. "Mitch doesn't want to repair our country. He only wants to see it destroyed. Why are you reluctant to allow our paths to diverge? Don't say it's just because of Jaycee. As far as I'm concerned, she's welcome to stay with us even if we cut ties with Mitch. We can resist and work for change in tandem with the salvageable parts of the existing government."

"The Resistance needs you! You'll weaken our chances for change if you disaffiliate from the group. You'll leave Tommy vulnerable. And Careen. David, Grace, and Trina too. Everyone you so nobly went to the capital to try and protect."

"But I can't continue my association with Mitch. He has no qualms about sacrificing other members of the Resistance. Don't forget, he staged a number of terrorist attacks and blamed them on me. He expressed no remorse when Careen was taken into OCSD custody. Since his brother's death, he doesn't seem to care about anyone, including Jaycee. He's too great a liability."

She seemed desperate to change his mind. "But the State of the Union address is the perfect forum for Trina's part of the plan. It's all going to come together. Just work with Mitch until Madalyn's out of power. We all want the best possible outcome."

"Lara, is there something going on between you and Mitch?"

"No. At least nothing personal, if that's what you mean. It's complicated."

"Don't you think we should be honest with each other?"

She pressed her lips into a hard line before she nodded.

He stood. "Good. Though it's going to have to wait until after I return. If I'm apprehended, the less I know about your secrets, the better." His kiss on her forehead was perfunctory.

2:20 PM

Jaycee Carraway braided her unruly, rust-colored hair into one long braid and fastened the clasp on a glass vial necklace she'd found on Tommy's nightstand. Then she pulled on a dark gray sweater of his, which hung almost down to her knees. It was her first mission for the Resistance, and she knew she should feel excited, but instead, she was dead inside. The Resistance wasn't noble, like she had always believed. Their leader was liar and a murderer. He was also her father.

She'd learned Mitch had been behind the bombing that had killed Careen's dad when she'd been eavesdropping on Tom and Lara's conversation the previous Saturday night. Now that she was a spy, she had to be able to control her emotions and act as though nothing was wrong. She made a face at herself in the mirror and then practiced looking calm and unconcerned before she headed down the hall. When she heard voices below, she paused out of sight at the head of the stairs.

She heard Tom say, "I'm not sure I want any part of Mitch's plan from here forward. Is it right to put Jaycee in danger when we don't have to?"

Lara responded, "There's no reason not to go along with this part of the plan. The objective is to get the coins into circulation. The danger is minimal."

"Coins are contraband. If she's not careful, she could be arrested."

"Eduardo will be there to watch over her."

Jaycee started down the stairs and Lara looked up, smiling brightly. "Ready to go?"

The girl nodded and went out the back door to meet Eduardo, who was waiting in the truck. Neither spoke during the short trip to the university, but as they drew near to the outdoor market, she stared at the people grouped around the stalls. This crowd, in her experience, was second only to one that had thronged the distribution hub at the memorial service in OP-441—and it looked like lots more fun. A smile broke out on her face, but she quickly sobered.

Eduardo pulled into a parking space and cut the engine. "Remember—don't come across as too knowledgeable or bargain too much. You're a young girl, not an expert."

She nodded, got out of the truck, and threaded her way through the crowd. She stopped in front of a booth where a gray-haired woman had laid out trays of cinnamon rolls and an eclectic mix of clothing and household items Jaycee assumed she'd taken in trade.

Jaycee rubbed the fabric of a brightly colored scarf between her fingers. "This is pretty. Do you take"—she cautiously showed a handful of coins from her coat pocket—"cash money instead of trade?"

The woman smiled. "Where did you get cash money, sweetheart?"

Jaycee shrugged and fibbed. "We found a jar of these coins in my grandpa's things when he passed. I figured it couldn't hurt to try."

"I see. Several people have been interested in trading for coins lately. I'm sure you and I can strike a bargain."

Jaycee laid the scarf and a wooly knit cap on the table, and after a swift look around to make sure there were no marshals in sight, she counted out coins until the woman nodded. The woman scooped the coins into a pouch at her waist, and Jaycee pulled on the cap as she turned away from the booth. She tucked her braid inside her collar and wrapped the scarf around her neck. This mission was going to be fun.

Over the next few hours, Jaycee was aware of Eduardo watching her from a distance as she added two sweaters, a pair of jeans, a messenger bag like Careen's, and a dozen assorted pastries to her purchases. She layered on the sweaters and slung the messenger bag across her body. She'd tried to spread out her purchases among many vendors, and she was down to her last handful of coins when she spied a dinner plate in the same pattern as the ones of Lara's that had been smashed during a QM raid.

She gave the man at the booth the rest of her coins and two of the pastries in trade and concealed the paper-wrapped plate inside her new messenger bag. She couldn't help doing a little hoppity-skip as she headed back to the truck and was passing between the stalls when she heard raised voices. She ducked behind a display of handbags and watched as a quadrant marshal grabbed something out of the woman's hand at the booth where she'd made her first purchase.

"This is contraband," she heard him say to the vendor. "Why did you accept it? Who passed it to you?" The woman tried to back away, but the marshal grabbed her by the arm, ripped the apron from around her waist, and dumped its contents on the table.

Jaycee watched the scene in horror, clutching the upright post in front of her. She recognized that marshal. He'd acted a lot nicer when she'd met him at Wes's funeral. Someone clutched her arm and she jumped, smothering a scream. Eduardo shushed her and drew her away with him.

"*Vamos*. You cannot help. Your part of the mission is done."

Chapter 7

Tommy carried the books they'd selected back to their room and stacked Careen's on the desk next to his. "You up for more of the tour?"

She glanced at the books and shrugged.

"You're going to have plenty of time to read. Come check this out."

She followed him into the hall again, and this time he led her away from Command Central to the outer edge of the building. "The day Atari Linked you, we began to put together a plan. We were going to extract you during the Inaugural Link Ceremony."

"Really?"

"Who do you think set off the explosion? That's Atari's signature move. Anyway, it was so hard to stand there in the crowd watching you. I thought you recognized me, but I guess you didn't. I looked different, but so did you. You looked older in a business suit."

"I don't understand."

"Atari was the photographer. I was supposed to grab you in the confusion after the explosion, but I missed my chance. The guards got you out of there too fast."

She seemed bewildered. "Why didn't I recognize either of you?"

"I'll show you." Tommy opened the door to Wardrobe. "Welcome to another of Atari's playgrounds. I've been out of the safe house twice so far in different disguises, and no one recognized me." He motioned her inside. "Who do you want to be today?" She hesitated before she wandered into the racks of clothing.

The elevator key and Logan Daniels' ID badge, which he'd used to gain entry to the OCSD, were on the dressing table where he'd left them. He picked up the short brown wig and glasses he'd worn to the Inaugural Link ceremony. This time when he put them on, the guy he saw in the mirror looked familiar.

She came back wearing a shapeless pair of coveralls.

"That's a little utilitarian, don't you think?"

She folded her arms. "I'm an anonymous member of the custodial crew. You look like Clark Kent in those glasses."

Tommy stuck out his chest and grasped the front of his sweater as if he was about to rip it open. "You should see what I've got on under this. I'll show you if you show me what you're wearing under that uniform thing."

She frowned.

"Or leave it on. I'm only kidding. You look better in it than Atari does." Her face fell even more, and he stopped joking for a moment. "It's all right to have fun for a few minutes. Why don't you take a break from being Careen Catecher? Pretend to be someone else."

She disappeared back into the depths of the hanging clothes, and when she returned, she was dressed in a hot pink top, jeans, and boots.

She chose a shoulder-length, light-brown wig from a stand and looked in the dressing table mirror as she tucked her ponytail inside.

"See how simple it is? You could go out like that, and no one would know it was you." He stood beside her. "No one would know it was either of us. When we eventually get out of here we may have to rely on disguises."

She pulled up her cuff to show the flashing light at her wrist. "The Link will know. I can't pretend to be someone else, and, honestly, the only person I want to be is me."

"Don't pretend for me. Ever. Because I can't pretend that I don't care about you, or that I don't find you intriguing—no matter whether you're happy or sad, or what you look like, for that matter." He brushed a strand of the light-brown hair off her cheek. "I'd know you anywhere."

She took a step back. "Please don't do that. I can't have a future with you, even if I decide that's what I want. I'm Linked. You're not. I'm in the inner circle, and you're an outlaw."

"Whether we have a future together is not going to be decided by a stupid piece of plastic."

He tossed the glasses on the dressing table, pulled off the wig, and shook out his blond hair.

She eased off her wig and put it back on the stand.

"May I keep these boots?"

"Yeah, sure. Keep whatever you want. But Atari doesn't need to know we've been in here. He's got secrets, and it won't hurt to have a few of our own."

5:43 PM
Quadrant OP-439

Danni looked up from her phone when she heard Jude's key in the lock. He staggered into the room, one arm wrapped around his torso, and she hurried to his side.

"What happened? Are you all right?"

"Just a little dustup with some QM over at the market." He slumped into a pub chair at the kitchen island, strength apparently sapped. "One of the marshals beat up a woman for having contraband. It was a handful of old coins. Big deal."

"Let me take a look. Do we need to get you to a hospital?"

"No, I don't think it's that bad."

She reached inside his coat and laid her hands against his ribs, and he flinched. He helped her pull his shirt out of the waistband, and she ran her hands over the fresh bruises that marked his stomach and back, pressing gently here and there. "Can you take a deep breath?"

He tried to comply. "Sort of. You know they've closed the university until further notice? Classes aren't canceled for our safety. They're canceled because they want to keep us away from each other. They don't want us to know who's been arrested. They think we won't communicate or organize if they isolate us."

He pulled his shirt back down. "They tried to keep CXD from becoming a thing by ignoring us. Then they tried to force us to stop by using military-style attacks in suburban neighborhoods. They think they can intimidate us. But it's too late for that now. The CXD network is stronger than they realize."

"This was bound to happen. They've had you in their sights since you gave that speech the day after the university bombing."

"It's not about me. In a few weeks, the Essential Services mandate will be lifted and people will be allowed to pull out of the program. ES will be done for, so they're trying to scare us into believing we'll starve without them. The OCSD thinks they can stop us from supporting the market by keeping us off campus, but we'll keep showing up. We'll keep having meetings, and we'll take the CXD message farther than they ever thought we could." His mischievous grin turned into a grimace of pain. "Weren't they ever young? Don't they remember outsmarting adults to get away with stuff?"

"Slow down, college boy. You can't save the world in one day." She frowned at him. "You should have called me. I would've come to get you."

"I can't risk throwing suspicion on you because you're with me. I don't want you to get in any trouble."

"You're the only person in my life who's ever said that to me."

"You need different people in your life."

"I think you're right."

His hands slid up her arms and he leaned in. She'd never kissed anyone and wanted it to last.

7:02 AM
Thursday, December 21, 2034
Quadrant DC-001

Pete Sheridan sidestepped through the door to Editing Bay Ten and held the door in place while he examined his primitive security system: a pencil, taped to the door beside the hinge, point touching the floor. The arc drawn by the pencil did not extend beyond its current location. No one had opened the door since his last visit.

The equipment in this particular editing suite was so old it predated the OCSD itself. No one ever used it, and that made it perfect for his purposes. He locked the door and set to work.

Since he'd read the news story declaring the end of the food shortage, PeopleCam had received reports from twenty affiliates in rural and lower-income quadrants who claimed their food shipments had never resumed, and the people there were relying solely on private food distributors for sustenance. The stories had all been rejected and would not be aired.

In the past two days, he'd received dozens of uploads from Resistance fighters who'd videotaped themselves hijacking shipments of Links.

To top it off, the QM reported arrests for possession of contraband coin in fifteen quadrants, all at the new public markets where citizens did business with former black market dealers. There was talk of reinstating the Restriction against private citizens selling food because it had led to people flaunting other Restrictions.

Pete turned on the equipment, loaded the new reports into his archive, and uploaded it to the computer. He keyed in an Internet address that was blocked under the current PeopleNet system and hit Send, feeling as though he might as well have sent a message in a bottle out on the tide.

1:45 PM
Quadrant OP-439

Lara put on her headphones and connected to Mitch's call on her laptop. She'd decided to delay delivering the intelligence she'd been gathering until she had a chance to talk to him. Maybe there was still hope to bring the Resistance—all of it—together to achieve their mutual goals. "Mitch, I know you believe that full-scale revolution is the only way to go, but wouldn't it be better to achieve your goals through legitimate channels?"

"Where's the fun in that?"

She waited for a chuckle that didn't come. "A nonviolent revolution of sorts is possible, if we can find enough support within the current government."

"You sound an awful lot like your husband. Didn't know you let him feed you your opinions."

"Stop trying to tick me off. I want the Resistance to succeed. I've got the research you requested nearly done."

"And what's the verdict?"

"You can guess how the scales tip. The vast majority of our elected officials are scratching each other's backs in some way, shape, or form. The networks and the kickbacks are mind-boggling—as tangled as last year's Christmas tree lights. There are few saints among the people in the capital quadrant, and they can't seem to behave in the nonpolitical areas of their lives either."

"So there aren't many worth trying to sway in our direction?"

"That's not true at all. A handful—junior members, mostly—have decent records and a few scruples. Overall, it's better than I expected."

She heard him sigh on the other end of the line. "They've all had time to do the right thing, and they've chosen to wallow around together and feed at the public trough. They've shirked their responsibilities and let first Stratford, and now Madalyn, run everything."

"Tom and Eduardo are in the capital meeting with the president, Chief Garrick, and Senator Renald. Incidentally, Renald's a good guy. He's at the top of my list. No scandals in his background, and he strongly agrees that the OCSD's powers need to be curtailed and the Restrictions lifted. We should stick together and keep to the plan. We can form alliances with members of Congress who recognize the disparity between the intent and the results of the OCSD's projects and want to see Madalyn ousted from the directorship. Things can change for the better. Don't go all Wild West on us. Not now."

"Lara, your job is to get me the intel, not tell me how to use it. Tom may say nonviolent revolution is the best solution, but I can't help it if I think he's decided to quit fighting and look out for his own long-term interests. He wants a cushy spot in the government. Maybe he's even after Madalyn's job."

She bit back an angry retort. The conversation couldn't end yet. "If we do this right, Madalyn's job will cease to exist, and the point will be moot."

"Maybe."

"And is everything else running smoothly?"

"Seems to be."

Whatever that means. "Good. Then I'd like to get in touch with my son."

Mitch grunted. "The less we communicate, the less chance there is of a message being intercepted. It's imperative to keep the safe house isolated and secret. It's for Atari's safety, and Tommy and Careen's too, now."

"I never expected to be separated from him for so long. It was impetuous of him to follow Tom in the first place. I understood his desire to help find Careen, but now that she's been rescued he still can't leave. He's sentenced himself to staying there indefinitely."

"Tommy knows why he's there. Time for you to cut the apron strings, if you ask me."

Her redheaded temper flared. "I didn't. And you haven't once asked about Jaycee."

"You said you'd look after her. Are you?"

"Yes, but—"

"Okay then. Good to know." Mitch disconnected the call.

Lara fumed at Mitch's lack of concern as she put away the laptop and headset. She could teach him a thing or two about responsible parenting.

Chapter 8

Tommy picked up the book he'd been reading for the last few days and settled into the club chair with his feet propped on his desk. He saw Careen give the cover another curious glance. "It was written way back in the 1940s, and it predicted a pretty bleak future in the year 1984, two years before my dad was born. The Link is like something that belongs in Orwell's world."

She ran her fingers over the plastic band. "The Link is the solution, not the problem. Madalyn says everyone will get used to it, and it will be a good thing."

He sighed. "You can't believe anything Madalyn says."

"Tommy, please stop pretending you don't know. Atari does. You're working with him, so you must know too."

"Know what?"

"As soon as the system is activated, my Link will tell the QM exactly where I am. So why isn't Atari worried about my Link giving away the location of a Resistance safe house?"

"Look … it's a secret, but the Link is never going to work. That's why."

She shook her head. "No, you're wrong. He's not worried because this building belongs to the OCSD, and he works for them. The Link is going to work. Atari's kept you in the dark, Tommy. I can't believe you didn't realize. I figured it out right away."

She said it with such conviction that he began to wonder if she was right. He protested, "Atari's Resistance! You know that. We met him before. He was there on our first mission."

"He might be involved in the Resistance, but he's really Madalyn's ally. He's fooled you all. The Resistance never could have won anyway. The OCSD is too powerful."

"How can you say that?"

"Oh, Tommy, think about it. The Resistance is disorganized. We weren't part of it for long, but their plans failed more often than they succeeded. Do you really believe they're capable of an elaborate kidnapping? I was closely guarded and protected, you know."

"Yeah, actually I do know. We tried three times to get you out of there before we succeeded."

"Before the OCSD *let* you succeed. Like I said, it's all part of the loyalty test."

He sighed in frustration. "The only one who's torturing anyone with loyalty tests around here is you."

"Just wait. You'll see." She took a pencil and one of her own books from the pile on the desk and curled up among the pillows on the bed, facing away from him. They read in the deafening silence. He had trouble concentrating, but she dove in, underlining passages and making notes in the margins, and devoured the short novel in a few hours.

When she finished her book, he tossed her the last bottle of water on the desk as a peace offering. She made no attempt to catch it, and it landed on the bed beside her.

"You should drink that. You'll get dehydrated. Hungry yet?"

She uncapped the bottle, but shook her head.

"Do you want to watch that movie I told you about?"

She took a few sips. "Maybe later." She took another book off her stack.

8:40 PM
Quadrant OP-439

"New leads in the investigation reveal that slain marshal Wesley Carraway knew both Tommy Bailey, the son of the purported leader of the Resistance movement against the OCSD, and Careen Catecher, the university student accused of both Lowell Stratford's murder and the university bombing. In fact, Marshal Carraway had arrested the pair just a few weeks before. They escaped and joined forces with members of the Resistance, who infiltrated the OCSD on the day Lowell Stratford was murdered. Speaking of Careen, why haven't we heard from her lately, especially on the eve of the Linking? It's anyone's guess."

Jaycee slouched low in her seat, wrapping her hands in their fingerless gloves around her steaming coffee mug. She'd concealed her fiery red hair beneath one of Tommy's knit caps and gone a little heavy-handed with the eye makeup; her dark jeans and oversized black sweater and coat were nondescript enough. She hoped she didn't look fifteen; she'd felt much older for some time. The pop-up coffee shop that had moved into an abandoned building near campus had become a popular gathering spot now that there was no student center. Everyone in the place was watching the PeopleCam broadcast, which was underscored by a buzz of conversation. They all seemed to have a theory about what had happened on their campus, no matter how much it varied from the official news reports.

Jaycee trained her ear on a table of kids wearing CXD sweatshirts. One of the guys gestured at the television. "Careen was with the Resistance at the OCSD the day she killed Stratford. So that's all on Carraway, right? Because he let them escape."

One of the young women objected. "I don't believe Careen killed anyone."

"We can't trust the QM. Never could, really. I heard that psycho marshal Carraway was obsessed with Careen and Tommy. He arrested them, and they outsmarted him and escaped."

This was met with a murmur of agreement, and he continued.

"Carraway was at OP-441 during the food riot—and that was in the official QM report on the news. After that uprising, he went looking for Tommy and Careen and found them hiding here, in OP-439."

Another girl chimed in. "He knew they'd be back eventually, right?"

"Yeah. He lured them into the student center, where he'd laid a trap. Trouble is, his plan backfired, and he was the one who died."

"So why is the official story almost exactly the opposite?"

"I don't buy the official story. Careen was all about solving problems without violence. There's no way she set off the bomb. No way she'd try to kill anyone."

A broad-shouldered guy in a letterman's jacket spoke up. "Yeah, but how does Tommy Bailey fit in? I played ball with him in high school. None of us knew that Careen girl he's with. And Tommy's the last guy you'd expect to turn criminal."

"It's always the last guy you suspect, though, isn't it? What if the university bombing was the Resistance, targeting the QM, getting revenge for arresting Tommy? Maybe he's been Resistance all along, and he's just a really good actor."

"He wouldn't have to be much of an actor to fool you."

Someone threw a wadded-up napkin across the table.

Jaycee rolled her eyes. None of them had it right. She hoped they'd all be at the CXD meeting tonight so she could set them straight. She'd noticed people going toward the restrooms in the back hallway, one by one; none of them had returned. Unless they were seeing how many people fit in the stalls, they had to be heading for the meeting. She walked back to the restrooms. Empty. She opened a door marked Employees Only and descended the stairs.

She hadn't been allowed in the Resistance's inner circle because her father thought she was too young. But she could be part of the CXD movement. The dimly lit basement was slowly filling with people. No one made eye contact with anyone else. As Jaycee raised her cup for another sip, someone clamped a hand on her arm, and she spilled the coffee down her front.

Whoever it was yanked her to her feet and dragged her into an adjacent room. Under the light of a single bulb, Jaycee found herself nose to nose with her cousin.

Danni hissed, "What in the hell are you doing here—and out in public? They're going to be Linking children, in case you didn't know."

"I'm not a child. For your information, I've already done a mission for the Resistance."

"You're under eighteen, so you're in danger. I can't believe Mitch let you out of his sight."

"He didn't have much choice. I left home. Came up here with Tom and Lara."

"And do they know you're at this meeting?"

"Not exactly." She glanced away before turning a defiant gaze on Danni. "I snuck out, okay? I want to know more about CXD. And I wanted to talk to you. I need someone to sign papers for me so I can get Wes's death benefit."

Danni put her hands on her hips. "You'd have to be on the grid to do that. No. No chance. Mitch would have my hide."

Jaycee thrust out her chin. "Fine. I'll get what I want with or without you. I just figured I could count on my cousin." She stalked up the stairs and out the back door into the darkness.

Danni ran after her. "Take it easy, okay?"

Jaycee hissed, "I'm here to help the Resistance. Tommy and Careen are the Resistance. They're spreading all kinds of lies about them and Wes on PeopleCam. I was listening to everyone—they think Wes was nothing but an evil QM. Don't you think we should tell the truth so he can be remembered as a hero of the Resistance? The CXD people don't know he was a really good person."

"You can't tell anyone who you are. Technically, you don't even exist. I'm taking you home. From now on, be a good girl and don't do anything stupid."

9:55 PM

Danni let herself into Jude's building. It was late, and she didn't feel like going back to the meeting. After she'd driven Jaycee to Eduardo's apartment, she'd stayed outside in the cold, peering in a window until she caught sight of her talking to Lara. Now that she knew an adult was present, she could be reasonably sure Jaycee wouldn't try to sneak back out to the meeting.

Wasn't it enough that she'd spent weeks on the road during the food shortages, dodging the QM as she worked to keep hungry people from starving? When did her life get to be about her?

She'd never met anyone like Jude. He had potential. He was passionate, funny, and smart. She wanted to see where this thing with a guy she'd never have considered her type—president of the Inter-Fraternity Council at a prestigious university, for crying out loud—would lead. She didn't want to take on the responsibility for her young cousin right now.

Mitch had warned Danni that she was one of the few people in the Resistance who knew that the Link was in Atari's control and not a bona fide threat. But Jaycee wasn't part of that inner circle.

She hoped fear of being Linked was enough to keep her cousin from playing spy games and getting in trouble with the QM.

She wandered into the kitchen. Jude's apartment was newer and a lot nicer than most places she'd been, and he kept a decent stock of liquor. She selected a bottle of whiskey, poured a few fingers, and gulped it down. She made another drink, brought the bottle with her, and curled up on the sofa. The whiskey calmed her enough that she didn't startle when he opened the door.

"I set up a schedule for the protesters starting tomorrow morning, and some people are coming over in a while to make signs." Jude shrugged out of his coat and left it lying across a chair. "Where did you go?"

She set her glass down on the side table. "My fifteen-year-old cousin showed up at the meeting. I didn't even know she was in this quadrant. Why does she want to get involved in the first place? She's too young. It's not like we need her. She doesn't understand what it means to be in the Resistance. I made her leave."

He didn't say anything, and she felt like she had to keep explaining. "One of my other cousins died in an accident; it was kind of my fault. Well, not all my fault, but everyone blames me anyhow. I couldn't stand it if something happened to Jaycee too. I've got no one to talk to about all the family stuff. No one who cares, that is."

"I care." Jude's dark eyes were full of sympathy as he sat beside her. "Your family and friends should be there for you when you're hurting."

Danni shrugged to dismiss his concern. "It would be nice if someone said they were sorry, instead of always expecting me to be the one who apologizes. Sometimes I'm not sorry. And sometimes I need someone to be sorry for me." She reached for the bottle, but he covered her hand with his own.

"I'm sorry for your loss, Danni."

"How long before the sign painters get here?"

"About an hour."

She kissed him, and when he responded she relaxed, knowing fooling around was the quickest way to get a guy to stop talking. Even though he had potential, she wasn't ready to fall for him yet. It was hard to keep him an arm's length away from her heart.

4:37 AM
Friday, December 22, 2034
Quadrant OP-439

Two-dozen college students tiptoed from Jude's building clutching the signs they'd painted, planning to divide ranks and meet back at the closest Distribution Center in a few hours.

"Do you think protesting will work?" Jude asked as he rinsed out the brushes in the sink.

Danni shrugged, loaded the last coffee mug into the dishwasher, and padded over to the couch. "How many volunteers do we have?"

He consulted a handwritten list on the kitchen island. "About a hundred people signed up. If we all take shifts, and no one loses their cool or gets arrested, we could block the entrances at all four Distribution Centers indefinitely. Maybe we'll even get some media attention."

Should she bring him into the Resistance's inner circle, and tell him that the fate of the Linked lay in Atari's hands, not Madalyn's? She started the dishwasher. "Look, you're an amazing organizer ..."

"But?"

She couldn't tell him. Not yet. "But nothing. You've done a lot for CXD and the Resistance."

7:10 AM

Jude left while Danni was still asleep, turning up his coat collar as he headed for the Distribution Center. There he joined the group of six CXD members who lined both sides of the walkway leading to the center, their homemade signs held high. Someone had brought coffee, and Jude gratefully accepted a paper cup of the steaming brew.

They stood silently in the faint light of the winter dawn, as though waiting for an opposing army to amass on the horizon. An hour went by, and no one else appeared. It felt anticlimactic after all their planning.

The girl who'd brought the coffee whispered, "Did we get the date wrong?" and others in the group giggled nervously.

Then a car pulled up. A middle-aged woman got out and scurried past them, unlocked the Distribution Center's front door, and locked it again from within.

Twenty minutes later, families started to arrive with their children in tow, and soon the line stretched to the sidewalk. Jude stood behind one of the other protesters and recorded the scene on his phone. Most of the parents averted their eyes from the signs. Those who spoke did so in hushed tones, as though they didn't want to draw attention to themselves.

At nine o'clock, the employee unlocked the door. The line inched forward, but she blocked them from entering and spoke into a bullhorn. "Demand for the Link has depleted today's supply. Come back tomorrow." She shut and locked the door, leaving everyone in stunned silence. Then the crowd surged ahead, and those at the front beat on the door, begging to be let in.

Chapter 9

Careen dragged herself through the routine of showering and getting dressed as if gravity had suddenly doubled its pull on her. She was getting lots of sleep, so why was her internal battery running low? Tommy had a protein bar and an apple ready for her when she emerged from the bathroom, and she obliged him by opening the wrapper and taking a few small bites.

"Do you want to go for a walk around the building? Stretch your legs a bit?"

"No. I'm so tired. How long did I sleep?"

"About twelve hours." He didn't have the heart to tell her that during that time, she'd had four gut-wrenching episodes of night terrors. He was as exhausted as she, but the difference was, she didn't remember anything. He couldn't erase the visions of her distress etched on his brain.

"What day is it?"

"It's Friday."

"What do you think is happening in the rest of the world?"

"I honestly can't say. I haven't kept up with what's going on since you got here. Atari'll let us know if anything big happens." Tommy closed his book and stretched. "How about we watch that movie now?"

She nodded, and he turned on the television mounted on the wall and scrolled through the database. "Here it is." He started the playback. "I'll go make some popcorn."

He dimmed the lights on his way out, purposely leaving her alone to watch the scenes of Harry Potter's early life in his abusive aunt and uncle's home. Maybe she'd find some truth in the fictional story. When he reappeared with the fragrant bowl of popcorn and some bottles of soda, she was hunched in the bed, knees pulled in to her chest, clutching the hem of the blanket under her chin. She flinched when he sat down beside her and scooted over as far as she could. He glanced at her sideways as he arranged the pillows behind his back and noticed a tear glistening on her cheek. He opened one of the sodas without comment.

About the time Harry left for Hogwarts, she began to eat mechanically, one piece of popcorn at a time. Other than the single tear, she displayed no emotion, though her eyes never strayed from the screen. Tommy found himself watching her more than the movie. He'd experienced a range of emotions when he'd seen the film the first time and hoped it would have the same effect on her. He understood what it felt like to believe your parents were dead and was thankful that, unlike Harry, the separation from his own hadn't been permanent. He waited for a sign that she'd identified with the kids who, inexperienced and seemingly outclassed, had to pit their wits against the greatest Dark Wizard of all time.

When the end credits began to roll, he spoke. "Hey, I read something funny the other day. Atari told me he chose the name Cerberean Link because Cerberus is the three-headed dog that guards the gate to the underworld, and the Cerberean Link is a multi-faceted security system, right?

"Anyhow, the name Cerberus derives from the Greek word *Kerberos*, which means spotted. So Hades, lord of the dead, named his dog Spot. Who knew Hades had a sense of humor?" He grinned, but she didn't act amused.

"I get what you're trying to do. I'm not oppressed. I'm not abused."

Busted. "I didn't say you were. Didn't you like the movie? I thought it was good."

"I brought it on myself."

"Bull. Kevin told us how badly they treated you."

"I only saw Kevin a few times. He probably doesn't believe that I deserved it."

"No one deserves to be beaten! I can still see the bruises on your face, and I know someone did that to you. If they were from the explosion, they would have faded by now. The ones you're hiding under your clothes were even worse."

She shrugged. "It's over now."

He decided to push back a little. "No, it's not over! What if Jaycee ends up there in your place, and they treat her the same as they did you?"

Her eyes widened. "Could that happen?"

"Yes!"

She chewed on her bottom lip and didn't answer.

"It could happen to anyone. That's why we have to fight back." He let that sink in before he changed the subject. "Do you want to watch the next movie?"

"Yes."

6:17 PM
Quadrant DC-001

Madalyn hurried into the Green Room at PeopleCam studios. Kevin was waiting for her, and together they moved into the backstage area to wait for her segment. One of the many monitors showed cover footage shot at the Distribution Center in DC-001. There were relatively few children in the crowd, which appeared to be comprised mostly of college-aged young people who stood on either side of the walkway. Silent and orderly, they held hand-lettered signs bearing the messages: FOREVER LINKED TO THE OCSD; YOUR CHILD IS NOT THE OCSD's PROPERTY; TRUST NOT LEST YE BE LINKED; ALL THE BETTER TO SEE YOU WITH, MY DEAR; and WHO'S WATCHING YOUR CHILDREN?

DC-001 was one of the few quadrants that had an adequate supply of Links. Why were so few families lined up outside? As she watched, a family approached, and upon seeing the protesters and their signs, halted and appeared to reconsider. She tapped the director on the shoulder. He pulled off his headset, and she held up a warning finger. "You will *not* air any of that footage. Do you understand?"

Kevin, ever at her side, whispered, "You're on in two minutes."

She fought down her anxiety and fired off orders. "Contact the PR department right away. Have them go to the temporary hiring pool and get people to protest the protesters at the Distribution Centers."

"Did you say 'protest the protesters?'"

"Yes! You know what I mean. Have them carry signs. Make them look authentic. The actual distribution workers can't do it. They're busy."

"Right away."

Madalyn turned her attention to Pete Sheridan and Sheila Roth on the monitor as Pete read from the teleprompter. "Looks like our next story takes us back to beleaguered OP-439. Again."

Sheila looked concerned. "What's going on there now?"

"Jeremy Howard, our OP-439 correspondent, is live with the story."

The young reporter held out his hand to show the camera. "Coins. Here's a quarter, and this one's a … dime. Anyway, no one's seen coins in circulation since the Restriction went into effect years ago, yet I got these at a pop-up market just a short while ago. Where are they coming from? And how do people know how to use them? Could this be resurgence of the use of coins? If so, can old-fashioned paper money be far behind?"

"It sounds like pandemonium out there, Jeremy."

"You'd think so, but that's not the case at all. The people I observed at the market today seemed eager to obtain and use coins."

Madalyn turned to Kevin. "Where in the world are coins coming from? We did away with them years ago. As soon as I deal with one problem, something else crops up. This is getting ridiculous!"

Kevin laid a hand on her arm. "Don't let it rattle you before you go on."

On the monitor, Sheila cooed, "Up next, we have OCSD Director Madalyn Davies live in the studio!"

Madalyn shook him off and strode into the next room.

The floor manager clipped a lavaliere microphone to her blazer's lapel and placed a chair for her between Pete's and Sheila's at the news desk. She had barely settled into her place when the red light glowed on the center camera.

Sheila laid her hand on Madalyn's. "Madam Director, we are thrilled to have you here with us today. Let's start out with a question that's been on my mind."

Madalyn looked at the camera and said with false brightness, "Thank you, Sheila. I just came from the Distribution Center in DC-001, and the line of recipients was out the door and around the block! The demand for Links has far exceeded the supply in many parts of the country. Anyone experiencing a delay today should come back again Monday, and rest assured that we at the OCSD are doing everything in our power to Link your children as soon as possible."

Sheila seemed taken aback and, to Madalyn's dismay, doggedly turned the focus back to her chosen topic. "Oh, of course that's wonderful news, Madam Director, but I had a different question. After all the hype and controversy when you allowed terrorist Careen Catecher to avoid punishment for her crimes and then rewarded her with a coveted job at the OCSD that anyone would be crazy to turn down, well, we've noticed that she has disappeared from public view."

"Yes."

Sheila purred, "Before you got here, I talked with Assistant Director Kevin McGraw, but I couldn't get much out of him. It seems Careen is currently being kept out of the public eye for her own safety. Tell me, who has made threats against the poor girl?"

When Madalyn hesitated, Sheila prodded. "I understand if you don't want to name names, but it's no wonder she's in danger of a public lynching. She's been allowed to get off scot-free, and people are clearly disgruntled about it."

She turned back to face the camera. "How long could she expect to be allowed to escape punishment for her terrible crimes? I'd feel safer knowing she was locked up where she couldn't hurt anyone else."

Before Sheila could ask another question, Madalyn turned to Pete. "I'd like to say a few words about your last story, if I may. The one about the use of contraband coin."

He gestured toward the camera. "By all means."

"The use of coins is a slap in the face to the progress we've made. It's dangerous. It enables one of the worst of all rebel habits—trading in stolen goods and contraband—with no way for the OCSD to track lawbreakers."

"How do you know they're breaking other laws?"

The question was incredulous, and Madalyn's response was heated. "Of course they're either taking part in terrorist activity or dealing in stolen goods. Why else would anyone choose to violate the Restriction? I promise you right now, anyone caught in possession of coins will be severely reprimanded and the coins confiscated. The person in possession will be placed on the dissident list and monitored."

Pete turned toward the camera. "You heard it here on PeopleCam. Thank you for stopping by, Madalyn Davies, director of the OCSD."

"Wait! I'm not finished yet."

6:40 PM
Quadrant DC-005

Atari stood in Command Central, staring up at Madalyn Davies' image on PeopleCam.

"I believe the American people have the right to know when they are threatened. The Resistance is determined to undermine our nation's security and pave the way to anarchy. They will achieve their aims by attacking your children.

"Link spokesperson Careen Catecher vanished without a trace last week and is feared dead at the hands of the Resistance. Though she was one of the first recipients of a Link, the system, not yet activated, is incapable of locating her. We are working diligently to bring the system online, and when the Link is activated, if Careen is still alive, we will find her. Careen's disappearance only proves that we must not waver in our resolve to secure the future of every young person in this country."

The camera cut back to Sheila Roth. "The perfect combination of safety and personal accountability is now within reach as the Cerberean Link program commences nationwide. For more details and directions to the Distribution Center nearest you, please check your quadrant's home page on PeopleNet. Stay tuned to PeopleCam for round-the-clock updates on this grave situation."

Atari wrapped his arms around his torso and rocked, eyes closed. His pulse throbbed in his stomach. He concentrated on breathing normally until his heart rate slowed and the tremor in his hands was almost imperceptible. "I'm still the smartest person in this fight. I can handle it."

He looked at his surroundings. Command Central was in a state of disarray, but such menial tasks as cleaning were beneath him and only to be done when the situation became intolerable. Hiring a maid, though preferred, was impossible. He fetched a cloth out of the closet, set to work, and soon the row of chess club trophies and action figures on the shelf above his desk was shiny again, each item spaced exactly two inches apart. He hauled out the vacuum, used the brush attachment to clean his keyboards and his Rubik's Cube, and then sucked up all the dust bunnies from under the desk. He lobbed several empty energy drink cans toward the trashcan and then retrieved the ones that had missed. The now-tidy surroundings did nothing to solve his real problems, and he cursed aloud as he settled in his chair.

Piercing the Shield that blocked the free flow of information in and out of the country was his real mission. Activating the Link was merely a means to that end, as it was necessary to take down the Shield to run the surveillance programs required for the Link. Without the Link as a distraction, he feared his efforts would be shut down before people had a chance to experience the freedom he alone could give them.

Mitch had insisted that the Link not be operational. In his eyes, it was nothing more than a boondoggle to further ruin Madalyn's credibility. But Atari's desire to test his skills had resulted in a prototype that actually worked. Had he intended to use it? No way. Not until now.

But as the accelerated timetable for the Link brought him closer to having to activate it, he'd realized that the accomplishment of which he'd been so proud had taken on a life of its own, and, like Frankenstein's monster, it threatened to surpass his ability to control it.

Chapter 10

9:45 PM

As their movie marathon continued, Careen refused Tommy's suggestion that she eat something besides the popcorn. He'd hoped the fresh fruit would tempt her, but she shook her head when he offered her a juicy section of an orange. She'd also refused to eat at Resistance headquarters when she'd been stressed and upset, and Tommy knew she'd make herself ill if he didn't press her. Her attention remained fixed on the story, but an hour and a half into the fourth film, gnawing hunger had overruled his own interest. When he excused himself to replenish their stores of food, she didn't react.

He put the orange peels, empty bottles, and the wrappers from other things he'd eaten into the bowl that had held the popcorn and carried it back to the kitchen. He thought about how to help Careen change the way she perceived her time as Madalyn's captive as he piled protein bars, bottled water, and a couple of hastily-made sandwiches on a tray. Trina wasn't a psychiatrist, but she was a doctor, and she'd done what she could to address both his mom's and Careen's mental health concerns while they were at Resistance headquarters. Trina knew more about how to help Careen than anyone he could think of. Maybe he could convince Atari to try to contact her now.

He heard Atari talking to someone as he approached Command Central, and paused just out of sight, craning his neck to see into the room.

"Of course, Madam Director. As you wish. I'll get on it right away." Atari slammed down the phone, grabbed the Rubik's Cube off his desk, and threw it across the room so hard it cracked one of the television screens.

Tommy, mesmerized by Atari's violent reaction, accidentally let a water bottle topple off the tray. When it hit the floor, Atari jumped like he'd heard a gunshot. He turned and caught sight of Tommy stooping to retrieve it.

He took a menacing step. "What are you doing listening in? Was I unclear when I told you I don't want you in my personal space?"

"Is everything all right?"

"Oh, just peachy. Never better."

Tommy could see Atari's chest heaving. "Can I help?"

"What makes you think there's anything you could do to help, Brainless?"

Tommy stood up and fiddled with the contents of the tray. "Umm . . . okay then. I guess not. Look, I really need to talk to Trina. Could you get in touch with Mitch and set it up?"

"No." Atari slammed the door.

Tommy hurried back to his room. Seeking help for Careen was of paramount importance. How could it wait until Atari was in a better mood?

He balanced the tray while he opened the door, and as it swung open, he nearly dropped everything. Careen lay slumped across the mattress, mahogany-colored hair spilling off the side of the bed.

He forgot all about Atari as he set the tray on the desk with a crash and knelt, pushing her hair out of her face. Strands clung to her wet cheeks, and she drew a shuddering breath.

"What happened? What's the matter?"

She wailed something incoherent and burst into sobs that shook the bed. He sat beside her and gathered her into his arms until the storm of tears subsided.

At length, she wiped her eyes and hiccupped. "He never knows who he can trust."

"What?"

"Harry. Every t-time, someone he trusts betrays him."

"I know. But he can count on his friends. Just like you can count on me."

Her temper flared and she pushed him away. "Bullshit! How can you say that? Wes died in the explosion. You left me behind. You didn't care if we were alive or dead."

His insides turned cold at her accusation. "I didn't even know you were in the building with Wes until it was too late. After the bomb went off, there were too many people around for me to go poking through the rubble." A lump formed in his throat. "You don't know how many times I've wished it had been me instead of you. Everything that happened—and everything they did to you—was my fault. I never should have gone along with Wes in the first place."

"Don't use your guilty feelings as an excuse to avoid what has to be done. Prolonging the inevitable makes things harder for both of us. If you ever cared about me, stop torturing me. Turn me over to Madalyn. Get it over with. Please."

"Not going to happen." He stormed out of the room and slammed the door. He'd make Atari get ahold of Trina, no matter what.

He opened the door and walked into Command Central without knocking. Atari, his back to the door, was wearing headphones that kept Tommy from knowing at whom he was shouting.

"Okay, just shut up, shut up, shut up! There isn't enough time. I've got eight million things on my to-do list.... Oh, really? I'm busy liaising with that she-wolf, and contrary to what you seem to think, she's easier to deal with than you are. Yeah, I heard what she's been saying on the news.... Your sabotage was a huge help. Not. I'm not going to have time to complete what you want me to do before the big showdown unless you send the rest of the video to me right away.... Yeah, well, you expect too much. Do you think I just whip up those videos in an afternoon? I haven't slept in two days. I never would've agreed to extract Careen if I'd known how it would affect the situation. To top it off, I'm stuck babysitting the teen edition of *America's Most Wanted*." He made a gagging sound. "From now on, I'm doing things my way.... Oh, yeah? I know about your agoraphobia. You don't have the guts to come up here and make me." Atari threw the headset across the room. Tommy backed away and eased the door closed.

He ran down the hall, burst back into his room, and locked the door. Careen shrank away from him as he grabbed the remote off the bed and turned up the sound on the television. He took her by the arm and hissed, "Listen. Something's wrong."

She tried to pull away. "Stop trying to scare me."

"I'm not kidding. Atari was having some kind of meltdown, yelling at someone on the phone. I think it was Mitch, but I didn't understand half of what he was talking about. It sounded like he's not happy about going along with the Resistance's plan anymore. I'm afraid you might be right about him—at least partly. I wish we had all the time in the world for you to be the injured party and to heal and all that, but we don't. I can't do this alone. I need your help."

She looked frightened, but she didn't refuse, so Tommy laid out his plan, half making it up as he went along. "Atari likes to be in control and believe he's the smartest one in the room. If we put him on the spot or see him freaking out, he'll get defensive and shut down. But if we let him come to us, he may tell us more than we want to know. So will you go out with me tomorrow night?"

"You mean out of this room?"

"Yeah, but also out, like, on an old-fashioned date. We can go spend time in the common area and act like everything is great between us. He'll get jealous if we're totally wrapped up in each other, because he needs to be the center of attention."

"I don't want him anywhere near me."

"I don't want him anywhere near you either. But since you flirted with him, he might try to impress you."

She sighed. "I don't know."

"He thinks we've been in here doing it nonstop since you arrived."

She curled her lip. "Eww. What makes you think that?"

"Umm, he's mentioned it a few times."

"Okay, but I'm only going along with this to prove I was right. What time are you picking me up?"

"Umm, how about seven? I need some prep time."

Chapter 11

Jaycee found a can of powdered cleanser in one of the kitchen cabinets, sprinkled it liberally, and then set to work on the soap scum in Eduardo's dingy stainless steel sink.

Lara came into the room. "You're not the maid, sweetie. You don't have to clean." She put the kettle on the stove and rummaged in the cabinet for teabags.

"It's all right. Gives me something to do." She applied herself to a stubborn spot. "Besides, Eduardo doesn't seem to have anyone but us to look out for him." Her own network of people was nearly as limited, and she meant to do something about that.

Soon the sink was sparkling clean, and she rinsed her hands and retrieved the clumsily wrapped gift from her messenger bag. "Here. I found this at the market and thought you might like it."

"For me? Thank you, sweetheart." Lara unfolded the paper and lifted out the plate. "It's in perfect condition!" Then she laughed. "I tell you what—we'll take turns eating off it, all right?" She set the plate on the counter, Jaycee still hovering at her elbow.

"Lara?"

"Yes, sweetie?"

"I asked you once before, and, well, I just wondered if you thought more about helping me find my mama?"

Lara bit her lip as she pondered the question. She knew how Mitch felt about Jaycee's mother. She'd promised him she'd look after the girl and protect her. But maybe giving Jaycee some options —and some perspective—wasn't the worst thing in the world. She picked up her cup of tea and motioned for Jaycee to follow her into the living room.

Lara settled on the sofa next to Jaycee and studied the girl for a moment before she spoke. "I just want to make sure you know you have … choices. Do you understand? We tend to go through life thinking and believing one way. It's okay to take a hard look at your life and realize you can make changes.

"You don't have to be part of the Resistance if you don't want to. It's good and healthy to reexamine our priorities and goals every so often. You're in a new place, and you're seeing the world differently."

"Oh, I want to be part of the Resistance. But I'd like to at least have the chance to know something about my mother."

"Do you really want the whole story?"

Jaycee's eyes lit up. "Yes!"

"Do you remember anything about her?"

"No. Daddy said the whole Resistance thing was too much for her, and she just took off one day. I was too young to remember her, and he wouldn't tell me anything more. I've never even seen a picture of her. I'm so tired of secrets."

Lara sighed. "No more secrets? That's easier said than done. Some of my own are so deeply woven into my life that it's almost impossible to talk about my past without dredging up a few. Can I count on you not to mention the things you hear today—at least not without asking me first?"

The girl nodded.

"When I was younger, my best friend and I shared all our secrets. She knew things I couldn't even tell Tom.

"One of those secrets was what I did at my job. When Tom and I started seeing each other, I told him I was a paper pusher at a boring administrative job, and because of the confidential nature of the material, I couldn't talk about it outside of the office, you know? But I was really one of the first generation of professional Watchers, back in the days before the OCSD took power. And I was assigned to watch Tom Bailey."

Jaycee gasped. "Really?"

Lara laughed and crossed her heart. "Scout's honor. He was my first assignment when I was promoted to field agent. I soon concluded that he was no terrorist. I found that I admired his convictions and his views on how to make the world a better place.

He was smart, and funny, and attractive. Tommy looks like his father did when he was younger."

Jaycee nodded.

"We fell in love and got married. I was his wife, but I was also the one who knew how to keep his secrets safe. Tom was a law professor at the university, and when I became pregnant, he was earning enough that he encouraged me to quit my job, at least for a while. I wanted to stay home with our baby, but I knew that by quitting, I wouldn't be able to protect Tom as effectively as I had in the past.

"After I left my job, there was a huge reorganization in the security and surveillance departments. Not long after Tommy was born, I was surfing online one day while he napped—"

"How do you surf on a line?"

"I believe I saw a set of encyclopedias at the boardinghouse?"

"Yeah."

"Well, it's like browsing through one of those, looking for information, except on the computer. We used to be able to have access to almost anything under the sun on the Internet. I stopped by the login page for my old job, typed in my password just for nostalgia's sake, and discovered that somehow, my clearance had never been revoked. I logged in, but logged back out right away, terrified that my office would contact me and ask what in the world I was doing. But they never did. Before long, I couldn't resist the temptation, and I logged in again.

"I used that administrative error to check every so often, to make sure Tom wasn't in danger of being arrested. He tended to speak his mind then, just as he does now, and many of his opinions weren't popular with the people in power in the government.

"I missed living in an adult world. Sometimes I found it hard to stay at home with a small child. Tom was a wonderful father, but he was also gone a lot. Tommy was a high-energy toddler, and when Tom noticed I was feeling particularly worn-out, he suggested a girls' weekend with my friend. Nothing fancy, just a road trip for a couple of days.

"Of course I was pleased that Tom had noticed I needed a break. My friend and I packed our bags and drove south, to what used to be known as Kentucky, and rented a cabin at a resort with a lake. Maybe you can guess the one I'm talking about?"

Jaycee nodded vigorously, her curls tumbling into her face.

"While we were there, we met a nice-looking young guy who worked at the resort. Even though he was a few years younger than we were, he started hanging out with us. I'm afraid I wasn't all that entertaining to be around. I was so tired, and I preferred to read a book on the dock and catch up on my sleep. By the time our stay was up, I felt rejuvenated, and my friend and that young man had become inseparable.

"What might have been nothing more than a weekend fling had lasting repercussions. A few months later, my friend told me *her* biggest secret. She was going to have a baby."

Jaycee twisted her fingers and bounced up and down on her seat.

"They got married right away. He had a big family who welcomed her wholeheartedly. Her family, on the other hand, didn't know what to make of her choice, and it wasn't long before she became estranged from them. After a while she stopped communicating with me, as well. I never opposed her marriage, and it hurt when she shut me out of her life.

"About a year later, she showed up alone. No phone call, no advance warning. I was delighted to see her, but she cried and cried and wouldn't tell me what had happened, just that it was over. She was sure she'd never be able to see her daughter again."

"What did you do?"

"Well, I couldn't get any more details out of her, so I dug around a little on my own. Mind you, I still don't know the whole story, just what I read in the official reports. A few years later, your dad contacted me. I thought he was ready to get back in touch with your mom and make amends, but instead, he wanted me to do some investigative work for him. He knew everything I'd shared with her about myself and about Tom.

"I agreed to help him, figuring it would keep my professional skills sharp and also keep the door open, just in case your dad really wanted your mother back but was too proud to say so. I never thought that what he knew about Tom and me could come back to haunt us someday."

Jaycee's voice was barely above a whisper. "Do you know where she is now?"

"Oh, yes. After some time had passed and it was clear your dad wasn't interested in reconciliation, Tom and I introduced her to a friend, and after a while they got married. She never had any other children. She lives about half a mile from here."

Chapter 12

Tommy wiped his sweaty palms on his jeans as he leaned against the wall outside Command Central. His nervousness was genuine and not just because of their plan. Atari stuck his head out the door and made an impatient face. "Why are you lurking in the hall?"

He shrugged. "Girls take forever to get ready."

"Ready for what?"

Tommy let the insinuation pass, determined not to let Atari bait him. "We have dinner plans."

"Well, you have to eat sooner or later to keep up your strength. You've been behind the Do Not Disturb sign ever since she got here." He wiggled his eyebrows. "So ... just between us ... was it worth the wait? Or is she too much for you?"

If Atari ever found out he'd been sleeping in a chair, he'd never hear the end of it. Tommy forgot he was playing it cool and responded with a rude gesture. "Hardly."

"Ha! I see what you did there. You don't have to get testy about it. By all means, ply the pretty lass with food. I've got better things to do." He slammed the door, and Tommy grinned at Atari's feigned disinterest. Was it really going to be that easy to draw him out?

At seven p.m. sharp, Careen emerged in jeans and an emerald-green sweater with a neckline that did more than hint at her cleavage. She'd swept her hair up into an artfully messy ponytail with a few loose strands framing her face and concealed the last tinges of yellow-and-green bruising around her eye with makeup she'd found in the well-stocked bathroom. She'd applied a hint of eyeliner and lip gloss and powdered over the nearly healed gash on her cheek.

"You look great." He lifted her chin for a strawberry-flavored kiss that lingered a bit longer than she might have liked. He knew he was taking a liberty, but Atari was certain to be watching. "Hungry?"

She nodded and took his hand, and as he led her into the dining area, she sniffed the air and her eyes lit up. "Did you make pizza?"

"Yeah."

"It's been—"

"Forever. I know."

He led her to a table in a corner of the room and pulled out her chair. She smiled, almost unwillingly, as she sat. He saw Atari duck back around the corner as he headed into the kitchen.

As Tommy returned, carrying the fragrant pizza aloft on his fingertips, he scratched the side of his nose with his other hand, which was the agreed-upon signal that they were being watched. She applauded as he slid the pan onto the table, and they both dug in as if they didn't have a care in the world.

Soon she popped a bite of crust into her mouth and wiped her fingers on her napkin. "You're pretty good at this first date thing. Should I be jealous? How many other first dates have you had?"

"Umm ... none. Not really. Unless you count our Essential Services smorgasbord on the day we met."

"I don't think you can have two first dates with the same person."

Oh, good. A little teasing banter. She really is in there, somewhere. "Fair enough. This one should count as our official first date. I've watched lots of old movies. Pretty sure this is what people did on dates when our grandparents were teenagers." He served them each another slice.

The video games whirred and chirped in the background as they ate. Careen looked over his shoulder into the gallery. He asked, "Have you ever tried any of those games?"

"No, I've never seen any of them before."

"Let's go play one."

They left the table and she wandered around the arcade-like room, looking at the brightly colored images on the screens. "How about this one? Asteroids."

"Okay." He stood close behind her, reached his arms around her to take the controls, and settled his chin on her shoulder. The first round was a tutorial, and he spoke near her ear as he played.

"The object is to break up the asteroids before they hit your spaceship. Use the roller ball to rotate the ship, and hit this button to fire." His lips brushed her cheek as he pushed the Reset button. "Your turn."

At first she giggled helplessly as the asteroids threatened, but it was so good to hear her laugh that he didn't care if she never caught on. As soon as she mastered the controls, her demeanor hardened until the competition felt more like a power struggle than a friendly game.

Seriously? No way was he going to knuckle under and let her win. He took his turn. "Ha! Beat you again."

She stuck out her tongue at him. "Fine. Let's try a different one."

"Centipede? Q-Bert? Pac-Man?"

"I want a fair chance. Which one haven't you tried? Or do you know how to play them all?"

"I've tried most of them. I've been here a lot longer than you."

"Okay, then let's play Centipede. The controls look the same."

"Yeah. Use the roller ball to move the garden gnome and shoot the centipede before it gets to the bottom of the screen."

"Me first." The game started off slowly, and she yelped when the pace increased. "Whoa! It just split in two!" She tapped the Fire button as fast as she could.

"Blast those mushrooms out of the way. That'll slow down the centipede." He smiled at the focus and concentration on her face. "Look out for the spider!"

She zapped it into oblivion, and when the game was over, she'd won by a lot. While she tried to figure out how to add her name to the list of high scores, he wandered over to the neon-lighted jukebox, flipped through the playlist, and made a selection.

She turned around. "All this and music too?"

"Yeah. Most of the tracks are pretty cheesy, but this one's good." He took her hand. "Wanna dance?"

She stepped into his arms and laid her head on his chest, and they swayed in time to the music. He waited a verse before he spoke. "I like your hair this way." He brushed his fingers against the side of her neck, and she sighed and nestled closer.

How could something as simple as slow dancing be so hypnotic? He wanted to freeze time until he was sure she felt it too. To hell with

Atari, Madalyn, and the rest of the world. Right now all he wanted was a lifetime of ordinary moments.

As soon as the song ended, she slipped out of his embrace and beckoned him over to the Wild Gunman game, where she posed with the plastic six-shooter. "We have to try this one." He watched while she drew down against caricatured desperadoes of all descriptions, until the guy in the serape was too quick. "See if you can win the tie-breaker." She held out the gun.

As Tommy hesitated, Atari's voice came from behind him. "Dude, when you gonna get back on that horse?"

He whirled around. "Mind your own business for once, will you?"

"What does he mean?"

Atari jaw fell open in exaggerated surprise. "You mean you didn't tell her?"

"I didn't tell you, so why would I tell her?"

Careen laid down the toy gun. "What are you talking about?"

"It's hard to keep secrets here." Atari flashed his wolf-like smile at her. "Careen, Danni's clothes flatter you. That sweater's a particular favorite of mine. Clingy. Sends all the right signals." Atari's eyes raked her, and she retreated behind Tommy, digging her fingers into his arm.

"Leave her alone." Tommy grabbed a handful of Atari's shirt, pulled him up on tiptoe, and stared down at him.

"Thought you didn't like video games." Atari twisted out of his grip and skulked away down the hall.

Tommy muttered to Careen, "Well, we called that right, even though we couldn't predict what he'd say to get attention." He pulled her back into their slow-dance cuddle.

She pushed against him. "The music's over."

"Doesn't matter. Please stay." After a moment she relaxed a bit, and they swayed on the spot until he mustered the courage to speak. "I never told you why I'm here instead of with the rest of the Resistance. Some bad stuff happened to me after the explosion too." He took a deep breath and kept his gaze fixed over her head. "A couple days after I got back to BG-098, they announced on PeopleCam that you were in custody and cooperating with the OCSD's investigation into the bombing. We figured the quadrant marshals would be coming for us sooner or later, so we made a plan to evacuate. My dad decided to turn himself in and give the rest of us time to get away. But I couldn't let him do that. He's too idealistic, you know?

"Jaycee and I got everyone else to safety, and then I took off after my dad. By the time I got back to the diner, marshals were already there. I hid in the bushes and watched. Apparently Dad managed to convince them he was on his own and that he'd never met Mitch before. A local marshal backed Mitch up, said there was no way he was in the Resistance, so the rest of them put my dad in handcuffs and took him to the capital.

"At least that's what Mitch said when I went inside. He didn't want me to go after my dad, but I didn't care. I was ready. I had the keys to the truck in my hand. Then, all of a sudden, one of the marshals was there. He'd thought something was fishy and doubled back.

"He held us at gunpoint and demanded to know where to find the others. Made some crack about looking forward to tracking down my mom." He shuddered. "Then Danni came through the door with a big box of groceries and startled him. There was no time to think about it. I drew and fired. And I killed him."

She stared, tears glistening in her eyes. He sniffed and turned his face away, trying not to cry. "It happened really fast. Before I knew it, Danni got me in her truck, and we were on our way here."

"You've been in hiding with Atari nearly the whole time?" He thought he heard a hint of a laugh. It broke the tension, and he sighed.

"Yeah. I had a chance to leave with my dad and go back to OP-439, but I said no. By then Atari knew where you were, and I wasn't going home without you. I've been stuck with Atari for weeks, and, believe me, I've suffered plenty." He took both her hands in his. "But there's no way to compare my situation to what you went through. When you pointed my gun at me, it freaked me out. A lot. I hope you can understand why I had to disarm you, even if it meant hurting you. I knew you were frightened, but so was I."

She looked like she was going to cry. "Can you ever forgive me?"

"It's not your fault. You didn't know."

"But it is my fault! I told the people who interrogated me how to find the diner. If I hadn't—"

"No." He fixed his gaze on hers. "That doesn't matter."

"I tried to protect you. I just ... couldn't."

"I know. You don't have to apologize. For any of it."

"But I am sorry. So sorry . . ." Her lips sought his, and as he clung to her, he forgot about Atari's treachery and the Resistance's revolution on the horizon. At this moment, there was only Careen, warm and soft and mostly unbroken, despite everything she'd endured. The video games around them chirped and whirred victoriously.

She whispered in his ear. "This was a good first date."

"Did you get enough to eat?"

"Yes. I really did."

"I'm still hungry." He'd seen a flicker of movement near where Atari had left the arcade, so he took her hand and led her across the lobby and down the hall.

She looked over her shoulder. "The kitchen's the other way."

"I didn't say I wanted food." He pulled her close and buried his face in her neck, whispering, "He's still watching."

She giggled and squirmed as though he was tickling her. He pressed her against the wall and kissed her deeply, letting his hands roam just a little, for effect, before he hurried her into his room. When they were alone, he kissed her once more for good measure.

This time, she pushed him away. "Slow down a little, okay?"

"What? You were great. It worked."

"I disagree. We already knew Atari thrives on voyeurism. We didn't learn anything about why he's panicking and yelling at Mitch."

"If we keep acting like we're having fun together, he'll butt in and try to ruin it by telling us something he thinks will upset us. I guarantee whatever he's yelling at Mitch about will upset us too."

She folded her arms. "I said I'd act like we're together when Atari can see us. That's all I can handle right now."

"So you weren't being sincere when you said you were sorry? You were pretty convincing. I thought we just had a moment out there."

"I am sorry about what happened to you, but I felt pressured to kiss you."

More lies. His anger flared, but he tried to keep his voice from showing it. "I didn't pressure you, and I'd never jerk you around like that. My feelings for you haven't changed. Don't you remember?"

She didn't answer.

"Okay, fine. Have it your way." She'd agreed to pretend to be in love with him. It was a start. Maybe someday it wouldn't be an act.

Chapter 13

It was all Lara could do to prevent Jaycee from leaving Eduardo's apartment before dawn.

"Sweetheart, she won't even be awake yet. No one is awake yet." She took a sip of coffee. "We'll go over in a few hours."

"What'll I say to her when I see her?"

"I don't know. I suppose you'll say whatever seems right." What, indeed? The same question had been troubling Lara ever since she'd offered to introduce the girl to her mother. Jaycee had no memory of her, and Lara had last seen her the previous July, on the night of the car accident that had torn apart her family.

Once her memory had returned, Tom had broken the news that his best friend had been an informant for the OCSD. That she believed. But was his wife complicit? *She was my best friend. I don't want to believe she would hurt me on purpose.*

Was she doing the right thing? She'd made the offer to introduce Jaycee to her mother while she was angry about Mitch's neglectful conduct. Had she overstepped her responsibility to care for the girl? Jaycee had a right to know her mother, but would she live up to her hopes and be a positive force in her life? Or was she merely the lesser of two evils?

Jaycee did her hair ten different ways before she was satisfied, and dragged Lara out the door the minute the clock struck nine. Lara kept to the alleys behind the houses as they drove the short distance in Eduardo's truck.

"Why don't you let me go to the door alone, first? I think it might be good if I prepare her for the surprise."

"All right." The girl could barely conceal her excitement and seemed sure that the surprise would be a good thing.

Lara pulled into the alley behind the house and parked the truck near the garage, out of sight of the main road. She wiped her sweaty palms on her jeans as she crossed the driveway. Her knees trembled a little as she climbed the porch steps and tapped on the back door.

Someone drew back the curtain on the door and one eye peered out. Lara heard her name and then the click of tumblers moving in three locks. Beth Severson opened the door and flung her arms around Lara, who staggered back a step.

Beth held her close and kept her voice low. "I thought you were dead! When did you get here? Are you all right? Where's Tom?" Then she grew silent, and her grasp on Lara loosened. "Who's that?"

Lara turned. Jaycee was waving out the passenger window.

"Beth, umm, as you can see, your daughter's anxious to meet you."

"My ... who?" She swayed on the spot and gripped the door-frame. "Are you sure?"

"Oh, quite sure."

"Does Mitch know she's here?"

Lara shook her head and motioned for Jaycee to join them.

Jaycee hurried onto the porch, where she halted behind Lara and ducked her head a little. "Pleased to meet you, ma'am."

Beth's chin trembled and she reached out to touch Jaycee's curls. "You're so grown up."

"I'm fifteen."

She glanced around and held open the door. "Come in, both of you. We shouldn't stay out in the open like this."

Lara looked over her own shoulder before she stepped inside and shut the door. "Are we safe here?"

"Of course."

"Where's Art?"

"We're not together anymore." Beth led them through the kitchen and the butler's pantry to the dining room. Soon, she was pouring coffee. Lara watched Jaycee take in the opulent surroundings with wide eyes. Unlike the Bailey home, the Seversons' had not been ransacked, and everything was neat and in pristine condition. Like a museum.

No one seemed to know how to begin the conversation. Lara's cup clinked against its saucer. "Would you two like some time alone to get acquainted?"

Jaycee nodded, curls bouncing around her shoulders, and Beth smiled. "Yes. I just want you to know, Lara, that I treasured the time Tommy and I had together after the accident. He's such a fine young man. I thought for a while it might turn into something more permanent, but"—Lara bristled without really understanding why. Beth tossed her head and continued—"well, I'm certainly glad you're all right. It did make me envious of you, not because of what happened, of course, but because you'd been able to watch him grow up." She picked at a perfectly manicured nail. "I guess what I mean is, thank you for doing this. I won't ever forget it."

9:25 AM
Quadrant DC-001

Pete Sheridan shook his head as he added new footage to his video archive. PeopleCam local affiliates from all over the country had been sending images of crowds massed in front of Distribution Centers, beating on the doors and demanding to be Linked.

The CXD protesters had bolstered their ranks, now that counter-protesters had showed up. The opposing groups waved their signs, shouting and chanting, their voices mingling with those of the frantic parents with their children in tow.

One young man made a heart with his hands for whoever was recording the video. "I just want to send out a message to Madalyn Davies and the OCSD—we stand with you! We pledge to do whatever we can to help get the Linking underway. Ask not what your country can do for you, right?"

Another man who clutched a sign and held his bare left wrist aloft, fist clenched, pushed him aside and spoke to the camera. "No! That's not freedom, man! The Link is like Big Brother. No Links! No Links!"

Someone shoved him from behind and the two protest groups spilled into one another. Signs wavered and fell like battle flags as their bearers were swept up in the melee.

How does Madalyn Davies do it? People are so willing to believe her lies. Maybe it's because most of them would be too frightened to see the truth, even if we were allowed to show it to them.

9:42 AM
Quadrant DC-005

Careen heard Tommy stir across the darkened room. For days she'd believed he was her assassin; now, her shattered trust had begun to knit, and an unfamiliar feeling stirred inside her. Optimism? Maybe. She let her lips form his name. Even without being able to see him, she knew exactly how he looked when he was asleep. Her face flushed, and she pushed away memories of kisses given and received a lifetime ago, chiding herself for longing for his touch. She'd agreed to pretend everything was great between them to help ferret out Atari's dark secrets, but she didn't trust her own judgment when it came to Tommy. She envisioned a short leap from acting like she cared about him to resuming their physical relationship. She didn't know if she'd ever be ready for that. It hurt too much to love people and then lose them.

She switched on the lamp. Tommy got up from the pallet he'd made on the floor, dragged one of the blankets around his shoulders, and sat on the edge of the bed.

"Hungry?"

"You always, always ask that."

"That's because I'm always, always ready for breakfast."

"Yes, you are. Today I am too."

"Good. First dibs on the shower." He tossed the blanket at her playfully, and she couldn't help casting an admiring glance at his broad shoulders as he headed for the bathroom. She held the still-warm blanket close. His scent lingered in the folds, and she smiled in spite of herself. *See? He did that on purpose.*

Steeling herself for another uncomfortable interaction with Atari, she brought the gun from under her pillow, climbed out of bed, and hid it between the folded clothes she planned to wear.

An hour later, she found herself casting more admiring glances Tommy's way as she helped him prepare bacon, eggs, and toast. He seemed so at ease, no matter what he was feeling inside, and it was easier than she'd expected to keep playing her part. She let him feed her a bite off his fork, and they were both laughing when Atari poked his head in the door.

"Don't you two ever give it a rest?" His clothes were wrinkled and stained, his lank hair greasier than usual, and as he drew near, Careen wrinkled her nose at the odor of stale sweat.

"What's up, Atari?" Tommy seemed not to notice the other man's appearance, and Careen followed his lead.

"Careen's back in the headlines."

Tommy grabbed Careen by the hand, and they ran past Atari and into Command Central. "I thought you said PeopleCam wasn't reporting anything about Careen."

Atari followed them. "A lot has happened while you were sleeping —or whatever it is you two have been doing. The press—mostly Sheila Roth, she's the only one who can get away with it—has been pushing to know why Careen's been out of the limelight. Once Madalyn figured out how to spin the situation to her advantage, she released the hounds." He made a snarling sound and bared his teeth in a more frightening version of his odd smile. Careen shrank closer to Tommy.

Atari started the playback of Madalyn's announcement. "It is with regret that I report that Link spokesperson Careen Catecher vanished without a trace last week. Though she was one of the first recipients of a Link, the system, which is not yet activated, is incapable of locating her. The need to expedite the Linking is clear. The Resistance is responsible for Careen's disappearance and for the delays that have threatened the security of the people who want to claim it for themselves and their families."

Atari snorted as he paused the recording. "They won't report that shipments of Links have been hijacked or show video of the protesters outside the Distribution Centers."

Careen went cold with the realization that she'd been right all along. Her supposed rescue was just part of a larger plan. Her disappearance was being used to prove the need to Link every child.

"So you brought me here and hid me away so I could be the Link's martyr figure?"

Tommy shook his head. "No, that's not it."

"It might as well be." Atari wiggled his fingers and made a scary face. "They need to frighten everyone into submission, so they've turned the spotlight on you again. Poor Careen, she's been kidnapped by the evil Resistance! When people panic and demand that their children be Linked, they'll do it because of you."

She shook her head and squeezed her eyes shut. "Why are you blaming me when you're the one who created the Link? You're trying to trick me and make me say something I shouldn't."

"Oh, Careen. You're imprisoned and your Link isn't even activated. The Resistance—"

Her voice turned accusing. "I don't believe you're working for the Resistance. If you were, you wouldn't let the Link exist. You're not fighting it. You're making it happen."

"I'm not making anything happen."

"I was right all along. You're going to force Tommy to kill me and dump my body someplace conspicuous, aren't you?"

Atari's temper flared, and he raised his voice. "Dumping bodies is not the Resistance's *modus operandi*. That's more the OCSD's thing. You still don't understand who the real enemy is, do you, chickie?" He seized a keyboard. "Let me show you proof."

Careen stared, uncomprehending, at the image that appeared on the screen. She saw a tangle of wet, dark seaweed flowing around something pale, with a spreading black pool of sludge beneath it. Tommy swore behind her. Then, through the seaweed, Careen recognized a brown eye that could have been her own, and she swayed on the spot. Black snow clouded her vision, and she gasped for air.

"Shot and killed while trying to escape from prison?" Atari snorted. "Oh, please. They don't even try to make it convincing anymore."

Chapter 14

10:00 AM
Quadrant OP-439

As soon as the door closed behind Lara, Beth took Jaycee by the arm and led her into the living room. "What did Lara tell you about ... everything?"

"She told me a lot. But I want to hear it from you."

"And your father?"

"My daddy never said much about you, except that you left because you couldn't handle life in the Resistance."

"I see. Well. Some of what I'm going to tell you is still a secret."

Jaycee nodded, sighing on the inside. *More secrets.*

"Lara wouldn't want Tom to know that he was nothing more to her than a work assignment. She was investigating him because he was in trouble for speaking out against the government. They wanted assurances that he wasn't going to start a revolution. Even after all these years, it would wound his ego to know she wasn't attracted to him at first." Beth giggled. "Lara actually fostered the relationship between Mitch and Tom, after years of keeping them apart. When she realized Tom wasn't going to let up in his fight against Lowell Stratford and the OCSD, she decided Mitch could be an important ally. Mitch needed a front man, and Tom needed a stronger faction behind him. Perfect Lara set the whole thing up."

"She and my dad are friends."

"Your dad doesn't have actual friends. Lara's afraid to get on his bad side. Secrets can hurt a marriage. She's not taking any chances." She picked up Jaycee's hand. Jaycee settled closer to her on the sofa. "Sometimes the things we say come back to haunt us. I learned that the hard way."

"When I left OP-439 to marry Mitch, Lara was one of the few people who supported me. Things were already starting to change in the more urban quadrants, and she encouraged me to go have lots of babies and raise my family far away from all the crazy things that were going on.

"That sounded like a good plan. When the OCSD rose to power, the changes were rapid and frightening. I wanted you to grow up unafraid. I thought we would have a good, simple life running a resort in the mountains.

"Wes and Danni were in elementary school. Your family was kind to me, and I thought you and your future siblings would have a wonderful life, surrounded by loving grandparents and lots of aunts, uncles, and cousins.

"Maybe I felt at home there because it was where your father and I fell in love. We loved each other very much, but I was still an outsider in the eyes of many of the locals. One afternoon I had gone into the nearby town to do some shopping. I'd called Lara, because we'd found out we were going to have a girl and I wanted to tell her. I made some joke about you being the latest outlaw in the clan, and said, 'I'd rather raise an outlaw than someone who kowtows to the OCSD.' I thought it was romantic and thrilling that his family eschewed the law and that they had, shall we say, a colorful history. Someone overheard me. They reported what I said, and the next day, troops raided the resort, looking for evidence of guns, drugs, and who knows what else.

"Mitch and I had taken Wes and Danni out on the lake, and we were too far away to be noticed. When we heard gunfire, we hurried back to shore. Mitch left me there with the children and ran home, but it was too late. Of Mitch's entire family, his mother was the only one present at the raid who survived."

Tears streamed down Jaycee's face. "No one ever told me any of this."

"Your father was devastated, and there was a dark cloud over the remaining months of my pregnancy. Your grandmother was slow to recover from the injuries she'd suffered in the raid, and I spent a lot of time being her nurse, while trying to keep an eye on Danni and Wes. Your grandmother insisted on acting as midwife when you were born, and we named you for her. She was so happy to have a granddaughter; she would have loved to watch you grow up, but she died when you were just a few months old. Then he and I were alone with three children. The neighbors stayed away, fearful that a close association with us would bring the law to their own doors. Your dad's grasp on reality seemed to slip. He became paranoid and angry.

"He insisted on keeping the children—all that was left of the family—together. Danni was in fifth grade then and Wes in the first. Mitch was still so young—far too young to take on everything the way he did. We tried to keep the resort going, but obviously our professional reputation suffered. We hoped the summer regulars would keep some money coming in, and we hired a few employees, but when the Travel Restrictions went into effect later that year, the rest of the business dried up, and we had to close down.

"So there we were, with a huge, empty park and a diner—and no income to speak of. He brooded and questioned why his family had been slaughtered for seemingly no reason, until one day I broke down and confessed that something I'd said could have sparked the raid." She wiped away a tear. "He got so angry. He ordered me to get out, and swore he'd never let me see you again.

"I didn't know what else to do but come back home. He raised you children on his own, ran the diner, and apparently planned a revolution in his spare time. I never told my second husband about any of it."

Jaycee chewed her bottom lip. "What did Lara think of all this?"

"Lara's always had a good poker face."

"Why didn't you tell her what happened? She was your best friend. She would have understood."

"Over the years, she pieced a lot of the story together. I thought it was my problem, and my shame to bear. I'm sorry I wasn't there for you when you were younger." She wrapped her arms around the girl. "I've missed out on so much of your life."

"There is something you can do for me." Jaycee reached for her coat and pulled the folded pages out of the pocket. "This is all I need for my future. Right here."

Beth glanced through the death benefit forms. "I'll sign them, but we'll still have to set up a debit account before you can get the money."

"Can't you just put the money in your debit account and then give it to me?"

"How, sweetheart? There isn't physical, touchable money to give you. It's all done electronically."

The girl's face fell. "Yeah, you're right."

"Give me some time to think about how to take care of it. Will you come back say, Wednesday?"

She nodded and stepped into her mother's arms. Beth held her for as long as Jaycee would allow and then watched her leave by the back door.

Chapter 15

"Oh my God, that's my mom!" Tears sprang up in Careen's eyes. She covered her face with her hands and turned her back to the screen. Tommy reached out and touched her shoulder, but she sidestepped him and turned a venomous gaze on them both. "It's all your fault for getting her involved. The Resistance might as well have killed her!" She bolted from the room.

Tommy advanced on Atari, arms wide in disbelief. "Tell me why that was a good idea."

Atari shrugged. "She had a right to know."

Tommy slammed his fists into Atari's stomach and kidneys and finished with a stinging right cross to the jaw. Atari fell back against the desk, protecting himself with his arms.

"That sums up how I feel about you. You could've figured out a better way to tell her." Tommy pointed a threatening finger as he headed for the door. "We are not finished. Understand?" He turned the corner and ran after Careen, and saw her skid to a stop on the far side of the lobby, jabbing the button to summon the elevator. The gurgle of the fountain masked the sound of his approach, and she jumped when he spoke behind her. "The elevator doesn't work without the key. It's too cold to go out without shoes or a coat. Where are you headed?"

"Anywhere but here. You should have left me with Madalyn. Then none of this would've happened."

"Why don't you get it? Leaving you with Madalyn was worse than any of the fallout we're facing now. You may not even realize what it did to you, but I can tell by your night terrors that there's a lot of stuff you're not acknowledging or dealing with."

He took a step closer, and she pulled the gun from her waistband. "Get away from me. I meant to fix things with my mom. Now I'll never get to tell her I was sorry."

"It sucks, okay? We didn't mean for this to happen. She wanted to help you. She knew what she was getting into—"

She swung the pistol at his head. He ducked, and as he recovered, she gasped in surprise and brought her free hand up to her face. A moment later, her eyes rolled back in her head, and she fell forward into his arms. The gun clattered to the floor as he caught her, and he staggered under the unexpected burden. Atari joined him, clutching a thin bamboo stick, and Tommy's voice reflected his panic. "What happened? Did she faint?"

"Dude, she pulled a gun on you! I believe thanks are in order." Atari cupped Careen's chin in his hand and plucked something small and feathered that was stuck to her neck just below her ear. He held it up with a grin. "Malaysian poison blow dart. I'm an excellent shot."

"What the—poisoned dart? What did you do to her?" He shook her to try and rouse her, and her head lolled from side to side. He put his ear close to her face, and his own heart seemed to restart when he heard her take a breath. "She's not dead!"

Atari waved the bamboo stick. "Of course she's not dead. Her Link is still flashing, see? Chill! As for this, it's like a glorified peashooter. The dart was tipped with CSD, to calm her down." He regarded Careen with curiosity. "I see she's lost her tolerance for Phase Two."

"She never took Phase Two at all!"

"No big deal. She'll sleep it off, and tomorrow she won't remember a thing."

"Give it." Tommy shifted Careen so he was cradling her in his left arm and held out his hand for the bamboo shoot. Atari surrendered it, and Tommy dropped it on the floor, where he smashed it beneath his heel. "The gun wasn't even loaded, you idiot. Just quit trying to help when you have no idea what's going on." He lifted her into his arms, cradling her against his chest, and carried her out of the lobby.

Careen came back to a semiconscious state with a sigh, and tears welled up in her eyes when she recognized him. "Tommy. I looked for you everywhere, but I couldn't find you. Where's Wes?"

Tommy bit his lip. "Wes got out the other way."

She looked back over his shoulder. "We have to hide. The marshals are everywhere."

"We can hide in here." He set her down in their room and then turned back to lock the door.

She shook her head slowly, her face reflecting the effort it took to concentrate. "No, wait. That's wrong. The explosion was a long time ago, wasn't it? Wes is dead, like my dad. And now my mom, too."

"There have been a lot of accidents."

"Poor Wes. He kissed me. He asked me to choose him, but I didn't, because I love you. And he died."

She spoke as though she was recalling something she'd been told, and wasn't sure if it was real or imagined. The effort of dredging up her thoughts seemed to burden her.

"I lied to protect the Resistance, and that made Madalyn angry. I could hear her shouting in the hall outside my hospital room. The next time I woke up, I wasn't at the hospital anymore.

"The people who interrogated me made me stand for hours at a time with a hood over my head. Other times I had to watch news reports about the food riots while they told me the riots and the resulting deaths were my fault. They shouted and hit me a lot. I wasn't allowed to sleep. They said I was stupid to think you cared about me, and I believed them when no one came to help me. The torture and the humiliation would never end, they said, until I told where to find Trina and Resistance headquarters. After I did, they didn't hurt me as often."

Tears stung Tommy's eyes. *She's not going to remember saying any of this, and I'm never going to be able to forget it.* He wanted to hold her, but he realized any gesture would be for his comfort, not hers. He clenched his fists.

She held up her hand and examined it, and waved her fingers. "Pink is coming out of my fingertips, like when I was on CSD." She eyed him suspiciously. "Is that why I feel so strange?"

"Atari dosed you with Phase Two. You're going to be all right in a while, but you probably won't remember this."

She nodded without emotion. "That makes sense. You never remembered either."

That made him wonder what kinds of things he'd said when their situation had been reversed.

"Tommy?"

"Yeah?"

She scrutinized his face. "Do you want to kiss me? You look like you want to kiss me." She was leaning in, lips parted, when he stopped her. The CSD had definitely compromised her filter.

The come-hither look on her face reminded him of Atari's fantasy Careen in the dating sim video, and he tried not to laugh at the change in her. "That's usually a safe bet." She seemed to take that to mean it was all systems go and lunged at him, but he managed to turn the kiss into something that could have passed for brotherly. "Wait, stop." He brushed his fingertips across her cheek and traced the nearly healed scar. "If I kissed you right now, it could lead to a lot more. You're not ready. When it does happen, I want us both to remember it."

"Oh. All right." She nestled against his chest and sighed when he put his arms around her. "You don't have to sleep on the floor tonight."

He chuckled. "You'd better leave yourself a note in case you forget that you invited me to stay."

"Good idea." She climbed out of bed, crossed the room and wrote something on the notepad on the desk. She signed it with a flourish, folded it, and put it in the pocket of her jeans.

"What does it say?"

She shot him a look of drunken shrewdness. "You'll have to wait until tomorrow to find out."

She yawned, climbed back into bed, and was asleep in his arms in less than a minute.

11:45 AM

Atari wrapped a handful of ice cubes in a towel and held it to his swollen, bleeding lip. When his phone vibrated on the desk, he looked at the number on the display and chose to ignore the call from Mitch.

What was the logical next move? He stared at the checkerboard of monitors on the wall, but nothing came readily to mind. *This must be what writer's block feels like.*

The Link around Madalyn's wrist should have been a way for him to control her and force her to make decisions that worked with the Resistance's agenda. He'd been sure she'd want to scrap the whole program to avoid having her secrets made public. The transparency that was part of life with the Link should have damaged her image.

But somehow it had backfired. Even though the Link wasn't active and Madalyn lied with impunity, people now perceived her as honest and responsible because of the red plastic band on her wrist.

Expanding the Link program to include anyone who was arrested had caused a public outcry—but again, not about what he'd expected. He put his head in his hands, frustrated by the irony of the situation. Protesters and so-called dissidents who'd been arrested and Linked that week had fueled the anger of a growing number of adults who wanted Links for themselves, and left them more determined than ever to have them. The pro-Link segment of the population believed that they deserved the Links over criminals who were undermining the chance at security for the righteous and the blameless.

Even the shortage of available Links had worked to her advantage.

He designed video games that presented players with options and choices. The ones who made good choices could win. For those who made mistakes, it was game over.

He laced his fingers and stretched, cracking his knuckles. Too many people had made the wrong choice, and now Frankenstein's monster was on the loose.

Chapter 16

Madalyn stood at a podium in the Essential Services building's lobby, with the OCSD seal in front of her and a mural of a wheat field behind her. "Victor Martel's promise to the American people was misguided. Everyone believed him when he said the opt-out of Essential Services deliveries would begin on January first, but we are not prepared to transition. There is inadequate food available in the private sector. Essential Services will continue to provide sustenance for every American in 2035. Maybe change will be possible sometime in the future—just not now. No questions at this time."

Security guards flanked Madalyn on both sides and rushed her out of the building. As they emerged into the wintry day, protesters surged toward them. *Splat.* Something landed in her hair, and she glanced around. Pieces of rotten fruit clung to the security officers' black jackets. Something wet hit her cheek, and she held up a hand to protect her face. Shouting and chanting filled the air, but she didn't understand the words. The guards held her by the arms as they hustled her to the armored SUV. The door shut behind her and muffled the roar of the crowd. She exhaled.

Her phone rang and she dug it out of her purse. She'd missed another call from this number a few minutes before. "Hello?"

"Your payment is ready. It will be delivered to your office." It was the man who had approached her about buying the CSD formulas. His accent sounded foreign, though she couldn't place it.

They had never nailed down the specifics of how she would be paid. Madalyn felt her panic level rise again. "Don't you think a little discretion is in order? I thought you'd simply deposit it—"

"In your government account?" He harrumphed. "That would be too easily traceable. Payment will be made ... indirectly. What you do with it is up to you. But first I must have the formulas. All three phases of the Counteractive System of Defense, as you call it. Phase Three will give me total control over those who use it, correct?"

"Yes, yes of course. Total control. I can send the file from here." She sent the email she'd drafted. There was a pause on the other end of the line before he spoke again.

"It has arrived. Everything appears to be in order. Obviously, we will not be in contact after we terminate this call."

She cleared her throat. "Agreed."

"I hope we have no occasion to meet in the future." There was a beep, and he was gone.

The SUV pulled up in front of the OCSD building. "Everything all right, Madam?" the driver asked.

"Yes. Wait for me. I may be going back out after I freshen up." Madalyn slammed the car door and stomped inside. She ran her fingers through her hair in an attempt to remove the bits of food that clung to her golden coif and wrinkled her nose as she brushed at something sticky on her coat sleeve. She unbuttoned the coat, intending to have it sent to the laundry. She was wriggling out of the sleeves when a young man dashed into the building and headed straight for her. She screamed, and two security guards dive-tackled the man, pinning him to the floor at her feet.

"Ow! Jeez! I have an envelope ... urgent message for Director Davies. It's in my bag. I was supposed to deliver it ten minutes ago, but I couldn't get through the crowds in front of the Essential Services building."

One of the guards spoke from the pile. "You got a work ID?"

"Yes ... ow! I'm a courier for Get it There Yesterday. We deliver all over the capital quadrant. I've been here dozens of times before. Let me up."

The guards released him, and he pushed himself to his knees. As he reached inside his windbreaker, the guards drew their guns. He raised shaking hands above his head. "Chill! How am I supposed to show my ID if you won't let me get it?"

The guards slowly lowered their weapons, and the courier produced a laminated ID card on a lanyard around his neck. The guards hauled him to his feet. One of them rummaged in the man's bag and pulled out a large envelope. Madalyn extended her hand. "I'll take that, please. It's addressed to me."

The guard held it out of her reach. "No can do, Madam Director. Anything that arrives for you has to be inspected first." He eyed the envelope suspiciously and held it at arm's length as he carried it to the x-ray machine at the security desk and laid it on the conveyor belt. Madalyn followed him, and watched it trundle in one side and emerge on the other.

"Now will you kindly give it to me?"

"No, ma'am. We have to open it. I wouldn't be worthy of protecting you if I didn't follow protocol."

She considered snatching it out of his hand, running away, and locking herself in her office. How much information was in the envelope? How would she explain a receipt for a transfer of funds from a foreign country? She tried to appear calm as he painstakingly slit the envelope and drew out a single sheet of paper.

"It's a receipt." His lips moved as he read it to himself.

She made another grab for it. "A receipt? For what? Give it to me. It's my private business."

He finished reading and handed it to her. "There's a package on hold for you at the post office." He headed behind the security desk and muttered to himself as he pecked at the keyboard. "Nothing in the employee handbook about how to handle this." He picked up the phone.

Madalyn left her coat lying on the floor and, clutching the receipt, ran outside. Her driver was waiting at the front of the building and hurried around to open the car door for her. As soon as they were settled, she spoke. "Driver?"

"Yes, Madam Director?"

"Have you ever been inside a post office?"

He laughed. "Oh, yes, Madam. I spend lots of time standing in line."

"I'll have to stand in line? Oh, of all the ridiculous, time-wasting.... " She scanned the receipt for clues. It said nothing about the sender or what the package might contain. She handed it to him.

"Take me there right away so I can get this over with."

Wooden barricades sealed off a perimeter around the capital's main post office. The driver nudged the car close to the curb and parked. Just ahead, marshals in riot gear swarmed from SWAT team vehicles and patrol cars like a colony of invading ants headed for the front of the building.

Hoyt Garrick, walkie-talkie in hand, approached her car. She rolled down the window.

"Madam Director, OCSD Security mobilized the bomb squad and SWAT to deal with your suspicious package."

"There's ... I just want ... whatever it is." She handed the receipt out the window.

He scanned it and gave it back to her. "I understand, but in light of the current situation, it's prudent to let the bomb squad check things out first."

"Current situation?"

"People are angry about you reneging on the Essential Services opt-out. You were just attacked by a mob. We can't be too careful."

Madalyn got out of the car, hugging herself against the chilly December air, and watched customers and uniformed employees, ushered by members of the SWAT team, exiting the building.

A PeopleCam news crew's producer elbowed his way through the crowd, making way for the camera operator and Pete Sheridan. The toothy anchorman tugged a postal employee in front of the camera and, arm around the other man's shoulder, held out the microphone. Madalyn was too far away to hear what they were saying.

Her driver offered her his overcoat, and she draped it around her shoulders. After thirty minutes of standing in the cold, watching everyone rushing about, she retreated inside the car and folded her arms across her chest. How long was it going to take, anyway? She jumped when someone tapped on the window. It was Garrick. She rolled down the window.

"Here you are. I'll bring the rest of them out to you as soon as I can."

She got out and accepted the box. It was unexpectedly heavy, and she set it on the trunk with a thump. "The rest of them? I don't understand. How many are there?"

"Forty. Says so on your receipt. Apparently they're all that heavy. The bomb squad is checking them out, one by one."

"Well, what's inside?" Did she detect the hint of a smile? She tried to conceal the unease that welled up inside her.

"They didn't say." He chuckled. "Thought they might be a Christmas thing, or an early birthday gift of some kind. You have the big four-oh coming up this week, don't you, Madam Director?"

She ripped off the packing tape and dug in, pulling out a dusty, dented metal coffee can. Her hands were cold, and she nearly dropped it as she peeled back the lid and poured out a handful of old American coins. She dropped them back into the can and felt around in the box, counting three more cans wedged into the wrapping paper.

If this was her payment for the formulas, it was worthless. It was worse than worthless.

Forty boxes of coins? I can't spend them. I can't deposit them. How will I explain where they came from?

She struggled to shove the first can back into the box, but in her haste, she knocked the box off the trunk, and the contents cascaded out, clinking and clanking and rolling everywhere, like a spreading silver puddle.

She stooped, intending to somehow scoop up the coins and hide them, but there were far too many. Flashes from cell phone cameras went off all around her. By the time she stood and faced the crowd, there wasn't a phone in sight, but the averted eyes had all borne witness to the contents of her package.

Madalyn skidded through the spilled coins as she retreated to the car. "Take me back to the office!"

As soon as they were underway, she dialed the number of her last incoming call. A recorded message declared that the number had been disconnected.

She threw her phone to the floor and clenched her fists, unable to voice the scream of fury that threatened to come out. But then a calming thought swept over her. That terrorist thought he'd double-crossed her, but he was in for a surprise. He'd procured the CSD formulas because he wanted unwavering obedience from his minions. When he distributed doses of Phase Three, he'd decimate his own followers with Trina Jacobs' poison, and, once again, Madalyn would emerge the victor.

Chapter 17

Someone rattled the knob at Beth Severson's front door. Had Jaycee come back? She flew across the foyer and threw it open. Her smile turned into a scowl. "What are you doing here? I hoped I'd never have to see you again."

Her husband stepped over the threshold. "Missed you too, dearest." She sidestepped him when he tried to kiss her on the cheek. "Relax. I just stopped by for a few things."

He wandered into the dining room, and she hurried after him.

"I was on my way here when I got a call from an old friend. Said he had something I'd want to hear." He pulled his phone from his pocket and inserted a chip drive. She recognized her voice, and Jaycee's, on the playback.

"How dare you bug my house and listen in on a private conversation!"

Art pocketed his phone. "Don't forget it's *my* house. I had it bugged after you threw me out. I hoped the Baileys would get in touch with you, and it seems I've hit the jackpot. Why didn't you tell me you had more than one connection to the Resistance?"

She shrugged. "What's a marriage without a little mystery? I don't recognize you at all anymore. The Baileys were our friends. It was you who betrayed them."

"Tom's nothing more than a giant thorn in my side. Delivering him and Lara back to Madalyn would have been enough to cripple the Resistance and assure my future at the OCSD—even without a close connection to another Resistance leader."

He picked up the sheaf of papers Jaycee had left behind. "She's coming back for these, I believe?"

She folded her arms. "You know she is."

He nodded. "I imagine Mitch Carraway would come out with guns blazing, so to speak, if his daughter was in trouble."

"Leave her out of this."

"What's in it for me?"

"Go back to the capital. You said the Baileys would be enough to keep you there. Take Mitch later if you feel you have to. Just let me have Jaycee. I don't have anyone to love. Promise me you'll wait until she's here, and safe, before you go after the Baileys."

The life she had envisioned for her daughter all those years ago could never be. Now, she had to protect her any way she could.

10:25 AM
Quadrant DC-005

Careen rolled over and draped an arm over her eyes to shut out the light from the bedside lamp. Her head pounded, and when her stomach lurched, she kicked away the covers and ran for the bathroom. She heaved over the toilet; the spasms brought up nothing but clear bile.

After her nausea passed, she came back into the room where Tommy occupied the far side of the bed. She shot him a what-do-you-think-you're-doing look.

He folded his arms to make it clear that he wasn't going anywhere. "My permission slip is in your back pocket."

"Permission slip?" She looked down and realized she was still wearing yesterday's clothes. She drew the paper out and unfolded it. "'Just in case you don't remember when you read this: Madalyn lied about everything. None of the Resistance is in prison. Atari has control of the Link. You really are safe here. P.S. Don't be mad at Tommy. You said it was okay for him to sleep in the bed last night, but it could have been the Phase Two talking.' This is my handwriting. What's going on? What did I mean by Phase Two?"

"Atari, um ..."

"Did you let him dose me?"

"I didn't let him anything. I never saw it coming, and neither did you." He cringed away from her, as if he expected her to unleash her wrath on him. "He kind of … shot you with a blow dart tipped with CSD."

"I don't believe you could make that up, so it must be true." She crawled back under the covers and pulled the pillow over her head. She lay silent for a few minutes, and when she spoke, her voice was muffled. "That's why I feel so awful. I'm not done puking yet, am I?"

"Not even close."

As if on cue, she suppressed a burp, scrambled out of bed, and ran back into the bathroom. Between the bouts of nausea, she lay with her cheek pressed against the cool tile floor. When she was sure it was over for good, she rose and brushed her teeth before returning to bed and propping herself up against the pillows. "Last night I dreamed my mom was dead." Her heart sank when he didn't answer. "It wasn't a dream, was it?"

He shook his head and pushed himself up to sit beside her.

She buried her face in her hands. "The last thing I ever said to her was that I wished she'd died instead of my dad."

"You didn't mean it."

"Yes, I did." She sniffled. "I absolutely did mean it. But now I wish I could take it back." Her tears spilled over, and he held her while she cried.

When at length she drew a shuddering breath and wiped her eyes on the sheet, he got up and tossed her a protein bar and a bottle of water from the pile on the desk. She sipped some water. "She thought I hated her."

"No. She knew you didn't hate her. When Atari and I met with her, she was worried about you, and she didn't hesitate when we asked for her help."

"When she showed up at PeopleCam, I never suspected what she was trying to do. It was brave, and I wish I could let her know I appreciate it." Her tears started again. "I'm an orphan. I never had the kind of family I wanted. Now I don't have anyone."

"But you do—you have all of us in the Resistance. We're a great big dysfunctional mess. The very definition of family."

That made her weep harder. "I nearly destroyed the Resistance too. I mess up everything."

He wrapped his arms around her. "No, you don't. You need to stop torturing yourself. Rewrite your story. Change the history between you and your mom. Change it between you and Madalyn. Hell, change it between you and me if you need to."

"I told the QM where to find Resistance headquarters."

"But that doesn't matter, because the QM never arrested any of us except Dad, and he turned himself in, so that doesn't count."

She sniffled. "So what you're saying is, I sent the QM on a wild goose chase after the Resistance?"

He nodded. "Yeah. Exactly."

"I knuckled under and did what Madalyn said ... for self-preservation. I didn't let her break me. I survived until you helped me escape." She pounded her fists on her knees in frustration. "Still I kept demanding to go back."

"But you didn't go back! You're still here. Still fighting. And you're getting more like your old self every day. Last night, you proved that you're able to express your true feelings."

His smug tone made her nervous. "What did I do?"

"Well, you tried to kiss me and gave the impression that you were up for just about anything."

She ducked her head, too embarrassed to look at him.

He nudged her with his shoulder. "But I convinced you the timing was off. All we did last night was sleep."

"I wish I could change what happened when you helped me escape."

"How?"

"I'd want you to take off your mask right away so I'd know it was you. And I'd say thank you."

For the first time, the Link on her wrist felt like a threat to her autonomy. She picked at it, but of course it didn't budge. He seemed to understand and covered the plastic band with his hand as if to make it disappear. The warmth of his touch and his nearness flooded her with the will to act on her feelings, and as she lifted her face, his blue eyes locked on hers.

His lips were tantalizingly close. "I want you to remember this moment, okay?"

She nodded. His request puzzled her, but the kiss that followed made perfect sense.

Chapter 18

11:15 AM
Quadrant BG-098

Trina, Grace, and David ate while watching PeopleCam. They had been in the bunker for weeks and hadn't made a dent in the seemingly endless supply of MREs. Trina often dreamed about Lara's lasagna and craved salads and fresh produce. Today, as she took another forkful of the "Meatballs, Beef and Rice" on her plate, her thoughts were on the Christmas dinners she'd shared with her family as a child.

Sheila Roth read from the teleprompter, "President Christopher Wright's final State of the Union address will be delivered on New Year's Eve at nine p.m. Eastern time." She turned to Pete. "Seems unusual, doesn't it? But I suppose there's no better day to evaluate the past year and look toward the future. President Wright is expected to discuss the continuing role of the Essential Services Department and recent changes to the pending Cerberean Link program."

"Perhaps we'll all want a stiff drink to ring in the new year when he's done speaking, Sheila." Pete turned toward the camera. "And in other news, could it be that the OCSD director senses a coming *change* in 2035?" Pete Sheridan's voiceover accompanied several still photos of Madalyn opening a cardboard box, taking out the coins, and bending over in her high heels to try and scoop them up after they had spilled in the street. "Madalyn Davies was summoned to the main post office in DC-001 to pick up forty mysterious packages full of contraband coin. When she was here on PeopleCam just days ago she had some pretty harsh things to say about people who keep or use outlawed American coins. Wonder how she's going to explain this away?"

Grace asked, "Did Mitch really give Madalyn a hundred and fifty coffee cans full of his life's savings? He could've at least filled some of them with buckshot or something."

David chuckled. "Buckshot's worth more than the coins, and I'm pretty sure some of the cans were full of rocks, if you want to know the truth. But rocks spend just as easily."

"Yes, but"—Trina couldn't let it go—"doesn't it seem kind of fatalistic of Mitch to give away all his money? Am I the only one who's worried about him?"

On the screen, Pete gathered his papers and then suddenly burst out laughing. "Forty boxes of coins! And COD on top of that! Wonder what it cost for shipping and handling?"

"Well, of course she's not going to pay for someone to ship her boxes of contraband! The very idea. I don't think it's funny at all, Pete."

"Sheila, if I had a dollar for every time you saw the humor in a situation, I'd be broke."

As Sheila began a heated retort, video cut off abruptly. Black and white snow dominated the screen for a moment before a message appeared, advising "Please Stand By. Experiencing Technical Difficulties."

11:40 AM
Quadrant DC-005

"Okay, that was ... wow!" Tommy sank back against the pillow, and Careen snuggled against him.

"I promised myself if we ever had another chance to be together, I wouldn't waste it."

He burst into laughter and sat up, clutching his stomach. He laughed for so long that she started to get mad, and finally he wiped his eyes and composed himself. "I'm sorry, but seriously? You've missed at least a dozen other opportunities so far, and those are just the ones I can think of off the top of my head."

She slapped his shoulder but couldn't help smiling. "Maybe I did, but I had to make sure I could trust you."

"It was worth every second of waiting." He pulled her into his arms again, and she laughed with him.

"Okay, all right. No more holding back. So what are we going to do about Atari?"

He glanced around. "Kick him out of our bed, for starters. He doesn't belong in here, even in our conversations."

"I'm serious. Should we leave? Maybe we can use our disguises and make it back to OP-439 without being recognized."

"How about we try to clear the air with him first. We still don't know why he and Mitch are so mad at each other. It might be even worse if we leave. We have no idea what's going on in the world."

She sighed. "I wish we never had to face the rest of the world."

"I wouldn't mind hiding out somewhere with you forever, but I hope one day soon we won't have to." He looked serious for a moment, and then a playful quirk of his eyebrow made her smile. "Before we talk to Atari, can I interest you in another act of rebellion against the OCSD's pathological need to control us?"

"Wow, that's some proposition. Why not woo me by professing your undying love and affection? Or suggesting that it would be fun?"

He gave her a squeeze. "Oh, fun is definitely on the agenda."

"I never know when to take you seriously."

"I'm one hundred percent serious." Their eyes met, and her pulse quickened at the intensity of his gaze. "I love you, Careen. I never stopped—not for a second."

"I love you too."

His face relaxed in a grin. "Just so you know, I've never said that to anyone before, except my family."

"Me either."

She turned her face up to his, and the touch of his lips was so gentle that she was the one who pushed the intensity up a notch. His kisses trailed down the side of her neck to her collarbone, and she shuddered as he whispered, "They don't own you, and they can't have you."

10:45 AM
Wednesday, December 27, 2034
Quadrant OP-439

On the drive back from the capital, Tom dozed off in the back seat. When Eduardo nudged him, he opened his eyes and the flashing lights brought him back to full awareness in an instant. He sat up and stared out the car window. Four patrol cars blocked the street in front of his house. Another was parked on his lawn.

Marshals in bulletproof vests swarmed around the perimeter of the property and through the front door, which had been knocked completely off its hinges.

He gripped Eduardo's arm. "Lara and Jaycee—"

"I don't see them anywhere. Let's hope they decided to stay at my place."

The driver maneuvered past the scene. "Looks like we need a different final destination for you fellas."

Eduardo recited his address.

When they pulled up in front of the apartment building, there were no signs of marshals about. They burst through the door and found Lara watching PeopleCam in Eduardo's shabby, but now spotless, living room.

Tom forgot he'd been angry with her. "Oh, thank God you're safe! They raided our house again this morning." He rushed over to embrace her.

She returned the hug. "Oh, no. Not again! There's nothing left for them to ruin. But yes, we're fine. We've been here the whole time. It's been quiet, actually."

"Where's Jaycee?"

"She's still asleep. How was your meeting?"

"Fruitful. We need to get some information to Mitch. Can you reach him?"

She opened her laptop. "I can certainly try. Do you want to talk to him on speaker, or would you prefer a more private conversation?"

"Speaker is fine."

She placed the call, and when Mitch answered, Tom shared his news. "Eduardo and I have just returned from the capital. We've got the perfect location and situation for Trina's part of the plan. The president will be giving his State of the Union address on New Year's Eve. That will give us a live audience as well as television viewers. Atari will need to have the video ready."

"Sounds like you've got it all worked out without me."

"I found the president quite willing to listen to our ideas, and I assumed we would all be participating."

"I don't like putting my trust in a politician."

"This is a good thing for the Resistance. Instead of being regarded as a crazy fringe group, we can have a voice and a chance to shape the future of the country in the post-OCSD era."

"Sounds like you're selling out to me. Hell, a few weeks ago you tried to cozy up to Madalyn."

"If you must know, I was negotiating with Madalyn only to try and curb your propensity toward violence. We're not supposed to be terrorists, yet that's how we're portrayed. People fear us, and they'll only listen to our ideas if we're sanctioned by someone like the president, someone they perceive as a legitimate leader.

"When Trina confronts Madalyn during the State of the Union address, it will bring Madalyn's treachery to light in a public arena. Best case, Trina and Careen will be cleared of wrongdoing. It could even lead to the abolishment of the Restrictions and take power away from the OCSD. It meets all our goals."

"Government's full of people you can't trust."

Tom clenched his fists in frustration, and Eduardo spoke up. "But can we count on you? We need you to carry out your part of the plan."

Mitch grumbled. "Nonviolent revolution hinges on compromise. We won't end up getting what we want unless we fight for it. Fighting's noble. It's the world's second oldest profession."

Tom sighed. "We're taking advantage of the opportunity presented. We'll expect you and Trina in the capital in time to get set up before the State of the Union address."

"I can do that."

Lara asked, "Do you want to talk to Jaycee? I'll go wake her."

"Yeah, sure."

Lara left the room, but she was back in seconds. "She's not in her bed."

Tom looked around. "Where could she have gone?"

Lara clapped a hand to her mouth.

"Did you lose my kid?" Mitch sounded less than pleased.

"No, of course not." Tom could tell she was lying. "I forgot she had planned to go visit Danni today. It's not far. She probably left while I was in the shower."

Jaycee walked down the sidewalk toward her mother's house, hands shoved deep in her coat pockets. Two workmen installing a scanner on the corner watched her pass. She felt their eyes on her halfway down the block. *They're wondering if I'm Linked, I bet. Will I show up on the scanner, or am I old enough not to?* She quickened her pace. *I'm old enough to take charge of my own life. It's none of their damn business.*

Beth greeted her at the back door with a hug.

"Did you sign the papers?"

"Yes, sweetheart. Come in." Jaycee followed her to the front of the house, where a man in a dark suit and Quadrant Marshal Henry Nelson waited in the living room.

The marshal eyed her. "I remember you. From the funeral."

Oh, crap. "I can come back when your company's gone." She tried to bolt for the door, but Beth gripped her shoulder.

The man in the suit spoke. "You're welcome to stay, young lady. In fact, we insist." Beth guided her to the sofa and sat beside her.

Jaycee whispered, "What's going on?"

Beth spoke rapidly. "Jaycee, listen to me. Your father has let his hatred of the OCSD blind him, and he's left you unprotected. What if something were to happen to him? Who would take care of you? I hope you never have to find out how hard it is to be alone."

"What do you mean, if something happens to him?"

"Hypothetically speaking, of course, if something happened to him you'd have no resources except your own wits. I can make sure you're protected and provided for. You need a debit account. We need to enroll you in school too."

She tried to shrug off the hand on her arm. "No, ma'am, that's not necessary. My daddy already saw to my education. I finished the high school requirements last year when I was fourteen."

"Well, then we can make application to the university. Perhaps there's still time to enroll for spring semester."

"I don't want to go to college right now."

The marshal's phone pinged with an incoming text. He read it and swore. "There was no one at the Bailey house."

The man in the suit glared at Beth. "Did you warn them?"

"No!" She shrank away from him, turning her body as though to shield Jaycee from a blow.

Nelson strode over and pulled Jaycee up off the sofa. "Where are the Baileys?"

"Wouldn't you like to know!" Jaycee sank her teeth into Nelson's arm. He roared in pain, and with a practiced motion she she threw an elbow at his solar plexus and then drove the heel of her hand into his nose. She ran for the door, but the man in the suit dragged her back into the room.

Beth stood, hands to her mouth, watching but doing nothing as Jaycee fought to free herself. Nelson, a trickle of blood running from his nose, stepped up and backhanded her across the face. Beth cried out as though it was she who had been struck.

Jaycee remained silent and faced the marshal like a cornered animal, prepared to die fighting.

The man in the suit nodded to Nelson. "Do it."

Beth stepped between them. "Wait. You said it wasn't necessary. You agreed to let her go."

Nelson wiped at his nose. "It's required now. She assaulted an officer." He took her by the other arm, and she twisted in their grasp, her feet lifting off the floor as they wrestled her into a chair. The man in the suit held her by the shoulders as Nelson pushed up her left sleeve.

Chapter 19

9:02 AM
Thursday, December 28, 2034
Quadrant DC-001

Sheila Roth sat alone at the anchor desk. "The response to the Link has been overwhelming! It's too bad it wasn't fully operational in time to save Careen Catecher, who has now been missing for ten days and is most certainly out of the picture. It won't be long until safety and security become the norm for every American child.

"In other news, OCSD Director Madalyn Davies was the victim of an annoying little prank this week. An investigation is underway to find the person or persons who mailed her boxes of contraband coin."

Pete Sheridan watched from behind the glass in the studio director's booth. When the broadcast cut away to the regional weather reports, he wandered down the hall and glanced around before locking himself into Editing Bay Ten.

As far as he could tell from the affiliate reports, there were no quadrants in which the supply of Links was sufficient to meet the demand. But that didn't mean everyone was on board with the Link program.

A reporter at a station in one of the northernmost quadrants in the Central Plains region interviewed families who, determined to prevent their children from being Linked, had kept them home from school until they could arrange passage to the nearest border. It was no easy task to defy the Travel Restrictions that barred most people from owning cars or traveling away from their home quadrant without permission. One family had traveled for nine days, only to be turned away by the border guards. After years of tense diplomatic relations, the neighboring countries to the north and south refused entry to those trying to flee.

The few remaining flights out of the country were reserved for business and government-related travel.

Pete understood people's fears for their children. He wished he'd been more proactive about protecting his son. He uploaded the new reports to his video archive and sent an email with a file attachment, even though connections to anything other than PeopleNet were blocked by the Shield, and then placed a call to Mitch.

"Hey. I don't know if you've seen the news this morning."

"Doesn't seem to be much going on. But we know that's not true."

"I've been suspended. I think I went too far with my jokes about Madalyn's currency problem."

"Sending her the coins didn't go off like I'd hoped anyhow. She manages to deflect everything we do to discredit her."

"I'm still working on the video archive."

"Good. It'll be seen someday."

"Yeah, I hope so."

9:08 AM
Quadrant OP-439

Jude stirred when Danni snuggled close to his side. The air in the apartment seemed particularly chilly this morning, and when his alarm went off a few minutes later, he had to talk himself into getting up and heading for the shower. He shivered as he dressed in a heavy sweater, jeans, and boots, wishing he could crawl back in and stay with her instead. She was on the phone when he came back into the room, and as he leaned over to kiss her goodbye, and she covered the mouthpiece and smiled up at him lazily.

"Have fun storming the castle."

"Always." Jude picked up his scarf and a long overcoat on his way to the door. He was scheduled to take part in the protests at the Distribution Center in neighboring OP-441, and it was a long walk over.

9:20 AM

As soon as Mitch was done talking to Pete, he placed another call. Danni answered, sounding half asleep. "Hey. What's up?"

"Where are you?"

It took a few seconds before she responded. He thought he heard someone else's voice and a door close. "In OP-439. At a friend's."

"You with the Baileys?"

"No. I said I was with a friend."

"All right. I need you to head up to visit Atari. Today."

She sighed. "You know, Mitch, I'm ready to move on from—"

"For crying out loud, I'm not asking you to throw yourself at him. He won't take my calls, so I don't know what the hell he's doing. Take some supplies to him and then hang around until you make sure he's on task with the video. I forwarded him most of the raw footage, and I haven't heard back. I'll get the last of it to him by tomorrow, and we're gonna need it in a few days. Not much turnaround time."

"All right, all right. Anything else?"

"Yes. Make sure he's not planning to activate the Link. I don't trust him any further than I can throw him."

10:27 AM
Quadrant OP-441

From his place on the lawn at the Distribution Center, Jude called, "Ma'am, don't sentence your daughter to a lifetime of constant surveillance."

Most of the adults with young children in tow pushed past the protesters and hurried inside. But when the woman who held a little girl by the hand hesitated, the protestors from CXD called out to her.

The woman looked around before answering, to see if she was being watched. "My daughter hasn't done anything wrong. She's here for her protection."

A young woman with a CXD button on her coat collar pleaded, "Who knows what laws they'll pass in the future? She'll never be free if she's got a Link."

Another young mother, clutching her two children by the hands, darted past them and up the steps before anyone had a chance to talk to her.

The woman who had spoken shook her head and drew her daughter toward the building. The child looked over her shoulder, glossy brown pigtails bouncing, not comprehending what all the fuss was about. Jude locked eyes with her. He needed to save her. He pushed through the crowd and dashed into the Distribution Center.

Large televisions screens in the vestibule played a video message in which a cartoon image of the earth turned on its axis. The perspective zoomed in to a pinpoint somewhere in the southwestern quadrants. *"The location of a missing child can be determined in less than five seconds using Link technology."*

A cuddly looking cartoon version of a three-headed dog bounded onto the screen, wearing a red collar with a flashing light and a name tag that read "Cerbie." The narrator said, *"Cerberus protects and guards you, night and day. Good dog, Cerbie!"* Cerbie's three heads barked in response.

Jude, mesmerized by the video, stood motionless in the queue as people edged past him. He watched Cerbie stand guard as fluffy sheep with a range of different wool colors frolicked in a green field dotted with flowers. The underscored music swelled, foreshadowing danger lurking nearby. A wolf waited on the other side of a hill for a lamb to wander close, but one of Cerbie's three necks stretched out and he grabbed the lamb in his mouth, bringing it back to the safety of the flock. Another lamb fell in a pond and sank, weighted down by is sodden wool coat. While the adult sheep bleated helplessly, Cerbie pulled the lamb safely to shore.

Happy music swelled, and children's voices rose in song: *"Cerbie, the three-headed doggie. Cerbie, he's our friend! He guards the gates and keeps us safe. Protection never ends!"* Cerbie brought food to the flock, spread it before the lambs, and then stood guard while they and the parent-sheep ate.

That had to be one of the creepiest things he'd ever seen. The cartoon image of the friendly Cerberus was inaccurate. Jude had enjoyed reading Greek mythology when they'd studied it in elementary school, and he remembered that Cerberus was the guardian that prevented the dead from leaving the underworld. Though the great dog fawned on people as they entered, he snarled if they tried to leave and would not let them pass. He wondered how many people knew the Cerberus of mythology and not just the convenient retelling being used to promote the Link.

He followed the queue and emerged into a gymnasium-sized room filled with another, longer roped-off line. People shuffled along, bombarded by another video message blaring from the giant screens on all four walls. He craned his neck to look for the little dark-haired girl. A video aimed at the adults was playing on monitors mounted on the walls. Several voices chimed in:

"They're tired of blowing up buildings. Now they're coming for your children."

"Why limit that protection and inclusion to your children, when you can also take advantage of the Cerberean Link?"

"Never miss out on anything that is rightfully yours."

"If there is another food shortage, your Link assures you won't be affected."

"Manage every aspect of your life from one convenient device."

"The Resistance has launched a war on children. Join in solidarity with the OCSD to protect them."

Jude's scalp prickled at the image of a little girl on the video screen. The child, wearing a flashing Link bracelet, clasped a woman's hand, looked up into the camera and whispered, "Mommy, I want you to be safe too." The video ended with children raising their left fists, showing their solidarity and their Links.

He took out his phone and recorded the looping video and sent it in a text to Danni and a few of the others in CXD. When he was done, he took in the rest of the scene. The father in the family at the head of the line was shaking his head, shouting at the distribution worker, but Jude couldn't hear what he was saying. A security guard hurried over and took the man by the arm, forcing him off to the side as his frightened family followed. It was then he saw the woman with the dark-haired child coming toward him in the next row. He reached across the rope and picked up the little girl. The mother's eyes darted about. He lowered his voice and tried one more time.

"Let's get her out of here while you still can."

"Give my daughter back to me!"

Jude felt a heavy hand on his shoulder. He whirled around and found himself face-to-face with a security guard, who took the child away from him and handed her back to her mother. The guard dragged him from the queue and into an empty hallway, where he slammed him up against the wall and zip-tied his hands behind him. He fished Jude's phone out of his pocket and took him roughly by the elbow.

As they emerged into the cold morning, Jude's heart sank. Marshals in riot gear had descended on the CXD protesters. He watched as they slapped the sign out of one of the young men's hands and twisted his arm behind his back. A few of the CXD group tried to run for it, but the counterprotestors surged forward and kept them surrounded until the marshals had them all in custody.

The security guard shoved Jude to the sidewalk, where he sat with his classmates, watching parents arrive with their children. None of them glanced toward the protesters. A siren *whoop whooped*, and the people picked up the pace as they headed into the building.

One of the marshals hauled Jude to his feet, led him toward a transport van, and shoved him inside. He managed to get a seat on the bench along the wall, and soon the space was filled to capacity. Someone yelled, "Where are you taking us?" and the guard slammed the door in response.

They rode in tense silence, and when the van came to a stop, one of the men who hadn't been able to fit on the bench seats staggered and fell across Jude's legs.

The rear door opened and Jude blinked in the bright light. One by one, the occupants were pulled from the van and, hands still zip-tied behind them, were ordered through the double security doors into the processing section of the OP-439 jail.

"ID card."

"It's in my wallet." As Jude struggled to extract it from his back pocket with his hands cinched together, he saw one of the marshals give one young woman's ID a cursory glance and then cut the zip tie that bound her wrists.

"Our apologies, Miss. You're free to go."

She gave Jude a sympathetic glance as she left. He looked around while the marshal examined his ID, and noticed others who had been at the protest were also being released. He wasn't so lucky. The guard tossed his wallet onto a pile on the desk and shoved him toward another set of doors.

Marshals lined the next hallway and watched the protesters file past. As Jude shuffled by, one of them seemed to recognize him and nodded with satisfaction as he passed. Jude met his gaze.

The man grinned and muttered to the marshal on his right. "Good thing we've got enough Links for all of them."

His voice was familiar. *I'm sure I've talked to him before. But when?*

"Yeah, just barely. Quite a roundup today."

Jude went cold with dread, wondering if he'd heard right. He was responsible for the fates of the other members of CXD who'd followed his lead. "Wait, what? Did you say Links? I'm twenty-two! I'm past the Linking age. We all are. The Link's only for kids."

"It's for kids *and* criminals. Makes me downright sick to say those two words together in a sentence, but that's what our world has come to. You all got arrested. Now you're getting Linked. Don't matter if you're a hundred and two. New policy."

"We haven't been charged with anything yet!"

"Don't matter. We Link everyone we bring in now, first thing. Soon we won't have anyone left who's stupid enough to risk breaking the law."

"Won't that put you out of a job?"

"Shut up." The marshal shoved Jude, and he fell against the young woman ahead of him in line. She, in turn, fell against another young man, and as they all struggled to stay on their feet, other arrestees shoved back in self-defense. That was all the provocation the marshals seemed to need. Within seconds, what had been a minor disruption erupted into an unprovoked attack. The marshals rained blows down on the backs and shoulders of the students, who tried to fight their way into the more protected center of the throng. Shouts and cries of pain filled the narrow space.

Jude ducked and managed to avoid the marshals' batons. He lowered his shoulder and shoved his way through the crowd toward the double doors. Just a few more feet and he'd be in the clear.

He emerged and hit the door at full speed, but it didn't yield. He slammed his shoulder against it again in a frantic and futile attempt. Something struck his back, and as he turned, he heard the *swoosh* as the marshal's baton missed his head by an inch.

He couldn't stay pinned against the door, so he launched himself at his attacker, driving him backward. The marshal shoved Jude aside, and he fell to his knees, cringing and trying to protect his head against the blows and the kicks that seemed to come from all directions at once. The force of the last one left him prone on the tile floor. As darkness closed over him, he tasted blood.

Chapter 20

1:45 PM
Quadrant DC-005

Careen, clad in one of Tommy's T-shirts, emerged from the bathroom and studied herself in the full-length mirror next to the bathroom door. He tilted his head to best appreciate the rear view.

She frowned. "I'll never be me again."

"You're the most beautiful—"

"Stop it."

"I'm serious! Who cares about a few scars? I've got plenty of 'em too. You're beautiful and brave and strong and smart, and if you wear nothing but my T-shirts all the time, I swear I'll never, ever complain."

She stripped it off and stood in her bra and panties.

"Or that. That's good too."

She ignored him and touched her reflection with her fingertips. "The scars don't bother me." She drew a sobbing breath and gnawed at the plastic band on her wrist, but it wasn't long before she stopped in frustration. Her teeth had left no marks. "It's this stupid Link. I can't ever get away from it!" She clawed at it with her other hand.

"Try not to obsess."

"Easy for you to say."

"You think I don't obsess over it too? You think I don't wonder what will happen?"

"Maybe someone will blow up the OCSD."

"Maybe someone will blow up this safe house and you'll have wasted your last few days on earth worrying." He caught her by the wrist and kissed the knuckles on her clenched fist. "Come on, get dressed."

Tommy led the way downstairs to the gym, which boasted an eighth-mile track, weights, and a variety of machines and equipment.

Stacks of shoeboxes rose on shelves against the wall. "Find a pair in your size. Atari keeps it stocked. Just like us, most people who show up here don't bring luggage or extra clothes."

He pulled a pair of boxing gloves and some sparring pads out of a bin near a wall of mirrors. "It felt really good when I socked Atari yesterday. So I was thinking it might help you to hit something too."

A small smile played over her lips as he helped her into the gloves. He slipped the thick pads on his own hands. "Jab, jab, cross. Okay?"

She channeled a lot of what was eating her into the first punch. He'd been expecting it, but still it drove him back a step. She moved into the empty space between them and kept up a steady rhythm until beads of sweat formed on her forehead and upper lip. The tendrils of hair that came loose from her ponytail clung to her neck.

As she threw punch after punch, her expression of determined concentration melted and she began to laugh, at first just a *ha* sound when her punches connected with the pads, but the laughter kept coming until it took over. She put her hands on her knees and gasped for breath.

"You all right?"

"Yeah. That was great. I think I broke my pinky."

Tommy dropped the pads and helped her ease the glove off. The light on her Link was flashing in time with her fast-pumping heart, and her knuckles were red and raw. He supported her hand in his as he examined her finger. "It doesn't look crooked. It might just be bruised. Let's tape it to the next one for support." He found the roll of athletic tape, and when he was done, she flexed her fingers, testing.

"That feels better. Thank you."

"You were awesome. Had enough for today?"

"No." Her eyes took in the expansive space. "Wanna do a few laps?"

He shrugged. "Sure."

He started off at an easy pace and she fell in beside him. His injured leg rarely bothered him anymore, but the metal plates and screws were there to repair some serious damage. His mobility and speed had improved a lot in the last five months, but he was never going to be a long-distance runner.

She, on the other hand, moved like a gazelle, effortless and graceful. They ran side by side for about a mile, and when it became clear she was holding back for him, he waved her on and trotted over to the water cooler.

She picked up the pace and ran another mile, ending with a quarter-mile sprint. She backpedaled to a stop and drew a cup of water.

He whistled. "You've been holding out on me."

She wiped her mouth with the back of her hand. "How?"

"You never said you could run like that."

"It never came up." She paced as she cooled off, hands on her hips. "Wow, that felt good. The only thing that's missing now is the sun. It's been so long since I've seen it. I understand why there aren't any windows in this place, and I love knowing that I have room to run, but I'm still shut away."

"Now that you mention it.... Come on, follow me."

He led the way up the stairs until they emerged in a rooftop solarium. The sunlight dazzled her eyes even under the tinted glass dome. "Wow!"

"Yeah, it's great up here."

He slid open the louvers in one of the windows, and fresh, chilly winter air rushed in. She breathed in blissfully and hugged herself. Then she wandered around the perimeter of the roof and gazed out over the quadrant from every angle. "I didn't realize we were right in the middle of everything."

He wrapped his arms around her from behind, and she leaned against him the way she had the first day they met, the top of her head fitting perfectly under his chin. Before them lay the panorama of the capital city.

She sighed. "It's so pretty."

"Yeah. Looks can be deceiving, huh?" She nodded, and he changed the topic. "Christmas was a couple of days ago."

"It was?"

"Yeah. I know most of the holidays have been downplayed until we don't really celebrate anymore, but I loved Christmas when I was little. I've been saving a gift, but today seems like a better day to give it to you."

"I don't have anything to give you in return."

"I have everything I want." He brought his mom's bracelet out of his pocket and fastened it around her right wrist.

"Last time I gave this to you, I told you I was going to make everything all right. I won't make that kind of promise again, but I want you to know that I'll stand by you, no matter what happens."

2:45 PM
Quadrant DC-001

"Balloons?"

"Why not? We have to do this thing big. I'm talking hundreds of balloons."

Kevin took notes on a legal pad while Madalyn's assistant, Nicole, perched on the edge of his desk. He'd enlisted her as an unwitting coconspirator in the final phase of the Resistance's plan.

He spoke in hushed tones while she pecked away at her tablet. "Umm ... order ice sculptures. We'll need one for each of the buffet tables. We should have extra security guards for the gift table too."

"How about a champagne fountain?"

"I was going to suggest chocolate, but heck, get both!"

Nicole giggled like a teenager and then shot a guilty glance at the open door as she stifled the sound. Kevin realized this was the most relaxed he'd ever seen her. Madalyn's constant berating of and finding fault with her sweet-tempered assistant was almost as bad as the torture she'd so gleefully inflicted on Careen.

Kevin shushed her. "She'll hear you, and then we'll both have some explaining to do. This is going to be one spectacular surprise party, but after all, you only turn forty once."

Madalyn's angry voice made them both jump. "Nicole! Why are you away from your desk?"

She gasped and sprang to her feet, hiding the tablet behind her back. "Madam Director. I didn't hear the phone. Did it ring?"

"No, but regardless, I need you at your post unless I send you on an errand. I can't be expected to hunt you down every time I need something. Get in touch with Atari and have him come over here right away." Madalyn waited until Nicole had scurried out of the room with her head bowed, and then turned on Kevin. "What are you two up to in here?"

He ignored the question, knowing it would make Madalyn all the more determined to ferret out answers. "There's no need to treat Nicole like that. She does a fine job."

Her voice took on a demanding and petulant tone. "Why were you laughing? Were you laughing at me?"

He resisted the urge to roll his eyes. *What is this, middle school?* "Can't you just leave it? Otherwise you'll ruin ... —well, let's just say you'll be sorry you did."

She glared at him, but he stood his ground. "It's nothing. Really! Don't you have enough to worry about with the Link?"

Chapter 21

"Your only hope is to take three drops of the antidote right away."
Trina held up a little amber bottle as she stood in front of the green
screen draped on one wall of the bunker's bedroom.

Mitch turned off the camera. "I think that's it. You satisfied?"

"Do you think this is believable? Oh, what am I saying? Stratford
fooled everyone with the same line a few months ago."

"Everyone except me, maybe. I wasn't fooled."

"Okay, present company excepted, then. I guess the only one I
have to fool is Madalyn." She glanced down at the rumpled flannel
shirt and sweatpants she'd been wearing for weeks. "You're sure
Atari can really change what I'm wearing? I'd feel more authoritative
if I could deliver this speech in a suit."

"Oh, yeah. No problem."

"Good. Then I can start worrying about the live portion of the
program."

The satellite phone buzzed at Mitch's hip, and he hurried out
of the room. *Why don't I ever get to know what's going on?* she
wondered as she hurried past David and Grace in the sitting room
and followed Mitch on tiptoe. She caught part of what he was saying
as he headed up the stairs.

"... take over the whole damn thing. They'll be distracted.
No matter how the vote goes, be ready to ..." The bunker door
slammed behind him.

*Hold on a second. The only plan I'm aware of is to force
Madalyn's confession and clear my name. I haven't heard anything
about a takeover.*

She hurried back down to the main room. "Grace, David, can y'all come here for a minute?" She beckoned them into the bedroom and shut the door.

"I think it's time for you two to think about leaving."

"Hallelujah! It's about time." David clasped his hands in delight. Grace shushed him. "Why? What's going on?"

"I need you to take a message to Tom and Lara in OP-439 but without letting Mitch know that's where you're going. Tomorrow we're unblocking the communication channels the old-fashioned way."

4:15 PM
Quadrant DC-005

Tommy rummaged through the cabinets in Wardrobe until he found a duffel bag. Careen put a change of warm clothing for each of them inside and laid their wigs, knit caps, and the glasses for Tommy inside and zipped it closed. He carried the bag back to their room while she followed with winter coats and gloves.

"What should we say to him?" Careen kept her voice low as they crossed the lobby, and Tommy shrugged. He'd been all over the safe house, but he'd never ventured down the hall that led to Atari's rooms. He'd never been encouraged to visit.

"He shot you with a blow dart. I mean, how do you trust someone after they do a thing like that?"

"I can't. I'm afraid to turn my back on him. We need to leave."

"He'll probably be glad to see us go. He never wanted either of us here in the first place."

He knocked, but there was no response. He put his hand on the doorknob. "Should we take a look inside?"

"No! What if he's in there?"

"He's not or he would've answered the knock. Aren't you the least bit curious?"

She giggled nervously. "All right. An invasion of his private space is nothing compared to what he did to me."

Tommy opened the door. Every surface in the room was glossy black. A neon blue maze lined with fluorescent yellow dots spread across the walls, floor, and ceiling.

"Whoa." Careen turned in a circle. "I'd get totally disoriented in here."

Tommy laughed. "It's ... a Pac-Man grid. His room is a life-sized Pac-Man screen. Look! There's Pac-Man on the ceiling." He pointed. "Do you see the ghosts? There, there ... and over there!"

"Oh my gosh. Can you say arrested development? I thought people quit having theme-decorated bedrooms when they were, like, twelve."

The only thing in the room that deviated from the video game theme was a dictionary of Greek mythology that lay open on the bed. Tommy picked it up and skimmed the entry on Hercules.

Careen wandered around the perimeter of the room. "There's another door. I almost didn't notice it. How would you find your way to the bathroom at night?" She paused with her hand on the doorknob, like she was about to reveal a prize on a game show. "I wonder how it's decorated. Wanna see?"

"I can live without seeing Atari's bathroom. Come on. If he's out of the building, we should be in Command Central. Maybe we can pull up PeopleCam or figure out how to send a message to Mitch or my parents."

They hurried back to the center of the building. The rows of television screens mounted on the wall in Command Central were all dark. A single white square moved across each screen, rebounding off edges and corners in an unending random pattern.

It's Pong, the first sports arcade game, released in 1972. Tommy shook his head at how much classic video game trivia he'd picked up while living with Atari. He wished he'd learned more about the computers instead. He pressed the space bar on each of the keyboards that ranged along the semicircular desk, to see if any of them were unlocked. "I'd feel better about leaving if we could get in touch with someone else first."

Careen started pressing random buttons, and the Pong image disappeared from the screens.

"Stop! You're not going to remember what you've touched. He'll know we've been in here if anything's different."

"I think it was this one." She pressed a key and every screen jumped to life. One replayed the video that had frightened her so much her first night at the safe house, and Tommy turned away as someone who looked like him shot someone who looked like her. Of the remaining screens, four showed PeopleCam, another six were hacked into the security cameras at the OCSD, and the rest were security footage from places Tommy didn't recognize. "Oops."

"Look." He pointed at PeopleCam, where a news story about Linking showed people lined up around the block at a Distribution Center.

"It's really happening."

"Damn right it is." They both turned, startled. Danni stood in the doorway. "What are you doing?"

Tommy sighed with relief. "Boy, am I glad to see you!" She crossed the room to hug him, and over her shoulder, he watched Careen raise her eyebrows and fold her arms across her chest.

Danni ignored Careen entirely and addressed him. "Where's Atari?"

"Out somewhere, we think. He never says when he's leaving."

"He hasn't been answering Mitch's calls for a couple of days. I thought you guys might need some supplies."

"He's been acting strange. I heard him yelling on the phone. I get the feeling Mitch and Madalyn are both leaning on him pretty hard, and he's cracking under the pressure. There's a chance Madalyn will convince him to activate the Link." Tommy gestured toward the computers. "Do you know how to download that"—he pointed at the doctored video—"onto a chip drive? Also, we need to get in touch with Mitch."

Danni took a fresh chip drive out of a box in one of the drawers and started the download. "Let me talk to Atari first, and then I'll put you in touch with Mitch."

Careen spoke up. "We don't have a whole lot of time. We're almost ready to leave for OP-439."

Danni popped the chip out of the drive and gave it to Tommy before she turned to look at Careen for the first time. "What? No, you can't."

"Why not? You can't tell me what to do. I thought you told me you never tried to stop anything from happening."

"That was a while ago." With a few quick keystrokes, Danni brought back the silent Pong screensaver. "There. Now we can hear ourselves think. Careen, I'm serious. You have to stay here. You could be the only thing that keeps Atari from activating the Link. He won't risk having you show up on the scanners and giving away the location of his safe house. Lock yourself in if you have to, but don't leave here under any circumstances."

Careen bit her lower lip the way she did when she was trying not to cry.

Tommy spoke up. "If the Link is going live, shouldn't we get Careen as far from the capital as possible? Head for the middle of nowhere so they won't find us?"

"They'd pick you up while you were still in the capital quadrant. Don't you know they have sensors and cameras with face recognition capability on every corner? They're busy installing more cameras and Link sensors in every quadrant, and soon there won't be any place to hide. Trust me, you're better off where you are.

"I guess Atari hasn't told you that the OCSD won't let PeopleCam broadcast anything about the riots and the arrests. Pete Sheridan was suspended for making a joke about Madalyn. The clashes between people who want Links and people who don't are getting worse. They closed the university in OP-439 last week to try to shut down the market there. Careen's our insurance policy. Things will get even worse if Atari activates the Link."

4:30 PM
Quadrant DC-001

Atari, incognito in a janitor's coveralls, bobbed his head in time to the music playing on his headphones as he pushed a bulky old photocopier past the rear entrance of the OCSD building on his way to the service elevator. His heart nearly stopped when the door opened and Madalyn came in, flanked by two security guards. He halted so they could pass in front of him. One of the guards cast a curious glance his way and slowed, motioning for him to take off his headset.

Atari kept his gaze off to the side as he hung the headset around his neck, still moving in time to the music. "Yeah?"

"Who roughed you up like that?"

Atari shrugged as though it didn't matter. Madalyn gave him a cursory glance and kept walking.

The guard laughed as he hurried after her. "You must have really ticked someone off!"

He gave a less-than-energetic salute and then trundled the copier onto the service elevator and pushed the button for the basement level. He emerged and headed down the low-ceilinged, maze-like hallway and swiped his ID to enter what had once been Kevin McGraw's office. He shoved the desk and chair against the far wall to make room in order to maneuver the outdated piece of equipment far enough inside to shut the door.

He opened the front panel to reveal a neat array of wires, blasting caps, and blocks of plastic explosives, and then glanced at his watch. Two days, plus a few hours, left until the president would deliver his final State of the Union address. He still had to finish the video Mitch needed for the plan, and he was adding his own twist to the evening's entertainment. If he timed it right, he'd have finished his job for the Resistance and be on his way before the dust settled.

He set up his supplies on the desk and whistled as he worked. Soon the connections were complete, the timer set.

When his phone vibrated in his pocket, he took a breath to transition from his janitor persona before he answered.

It was Nicole, Madalyn's assistant. "Madam Director needs to see you at once."

He coughed dramatically. "I'm afraid that's impossible at the moment. I'm indisposed."

"She'll still want to meet with you as soon as possible to finalize the preparations for the Link."

"I don't want her to catch my cold. I'll call her later." He hung up. There was no way he could return to the OCSD as Atari until his bruises healed. Madalyn was self-absorbed and not all that observant, but the evidence of Tommy and Careen's physical assaults on his person could definitely blow his cover.

Danni took the elevator down to get the food and supplies she'd brought with her. Tommy and Careen helped her put everything away, and they were making dinner together when Atari appeared in the kitchen doorway, dressed in his janitor uniform.

"To what do I owe this adorable domestic scene?" He crossed the room and planted an enthusiastic kiss on Danni. "I've missed you, baby!"

"I told you not to call me that." She stepped back and took a good look at him. His bottom lip was cut and swollen and stood out in bright contrast to the yellowish-green-tinged purple bruising around his nose and eyes. His hair was greasy, and she'd gotten a whiff of him when he'd kissed her. It was clear he hadn't showered in days.

She put her hands on her hips. "I understand you have something to say to Careen?"

He fidgeted and hung his head like a small boy. "Sorry I shot you with a blow dart. Won't happen again."

Danni turned her look on Careen, who matched her voice to the flat tone of Atari's apology. "Sorry I accused you of killing my mother."

Atari cast an expectant glance at Tommy, who shook his head.

"Don't even go there. I'm not sorry I hit you. We've overstayed our welcome. We're going to call the car service and go back to OP-439."

"Dude, you can't!" Atari's demeanor went from sullen to frenetic. "You gotta stay in the capital for New Year's Eve! It's gonna be a big blowout. You don't want to miss it. When the ball drops, new people will be in charge. New year, new you, right? Just hang out and chill. I honestly don't mind. In fact, I insist. Talk to you later." He grabbed Danni by the arm and hurried her out of the kitchen.

As soon as they were out of earshot, she pulled free. "What's going on with you?"

He sidled up to her again. "I was just hoping you'd be up for ordering me around some more. You know, like that one time?" He touched her hair. "I wasn't kidding when I said I missed you."

"You look like hell."

"You're the second person to comment on my battered visage today."

She sighed. "Why aren't you returning Mitch's calls?"

"Oh, I see how it is. You're just here to spy on me. And here I thought maybe you missed me too."

"I don't usually like people enough to miss them."

"Burn."

"Truth." She grasped his arm to make sure she had his attention. "Have you finished the video for New Year's Eve?"

"Yes. Yes! Almost. Mitch just sent me the rest of the video. Did you come up here to pepper me with questions? All work and no play, baby!" He tried to pull her closer, but she shook him off again.

"I'm here because rumor has it you're going to go against Mitch's orders and activate the Link. If you do, I'm screwed. Most of the people I work with are trying like hell not to get Linked. They're afraid. It's getting harder to get people to aid the Resistance. It's weakening our numbers."

"See, I heard just the opposite. People are clamoring to be Linked. They've had a sip of Madalyn's Kool-Aid, and now they're knocking kiddies out of the way to grab the ultimate personal security device for themselves. So I'm giving them what they want."

"That's not going to solve anything."

"The people who are crying for Links want to be taken care of and kept safe from harm—even though it's freaking impossible. They don't get it, and I'm giving up. Let them be Linked."

"You're insane."

"Linked will become the new normal. After a while, everyone will forget what life was like before."

"Do your job for the Resistance so I can do mine."

"You haven't been around lately, Danni, and that leads me to assume you've been doing *your* job on someone new. Pillow talk is when lovers—or whatever it is we were—share secrets. I could've told you that it doesn't matter how many shipments of Links you hijack. The Resistance might delay it, but no one—not even me— can stop it. So I'm going to do what I have to do. We're past the point of no return, baby. Mitch has no one but himself to blame. He put me on this project in the first place. So come on, sit back, and enjoy the ride."

"You son of a bitch."

His laugh was mocking. "Names will never hurt me. I know you crave power as much as I do, and I admire you for who and what you are. Come rule the world with me. I'd rather share it with you than someone weak like Careen."

She fled, and before she knew it, she was in her truck and roaring out of the parking garage. Helplessness and loss, emotions she'd vowed to keep permanently at bay, overwhelmed her, and she cried.

Chapter 22

7:38 AM
Saturday, December 30, 2034

Tommy hit the gym with purpose and went through a strength-training workout he'd done many times during his years playing football. Watching Careen run on the track was an added bonus. When he was done with his circuit, he joined her, and she slowed to his pace.

"I never thought I'd say this, but I feel so much better now that Danni's here."

"Yeah, me too. We'll finally get a chance to talk to Mitch. Want to walk together for a while?"

"No." She swatted his arm. "Tag! You're it!" She dashed ahead and he gave chase, working hard to catch up to her by the second turn. He wrapped his arms around her waist and lifted her off the ground.

"Oh, ow, ow!"

He released her immediately. "Shoot! Sorry, I forgot about your ribs."

"Just kidding. They don't hurt anymore."

"No fair!"

She threw up her hands in mock surrender. He laced his fingers with hers, pulling her closer, and kissed the side of her neck. She giggled and took off again. "Come on. I was going to run the stairs."

She led the way to the rooftop, where they burst out into the solarium.

She gasped with delight. "It's snowing!" She ran to open one of the louvered windows and took a deep breath. "It smells so clean!"

"It's real snow this time."

"Yeah, none of that black stuff I saw when we were on CSD."

They watched as the snowflakes struck the glass walls and ceiling, melted, and ran down in rivulets. She held her palms against the pane. "I can almost feel it." Without warning, she whirled around and pressed both hands to Tommy's cheeks. He yelped at the cold and pulled away, and she giggled as she advanced again and tried to put her hand inside his sweatshirt.

He laughed as he twisted away from her. "Okay, now you're asking for it."

"Oh yeah?" She dodged as he made a grab for her and stayed just out of reach as she led him across the solarium, grinning all the while.

He rushed her, feinted right, and when she turned to the left, he tackled her low and flipped her over his shoulder, reveling in her laughter and the way she shrieked when he pretended he was going to drop her. When he deposited her on a chaise lounge, she scooted over to make room for him and they snuggled close. Her kisses were warm and cold at the same time, and her frosty breath mingled with his as they clung to each other.

Ever since the day he'd tossed her over his shoulder and carried her across the PeopleCam parking lot to the getaway van, he'd been holding back, letting her set the pace for their interactions. Well, except for that first kiss. But that didn't really count. He'd gotten used to the feeling that she was going to throw on the brakes. But not for the past few days. Now when he kissed her it was like picking up speed while riding down a steep hill. He'd had no problem getting used to that.

She draped one leg over his hip, and he was ready to drop back the adjustable chair as far as it would go when Atari's voice echoed across the room.

"There you are!" He hurried toward them. "I've been looking all over for you. I thought you'd left too."

He sat up. "What? Did Danni leave?"

"Yeah, she's gone."

Careen's smile faded. "Umm … she didn't say goodbye."

"Yeah. She never does." Atari looked lost for a second, and then he snapped back to his usual brusque self. "Well, just wanted to check and make sure. Carry on. Or whatever." He left as abruptly as he'd come in. Careen sat up on the chaise, the mood definitely gone.

"She never told us what we should do. She didn't let us talk to Mitch or anyone."

"Hey." He tried to reclaim her attention.

"What?"

"Once, a long time ago, we didn't know what was going to happen to us when we ran out of CSD. We were so afraid we hid under the dining room table like little kids. Remember?"

"Of course."

"And what happened? Nothing. We didn't die."

"I wouldn't call it nothing. A lot of awful things have happened since then."

"And good things too. My point is, we're still here. I had fun this morning just doing normal stuff with you.

"When the OCSD makes decisions on our behalf, they say they're helping us. We know they're not interested in helping us. It's all about controlling us. We can't dwell on what we might not get to do in our lives. If we give up, we give those terrorists at the OCSD power.

"I'm not going to sit here and worry while I wait for something bad to happen. I want to make happy memories with you. I want to laugh. I want to kiss you in the snow—or at least in the solarium where we can see the snow, for now."

He claimed her lips and closed his eyes, feeling her warmth close to him and the chill of the air that swept in the open window.

She broke off with a little sob. "Until the Link means we can't be together anymore."

"We don't know that will happen." He took her by the shoulders and looked her in the eyes. "For now, we can keep training and prepare ourselves so we're ready to fight if we need to."

8:24 AM
Quadrant OP-439

Jaycee tried not to tug at the Link that was cinched tight around her left wrist. The marshal and her mother's husband let her go, and she knew they could reel her back in whenever they felt like it once the Link was activated. She'd run as fast as she could in the opposite direction from Eduardo's apartment, checking over her shoulder until she was sure no one was tailing her. Even now, almost a week later, she choked back the bile that rose in her throat as she imagined Tom and Lara's reaction. She couldn't bring herself to tell them. Not yet, anyway. As awful as that would be, it was dread of her father's reaction that made her wish she'd be struck down by lightning so she'd never have to tell him. She'd told herself to quit being a crybaby and had wandered through the market and past the shops around the university every chance she got, searching for the one person she could tell.

She found Danni nursing a mug of coffee in a booth at the pop-up coffee shop. At the sight of her cousin, her resolve to be brave wilted again. Danni was far tougher than she. Jaycee slid in across from her. "Where have you been? I've been looking all over for you for days!"

"What's the matter?"

Her chin trembled, and she didn't trust herself to speak. Without a word, she pushed up her coat sleeve.

Danni's voice was full of anger, not the sympathy she'd hoped for. "Oh, perfect! Glad to see you can take care of yourself."

"Help me."

"I can't."

"You've got to!"

"I don't know what you expect me to do."

"Call your boyfriend."

Danni blanched at the word.

"You know, the bomber guy. I heard Daddy talking about you and him. He's the only one who can help me." Tears ran down her cheeks, and she wiped her nose on her sleeve.

Danni handed her a napkin and hissed, "Stop sniveling. People are looking at you." She sighed and scooted out of the booth, and Jaycee followed her outside. "What happened?"

"It's kind of a long story."

Danni's phone rang, and she held up a hand for Jaycee's silence. When she answered, her tone was carefully neutral. "Hello?"

She listened for a moment. "He did? Where? Okay, I'll be there as soon as I can."

Danni led her to the truck. "Come on. Tell me what happened while I drive you to Eduardo's."

"I did the one thing Daddy told me not to do. Now I'll never be able to be in the Resistance. My life is over. Nothing matters anymore!" Jaycee fell into Danni's arms, sobbing.

"Monroe? Jude Monroe. Last call, Monroe, if you wanna get out of here."

Jude's first attempt to answer was nothing but a raspy croak. Only one of his eyes would open, and he squinted against the glare of the uncovered light bulb overhead.

He cleared his throat and called, "I'm here. Coming."

He tried to sit up, and the pain left him gasping. He clutched his ribs as he swung his legs off the bench one at a time.

"I'm here. I'm Jude Monroe."

The marshal who opened the door leered at him. "Fat lot of good resisting did you. Idiot."

Jude braced himself as he rose to his feet, and saw the flashing red light of the Link that now encircled his left wrist, visible just inside his coat sleeve.

"Stay outta trouble, kid, or you'll be back here before you know it."

Jude stood a little taller and forced himself not to wince in pain as he walked past the marshal. "Then I guess I'll be seeing you soon."

Danni was waiting for him on the other side of the door. She didn't reach out to hug him or react to his appearance. He tugged his sleeve down as he approached.

"What's happening? Have I been charged? When's my arraignment?"

"The charges have been dropped. Let's go."

As soon as they were out of the building and headed toward her truck, he tried again. "Now will you tell me what happened?"

"You were charged with disorderly conduct and assaulting an officer, and that's some serious trouble. It was hours before I could get anyone to talk to me. I bribed one of the marshals to drop the charges. Some of the others were able to post bail, and they were allowed to leave, too."

"Things are bad. I've got to get back to the Distribution Center." He eased himself into the passenger seat.

She came around to the driver's side. "Think maybe you ought to clean up a little first? Or go to a hospital?"

"No, I need to go as I am." He pulled back his sleeve, and tears sprang up in her eyes. It was the first time he'd seen her lose her composure. He beckoned for her to come closer and kissed her.

"I have to spread the word. They're Linking everyone who gets arrested, and you know they're not going to be broadcasting the fact on PeopleCam."

"You'll just get arrested again."

"So what? They can only Link me once. I have to do everything I can to fight until the day they activate the Links. I have nothing else to lose." Her face fell again. "Well, not nothing. If things were different...." He kissed her again. "But what I want—what we want—doesn't matter. This is my life, like it or not. I have an obligation to do what I can to warn people."

She wished with all her heart that she could tell him the Link wouldn't really be activated and be sure it was the truth. First Jaycee, and now Jude, was caught in the snare, and she was powerless to help them. "I'm sorry! I didn't know you were going to commit like this."

"Of course I was going to commit! Other than you, CXD is the most important things I've got going right now."

She squeezed his hand. "It shouldn't surprise me. You've been brave all along."

"Gee, thanks." He winced as she moved closer. "I gotta say, I'm glad I didn't know this was going to happen to me when we hijacked the shipment of Links. It would've taken the fun out of it."

Chapter 23

12:20 PM
Quadrant BG-098

The bunker's metal door opened with a creak. Trina pulled up the hood on the oversized sweatshirt she'd borrowed from Mitch and drew in a breath of the crisp, clean air that smelled like snow, pine needles, and dead leaves.

David and Grace followed her, blinking in the sunlight. She cautioned, "Now, quiet. We don't know if he's still around." Even though no one spoke, Trina was afraid the crunch of their footsteps could be heard miles away. It was easier to be quiet once they reached the downhill part of the hard, frozen trail. When the lake came into view David waved them to a halt and sat down on a big, flat rock with his hands on his knees.

Trina hadn't liked Mitch when they'd first met, but she had been forced to trust him. He'd been the one to dress the bullet wound in her arm, and he'd surprised her with his knowledge and gentle touch. Though he'd been adept at doctoring her, she didn't think he really cared about anyone. He'd had no qualms about encouraging the food shortage that had left millions of people without rations for over a week.

This business on the phone arranging some kind of takeover was scaring the hell out of her. She'd feel a lot better if she knew Tom was on board with it.

Once David was rested, they continued their descent, keeping close to the tree line as they had weeks before on their hasty flight into the woods.

Trina halted the party within sight of the barn. "He keeps all the keys on a hook by the walk-in. If he's inside, you know what to tell him."

Grace hugged her. "I wish we didn't have to leave you. Are you sure you're safe alone with him?"

"I don't think he'll do anything to sacrifice the plan. I need to be in the capital tonight, so we've got to leave soon anyway."

She watched them until they were out of sight and then hid in the underbrush to wait. If something went wrong and Mitch forced David and Grace back up to the bunker, she'd make a break for it herself.

Ten minutes passed, and then she heard voices.

"Revolution's a young man's game, Mitch. I'm glad you understand that."

Grace gushed, "I'm certainly willing to take our chances to get back to Virginia. I'm never going to call it by a quadrant number again. We're going home, and we're proud to have done our part. Now it's up to you, dear."

"Thank you for loaning us the vehicle."

"Be careful." Mitch's tone sounded normal.

She heard an engine start and listened until the sound faded away. Maybe if she waited, she could get a look inside his office in the rear of the barn.

"I hoped I'd find you here." Trina jumped at the unfamiliar voice. *Oh, Lordy.*

"Josephine?" Confused, Trina looked over her shoulder. "Wait, you're not—"

A young quadrant marshal, no more than a kid, stood on the path. His smile faded and his eyes widened as recognition dawned.

Trina tried to keep him calm. "Who's Josephine?"

"She works here. Her uncle's the one who died."

Trina jumped again as Mitch stepped up behind the boy and put him in a headlock, gripping him so fiercely that his feet lifted off the ground. "How do you know her? What do you want with her?"

The boy gasped, "I wanted to see if she was okay." Mitch forced him into the barn, Trina at his heels. He shoved the boy to the ground and shut the door behind them.

He cowered. "Look, mister, I never—"

"Where's your partner?"

"I'm off duty. This is—was—personal." Mitch's gaze turned murderous.

Trina grabbed Mitch's arm. "Take it easy." He turned that gaze on her, and her blood ran cold.

His voice was tight with fury. "It was pretty stupid of you to come down here. You do realize that now we're going to have to take him with us?"

10:29 PM
Quadrant OP-439

Eduardo, Tom, and Lara returned to the Bailey house after curfew to sift through the devastation left by the raiding QM. Tom and Lara had drawn the curtains in the home office at the rear of the house, and were poring over what was left of Tom's files when Eduardo heard a car pull up outside; the engine sputtered and was quiet. He hurried through the dark house and stood out of sight near the open front doorway, his flashlight raised like a club. "Who is it?" he said, his tone harsh.

"For heaven's sake, Eduardo! It's Grace and David."

Eduardo stood aside for the professors as they hurried inside, and turned on the flashlight.

"Oh my, what an adventure!" The beam reflected off David's thick glasses. "I haven't driven like that in twenty years."

"He lost those officers who were tailing us in the MG quadrants." Grace looked at her ex-husband with admiration, and they both giggled.

Eduardo led them down the hall into the office. "What are you two doing here?"

They sobered and seemed to remember the reason for their flight. David lowered his voice. "We came to warn you that the plan could be in danger."

"Grace, what about Trina?"

"Trina thought it best we come to you while she manages Mitch. By now, they should be on their way to the capital for her part in the plan."

David added, "We told Mitch we'd decided we were too old for the actual revolution, and that we were heading home to Virginia.

Then we beat a path to you. Mitch wouldn't give us access to any means of communication with the outside world."

Tom looked at Lara, and she shook her head. "He hasn't responded to the messages I've sent over the past two days."

"Then we'd better leave for the capital right away and make sure Atari has the video ready in time."

"Can you find the safe house?"

"Possibly, but it will be difficult without assistance. I hesitate to call the car service that brought me here. They might warn Atari of our approach."

"Don't call the car service. Danni can tell us how to get there. I'll get directions from her and be back soon." Eduardo pulled out his phone as he headed for the door.

11:21 PM
En route to DC-005

Lara huddled under a blanket with Tom in the back of the stolen mail truck as Eduardo piloted them into the endless darkness. Jaycee was asleep, curled up on a pile of mailbags.

Tom glanced at the girl before he spoke in a hushed tone. "You know I've had my reservations about Mitch for some time, since before we left Resistance headquarters for the bunker. President Wright, Chief QM Garrick, and Senator Renald stand ready to facilitate and work with us. I hope Mitch will still be willing to see through our original plan and make it impossible for Madalyn Davies to retain any influence or credibility."

"I hope he will, but I'm also disillusioned with Mitch. I don't approve of the direction he's taken with the Resistance. You're right, Tom. We can't trust him."

"I'm glad to hear you say that." Tom looked out the window. "Lara, don't you think it's time we were completely honest with each other? You've been keeping things from me, when we should be each other's strongest allies and confidantes. In the past few years, maybe I was too absent from our relationship. I wasn't seeing you the way I should.

"But I had a lot of time to think while we were held captive at the OCSD. I was more alone than I'd ever been, because you couldn't remember the bulk of our life together. You were so vulnerable, and I started to wonder what else might be hidden inside of you. The brain is capable of remarkable things—including self-defense. I began to fear you possessed information that would be useful to Stratford.

"I refused to tell him anything, because I wanted him to think I was the only one of us with secrets and that you were ignorant and therefore of no use to him. When he began torturing you, it nearly broke me, but I feared something even worse for you if he had any inkling that you were the one who possessed information that would be valuable."

"I'm sorry, Tom. For a long time, I've had to keep some things to myself. You and I couldn't be part of the same Resistance cell. Those were the rules. We weren't supposed to know who else was involved."

"But you knew of my involvement."

"Our roles were different. Mitch convinced me you didn't need to know. Then everything went haywire, and we all ended up at Resistance headquarters."

"I was certain you'd done sensitive work before, and I was afraid you might be involved in counterintelligence or even be some kind of double agent. I didn't know what Lowell Stratford would do if he suspected you were a threat to him in your own right, and not just my wife who could be used as a pawn.

"You know, Tommy seems to think you do all the heavy lifting in our relationship." He brushed back a strand of her hair. "But I stand ready to defend and protect you. Before the accident, I suspected you were keeping secrets from me. I was going to confront you and tell you it didn't matter what had happened to cause the chasm between us. I wanted to repair whatever damage I'd caused. I couldn't stand the thought of losing you.

"When Tommy was a child, I had no idea that you were involved in anything behind my back, but when they never took our car away, it gave me pause. I was no friend of the government, and, in fact, they probably would have been glad to invoke the Restriction and deny me the freedom that comes with being able to travel at will. I realized it when you taught Tommy to drive. You weren't afraid. We kept our driving privileges because of you.

"Maybe I made the wrong decision by not telling Lowell what he wanted to know when we were being held at the OCSD, but I was afraid I might implicate you and make things worse."

Lara nodded. "The agency where I worked was absorbed by the OCSD many years ago. Somehow—probably because I went on maternity leave in the middle of the agency transition—my security clearance was never revoked. I was tantamount to a professional Watcher when we met, and I was good at my job. I was on the list of those approved to keep their cars. I wasn't about to bring the oversight to anyone's attention."

"But how did you meet Mitch?"

"Through Beth. I believe she made some comment to Mitch about how she was torn between two extremes—a best friend who had been a professional Watcher and a fiancé who was a revolutionary."

Tom scratched his head. "So Beth ... and Mitch? He was her fiancé? So that makes Jaycee her daughter? You obviously remembered all this. Why didn't you tell me?"

"Beth kept a lot of the details from me. She was remarried to Art by the time I started doing work for Mitch."

"Does Jaycee know who her mother is?"

"Yes. I facilitated a meeting between them, at Jaycee's request. Mitch would have a fit if he knew, and, honestly, I don't think it went well. Jaycee doesn't seem to want to talk about it. Anyway, this all happened a long time ago. I was used to being at home with Tommy all day, and when he started school, I was bored. Mitch contacted me and asked if I could do a little work for him on the side, and I admit I jumped at the chance."

He looked wary, and she hastened to add, "At first, it was just background checks and arrest records. Later, I helped Mitch locate potential new members. The first time I logged in, I was a nervous wreck, waiting for someone from the OCSD to send an email or call and ask why I was accessing the database. But no one seemed to notice.

"It never occurred to me that you might want me to quit because you feared for my safety as much as I worried about yours." She smiled in the dark. "Silly me. I worried you'd shoot your mouth off and get into trouble."

"A realistic fear, so it would seem."

"I stood by you." She laid her head against his shoulder.

"Lara?"

"Yes?"

"Was your amnesia genuine?"

"Yes, it was. But I never forgot I was in love with you."

He lifted her chin and kissed her. She responded with the kind of enthusiasm that sent him back twenty years, to when their infatuation with each other had been at its peak. Her revelation about herself added a new, mysterious dimension to this woman he'd loved for so long and fanned the flames of his desire. His hands wandered, and she giggled like a teenager. They had hours ahead of them before they reached the capital.

He heard Eduardo chuckle. "You Baileys get more action in the back of mail trucks than anyone I ever knew."

Chapter 24

12:04 AM
Sunday, December 31, 2034
Quadrant BG-098

"Mitch, we're going to be late if we don't leave soon." Trina sat at the counter, a to-go box and a picnic basket beside her, watching him as he wandered through the diner like a cat patrolling his territory.

"We've got time." He ran his hand over the worn Formica as he went behind the counter and began rummaging on the shelves.

She glanced at the clock. "No, we don't. It's going to take forever to get to the capital."

"We'll make better time at night when the roads are empty."

"You haven't seen the condition of the roads in the MG quadrants. Nothing's been repaired there in ages, and to be honest, it's not much better in BG. We'll be lucky to make it in eighteen hours."

"I haven't cleaned the kitchen." He started for the swinging door, and she grabbed his arm.

"I did it while you were packing. The only thing left to do is get in the truck and go." She released him. "We don't have to take him with us, you know."

"And have him blow the whistle on us? No chance. I had everything under control. Why'd you have to mess it up by leaving the bunker too soon?"

"Don't change the subject. It's still time to go."

He looked at the floor. "It's been a long time since I left here for more than a few hours at a time."

"I know."

He came out from behind the counter and went down the hall, and his footsteps sounded heavy on the stairs. As Trina heard him moving around in the rooms above, she envisioned him taking one last look in both Jaycee's and Wes's rooms. He returned with the young marshal, whom he'd locked in one of the upstairs closets.

He dragged the boy outside to his truck and shoved him inside, then went back to lock the diner's front door.

Trina brought the food with her, and shot the boy a sympathetic look as she scooted in beside him. "What's your name?"

"Seamus. Seamus Owens, ma'am."

"I'm Trina Jacobs." She set the picnic basket on the floor at her feet and held out her hand.

"I know."

Mitch climbed in the driver's side and started the engine.

She handed Seamus the to-go box. "Here. I made you a hamburger and fries. Should still be warm." He opened the container and dug in with such relief that her heart went out to him. It couldn't hurt to be friendly. "So, how do you know Jaycee?"

He swallowed before he answered. "I met her when we notified her of her uncle's death."

"I see."

"Where've you been all this time? Seems like all we do is search the quadrant for you."

Mitch broke in. "Oh, for the love of Mike. Am I going to have to listen to small talk all the way to the capital?"

Seamus glanced his way. "No disrespect, sir, but do you have a travel pass?"

Mitch turned a threatening look on the boy. "Of course I've got a travel pass. I'm not stupid."

"I only ask because, well, QMs are everywhere these days. Even though I'm along for the ride, I might not be much help if you get pulled over and you don't have a pass. Why are we going to the capital?"

Trina spoke up. "I'll be glad to tell you the whole story."

10:38 AM
Quadrant DC-005

After breakfast, Careen followed Tommy into the stairwell. "Where are we going now?"

"We never finished the tour of Atari Land." He pushed through a fire door to the basement and flipped on the lights in the target range.

Careen looked around in amazement. "How big is this place anyway?"

"Now you've been everywhere that I know about. Look, I've come to respect a nonviolent approach to problem solving, but we both need to know as much as we can about everything, right? So are you up for learning how to use a gun?"

She nodded. "I had a lot of time to think about it too, and you were right. I need to know how to defend myself."

He opened a cabinet and selected a .22. "Let's start with this one." He released the magazine with a flick of his thumb, pulled it out, and handed the weapon to her. Her hand was shaking, but she accepted the gun with a look of determination on her face.

"I'll show you what to do." He gathered safety glasses, ear protection, and a box of ammunition from one of several metal lockers along the wall.

"Are there guns in all of these?" The thought of so much firepower made her nervous.

"In these three, yes. That one over there"—he pointed to a locker set apart from the others—"has explosives and some of his bomb-making stuff."

Tommy laid the .22 and the rest of the items on the shelf in one of the bulletproof booths. Careen peered out at the paper target of a man's torso hanging about ten paces away.

She slipped on her safety gear and watched while Tommy loaded the magazine, inserted it into the grip, and chambered a round. He motioned her into place. She picked up the gun and folded her hands over the grip. He stood behind her, one hand on her shoulder, and when he spoke, his voice sounded far away. She concentrated on every word.

"Feet apart; easy stance. Extend your arms. Line up the front and rear sights. Tip it forward a little, see? Breathe in and hold it before you pull the trigger."

He stepped back out of the booth. Careen locked her elbows, took a deep breath, and pulled the trigger. The force of the explosion was greater than she'd expected. An orange flame shot up from the rear of the gun's barrel, and a brass shell casing popped out, singeing her forearm before it fell to the floor. Even with the ear protection, it was loud enough to evoke flashbacks of the explosion at OP-439.

She laid the gun on the shelf in front of her and backed away, overwhelmed by the desire to curl up in a corner and cry. Tommy touched her on the shoulder and she jumped.

"Hey! Take it easy. That was a good shot. Look!" He pushed a red button on the wall and the target trundled toward them. She'd pierced it in the upper right torso.

"It was ... I wasn't expecting it to be so ... I can't believe I ever pointed a loaded gun at you. What if I'd—"

"Yeah, and this one's just a .22. A caliber that small barely leaves a dent." She looked up at him, wild-eyed. "I'm kidding! Don't think about what might have gone wrong. Concentrate on learning to use the weapon properly."

Her heart thudded in her chest. She chewed on her bottom lip for a moment before she nodded.

He sent the paper target back out and she stepped back into the booth, lined up the sights, and fired, hitting just outside the torso. She adjusted her position and tried again. A gut shot. Who knew it could make her smile? *Okay, I get why Jaycee hangs her targets on her bedroom walls.*

She worked her way through the first ten rounds, taking time to evaluate after each shot. When the magazine was empty, she laid the gun down again and stepped out of the booth.

Tommy had retreated behind the bulletproof glass window. She called to him, "Why don't you take a turn? Show me how it's done?"

"Nah, not right now. I'll help you reload though."

He supervised as she fed bullets into the magazine and inserted it into the grip. When she was ready, he hurried out again. She grew increasingly confident and obliterated six targets before she'd had enough. Her hands shook as she took off the eye and ear protection and fluffed up her hair, but she grinned, eager for his approval. He gazed down at her as he handed her a broom. "How about you sweep up all the shells while I put everything away?"

She watched him return the gun to the cabinet and take out a box of shells for the 9 mm. He filled his pockets as she swept the last of the spent casings into the dustpan and deposited them in the trash. Empowered by the experience, she threw her arms around his neck and stood on tiptoe to kiss him.

"You were great. But we have to go. Right. Now."

"Why? What's the matter?"

He didn't answer, but instead pushed through the fire door and took the stairs two at a time, as though he couldn't get away fast enough. She followed him, perplexed, all the way to his room. As soon as they were inside, he locked the door.

"Tommy, did I do something wrong?"

"No." He was still breathing hard from the pace he'd set on the stairs. "Watching you face something that frightened you and master it was the hottest thing … ever. It was like I couldn't go another minute without—"

When their lips met, she was already sliding her hands down his stomach, and they tugged at each other's waistbands and belts as though there was no established system for their removal.

She pushed his hands away, and like magic she was out of her jeans and he was on top of her and there was no need to think.

She saved the thinking for much later, when she rolled onto one elbow and pressed close to his side to gaze down at him. Since they'd resumed their relationship their intimacies had been all about hello, but this time the intensity suggested a prelude to goodbye.

Had admitting she loved him been a mistake? No amount of love given or received could alleviate the threat of the Link. Tommy's optimism and sense of humor kept her from taking herself too seriously, but would shouldering the weight of her problems end up crushing the qualities she most valued in him? He was half asleep, sated. She nudged him, and he opened one eye.

"Wow. I think you made me forget my name."

She didn't even try to look embarrassed. "My first night here, you said you'd wait until I was ready to go back to the way we were. Now we're together again, but Tommy, we can't ever go back. The Link will always be a part of my life. It doesn't have to be part of yours."

His eye closed. "Sounds like you're trying to get rid of me."

She knew she was making the moment too serious. "No. I just won't hold you to any promises. The Link complicates everything."

He sat up and rolled his eyes. "Yeah, because I hate complicated. Can't handle it."

"You might come to hate it, in time."

"If you really, really want something, you don't give up until you get it. I know what I want. It's time for you to make up your mind."

"Madalyn says the Link is the key to safety and security, but she's wrong. This is the safest place in the world for me." She touched her lips to his. "Right here."

"You're serious?"

"Yes."

He trailed his fingers down her side, following the curve of her waist, and let his hand come to rest on her hipbone. The light on her Link pulsed faster, in time with her heartbeat, and he studied it for a moment before he spoke. "You ever play Hot, Warm, Cold when you were a kid?"

That wasn't what she'd been expecting him to say. "Umm, yeah?"

"Well, I was thinking." He laced his fingers through hers and turned her wrist over. "Your Link will tell me if I'm getting warmer"—he kissed the hollow at the base of her throat—"or not." He gently closed his teeth over the tip of her nose.

She giggled. "Interesting twist on a childhood classic. Tell me more."

"First of all, no laughing." He shook a warning finger at her, and she pressed her lips together until her smile nearly disappeared. "It ruins the game if you don't take it seriously."

"I'm taking it seriously. I promise." The smile threatened to break through again and she bit her lower lip.

"That's better." Under the covers, he trailed his fingers in an undulating line across her stomach. "Hmm. Warm? Cold?" He wiggled his eyebrows and she burst out laughing. He reached for her left wrist and touched his lips to her skin just above the flashing light. "Lie back and close your eyes."

Her hair fanned out on the pillow, and her eyes fluttered closed. Her lips parted in anticipation.

Chapter 25

Madalyn stripped off a silk sheath dress and added it to the growing pile of discards on her bedroom floor. Her ensemble had to be businesslike for the State of the Union address and festive enough for a surprise birthday party given in her honor—without signaling that she'd known about the party in advance. A navy fit-and-flare with soutache flowers on the bodice was under consideration when her phone rang. She glanced at the caller ID and hastened to answer it.

"Madam Director? I have a surprise for you." The tone of Atari's voice jump-started her heart. "It's something, I mean *someone*, you want."

Hardly daring to hope, she whispered into the phone, "Is it ... do you know where she is?"

"You said no questions asked, remember?"

"Yes, only how did you find her without the Link?"

"Ah-ah-ah!"

She broke into a grin. This was going to be her best birthday ever. "Where is she? When can you deliver her?"

"First we need to discuss my compensation."

"We said one million."

"I believe it was five."

"Oh. That's right. So it was."

"I'll need it wired to an offshore account. Not here, obviously. As soon as I see the funds have arrived, she'll be delivered to you within the hour. That should leave plenty of time for you to trot her out before the State of the Union address. Are you ready to write down the account number?"

President Wright read aloud to Garrick and Senator Renald from the notes for his final State of the Union address. "The Office of Civilian Safety and Defense has proven itself to be a nonfunctioning and corrupt institution, and yet has suffered no negative consequences when it fails to achieve its purpose. It must be abolished to clear the way for a better system to emerge." He paused. "This could backfire and throw people into an even worse panic."

Garrick spoke up. "There are a great many people who cling to their belief that the OCSD programs help keep them safe, even when they're presented with evidence to the contrary. The people who've blindly followed Madalyn and Stratford don't realize how out of touch and out of control she is."

Senator Renald nodded. "Her supporters in Congress have proved over and over that they see no reason to break from the status quo. Maybe they'll change their minds when they witness this evening's entertainment firsthand. Garrick, are you ready to press charges against Madalyn?"

He nodded. "We have Madalyn's fingerprints on the vial of poison. The security camera footage doesn't actually show her switching the vials, but it does capture her reaction when Lowell collapsed. We'll depose Trina Jacobs and enter her statement into the record as soon as possible."

He glanced at his watch. "Speaking of Trina, I'm supposed to meet her and give her an escort inside. I downgraded security at the Capitol so she's less likely to be noticed. Don't want an overzealous guard getting trigger-happy. See you soon."

Renald stood. "You're doing the right thing, sir." He followed Garrick out of the Oval Office, leaving President Wright feeling as though he was mustering his troops for battle. The speech was a call to revolt against the OCSD, an agency he'd helped to attain its present height of power.

Throughout the nation's history, every president had surrounded him or herself with trusted advisors. Though people tended to either praise or malign the president as an individual, being president was a team effort.

He'd made the mistake of entrusting too much power to Lowell Stratford and putting his faith in the Office of Civilian Safety and Defense. He wished he'd made a different choice when he'd been new on the job and desperate to quell the people's fears. Stratford's overreach had not eliminated terrorist attacks. On the contrary, the OCSD's recent track record included two recent bombings, the murder of a high-ranking state official, unprecedented civil unrest, and the breakdown of government programs that had been established with the intent of helping the people.

Madalyn Davies did not have her predecessor's commanding presence. Why Stratford had insisted she be the one to succeed him, he'd never understand. She had no experience to prepare her to guide the nation out of peril; instead, she'd made matters worse. When it was over, he hoped he and the rest of the country would be out from under Madalyn Davies's manicured thumb.

5:15 PM
Quadrant DC-005

Tommy startled awake and sat up. "What was that?"

Careen stirred beside him.

The doorknob rattled, and someone pounded on the door. His adrenaline surged, and when Atari's voice rang out, it did nothing to set him at ease. "Intruders! Man the battle stations!"

"What battle stations?" Careen threw back the covers and grabbed her jeans off the floor.

"No idea. We never did battle station drills." He was already half dressed and balancing on one foot as he pulled on his boot. "Where's my gun?" He pushed a chair over to the closet so he could retrieve the magazine and bullets from the top shelf. As he jumped down, she tossed him the empty gun and pulled on her sweater.

The magazine clicked into place, and the spare bullets rattled as he poured them into his pocket. "Ready?"

"No, but let's go."

He unlocked the door and they hugged the wall as they crept toward the lobby. He heard the elevator bell chime and the door slide open, and he held the gun poised as he chanced a look around the corner. Then he laughed aloud. "Mom?" He stuck the gun in his waistband, and he and Careen ran across the lobby to meet her.

Lara's smile warmed him like the sun, and she gathered them both into a fierce embrace. Tears welled up in his eyes for a moment, and beside him he felt Careen draw a shuddering breath. When his mom released them, she kept a hand on Careen's arm. "I couldn't believe you were all right until I saw for myself." She hugged Careen again.

Careen swiped at the tears that trailed down her cheek. "I am now. I missed you so much."

Lara squeezed her shoulder, her gaze a mix of appraisal and empathy. Then she turned a stern gaze on Tommy. "You, on the other hand—sneaking away from the bunker and following your father to the capital was dangerous and unnecessary." Then she winked to show she wasn't really angry. "You couldn't let the grownups handle things, could you?"

He shrugged. "How else am I going to learn the family business?"

Only then did he notice Tom, Eduardo, and Jaycee had followed Lara into the lobby.

Careen brushed past him and threw her arms around the mailman's neck, and he spun her around. *"Carina! Como estás?"*

"Much better now, Eduardo."

Tommy's gaze took in all of them. "Boy, are we glad to see you guys." He winked back at his mom. "It'll be nice to have some backup."

Atari skulked in the doorway of Command Central. "More Baileys? Fantastic. To what do we owe the unexpected honor?"

Tommy caught his father's eye and shot a pointed glance in Atari's direction. Then they spoke at the same time. "We need to talk."

5:25 PM

Jaycee had hesitated beside the elevator while Lara spoke to first Careen and then Tommy. They were all smiling, and Careen wiped away a happy tear. She should have been happy, but she felt pushed aside and forgotten. She'd never had enough of a chance to make Tommy notice her, just as surely as Wes had never had a real opportunity to woo Careen.

Careen had hugged Lara and Eduardo first, but now she hurried to throw her arms around Jaycee. The younger girl kept her left arm at her side to avoid giving away her secret.

"I missed you!" Careen said.

"I missed you too." She lowered her voice to a whisper. "Your sweater's on inside out."

Careen glanced down and her cheeks colored. "Do you think anyone else noticed?"

"Uh, yeah." Jaycee pulled her a few steps away from the group. "Can we talk alone? There's something I have to—"

"I know where you got that."

Jaycee started guiltily. "What?"

Careen touched the vial necklace. "This was mine, but you can have it if you like it. I don't want it any longer."

"Careen, are you ready?" Tommy held the stairwell door open.

Jaycee followed at Careen's heels. "I'm coming too!"

Lara gave a quick shake of the head and addressed Jaycee like she was talking to a little kid. "Not right now, sweetheart. Look at all the games in there! Why don't you go check out the arcade, and we'll be done talking before you know it."

Careen glanced over her shoulder and made a sympathetic face. She whispered back, "Let us talk with Tom and Lara first, and then I'll find you, all right?"

Jaycee tried to conceal her hurt at being left out. *I'm not a baby. If they knew what had happened, they'd see fit to include me.*

She felt a little better when Tom blocked Atari from following them into the stairwell. "I'm sure you understand. We need to discuss some private family business. I'll want a status update from you shortly." Tommy's presence at his father's elbow gave additional weight to Tom's words.

He bowed. "As you wish."

Jaycee watched the strange-looking man turn away, his face angry, as Tom closed the door. A moment later, he put his hand on the door as if to follow, looked at his watch, and then changed his mind. He paced in front of the door as she took a quick look inside the arcade so she could say she had if Lara asked her. She regarded Atari from the doorway and tried to keep her voice casual. "Is it true that you invented the Link?"

When he startled before he turned toward her, she realized he'd forgotten she was there. He showed all of his teeth when he smiled. "Why, yes, sort of."

"Can I ask you something?"

"You already did."

Should she share her secret? This might be her only chance to get help. "How do I"—she pulled up her sleeve—"get this thing off me?"

He came closer, his eyes suddenly bright with interest. "Now why would you want to do that?" He reached toward her wrist with a trembling hand, and she pulled away.

"Because I'm Resistance, that's why! It was the only thing my daddy told me not to do when I left home. Now I've gone and ruined everything. You've gotta take it off."

"No can do, Little Red."

She bristled at both the denial and the nickname, and he threw up his hands in defense.

"Hey! Not my fault. I built the device for the OCSD, but your dad put me up to it in the first place." He leaned forward, a conspiratorial gleam in his eye. "But I can tell you something. The Link will go live unless someone gets rid of the OCSD once and for all." Then he glanced at his watch and shrugged as if to dismiss her. "Make yourself at home. I'm busy." He went back into the room with the computers and shut the door.

So am I. She had no interest in the kitchen or the video games, so she headed down another hallway. She opened a door to a room with a rumpled, unmade bed. *I'm glad I'm not the maid around here.* At the end of the hall was a room full of clothes, wigs, and makeup. She considered a pair of coveralls lying on a chair and held them up against her front. *But I could be a janitor.* She folded them and zipped them up inside her coat. An OCSD ID badge and a set of car keys she found lying on the table went into her pocket.

Back to the lobby and down a flight of stairs, she emerged in a workout room. There was nothing there she could use. But in the basement, she found what she'd been looking for. She loaded up a duffel bag and searched in vain for a door that led to the underground parking garage.

She dashed back up to the lobby, hoping the meeting wasn't over yet, and breathed a sigh of relief. No one was around. She tiptoed across the room and pushed the elevator button but nothing happened. In her whole life, she'd only ridden in a handful of elevators. Maybe there was a trick to it? Her heart pounded as she tapped on the door of the computer room and opened it a few inches. "Umm ... excuse me?"

"Done with the tour already?" Atari didn't turn around.

"Yes, sir."

"Did you go up to the solarium on the roof?"

"No."

"You should check it out. There's a great view of the capital."

"Okay, I will. Only, their meeting's taking forever, and I forgot something in the car. How do I get back down to the garage? The stairs don't go there, and the elevator doesn't work."

He spun around in his chair. "You need the key." He crossed the lobby and used a key that hung on a long chain around his neck. "Pull out the stopper on this button to hold the door open so you can come back up. See? The alarm will sound, but I'll know it's just you." He headed back across the lobby. "You really should check out the solarium."

"Yes, sir. Thank you."

She shouldered the duffel bag as the doors slid closed.

Chapter 26

Trina took over the driving about thirty miles outside the capital. Mitch hadn't let Seamus out of his sight, even to relieve himself, and now when they came out of a clump of bushes near the side of the road, he shoved him into the middle of the truck's bench seat before he got in on the passenger side. As Trina pulled out onto the highway, Mitch regarded the rolling hills with interest.

"Lot of American blood's been spilled in this part of the country. Manassas, Virginia. They don't call it that anymore though."

Cheery. Trina changed the subject. "It'll be strange to go back to my apartment after months away, but I'm looking forward to a hot shower and wearing some of my own clothes."

Mitch tapped the dashboard clock. "We haven't got a lot of time for primping."

"I know that, but I have to blend in at the State of the Union. I can't show up in your sweatshirt and these ratty pants. I wonder what Atari has me wearing in the video."

"Won't matter. Madalyn's the only one who's going to see it. She won't notice if your clothes aren't the same."

Trina laughed. "Only a man would say that. If anyone will notice, it will be Madalyn. How are we going to meet up afterward?"

He didn't answer.

"What? Aren't you going?" Still he was silent. *He's going to throw me under the bus.* No way was she going to let that happen. She kept her voice casual. "After all your hard work you don't want to be there for the payoff?"

Mitch snorted. "Hell, no. I wouldn't be caught dead there. I'll stay in contact with Kevin and watch the action from your place." He pointed a thumb at Seamus. "I've got to keep an eye on him so he doesn't spread the alarm."

Trina nodded and said no more. When they arrived at her apartment complex, she found the spare key on top of the doorframe where she'd hidden it months before.

Mitch hurried her and Seamus inside. "Nice place."

She looked around as though she was seeing it for the first time. It was a nice place. She'd been pleased to rent it when she'd started work at the OCSD, and it was just the way she'd left it back in October. She'd had no idea she wouldn't be returning home, but her mother had always insisted the breakfast dishes be washed and put away before the family left for the day, and now Trina was glad she had kept up the practice.

She motioned toward the television. "The electricity's on, so I assume the automatic withdrawals for all my utilities have continued in my absence. You can turn on PeopleCam. I'm ready for a long, hot shower."

Mitch picked up the remote. "Don't be too long. I'm calling the car service and telling them to be here in half an hour."

She headed into the master suite and stealthily turned the lock, showered, and dressed as fast as she could. After going without makeup for three months, even a touch seemed to make a drastic difference in her appearance.

Good enough for government work. She glanced at the clock. Six minutes left. She opened the medicine cabinet for tweezers, and then got her medical bag out from under the sink.

When she emerged she found them in the living room, watching television. Seamus was seated in a chair, hands tied, while Mitch glowered at him from the sofa opposite. Trina walked up behind Mitch. "Did you call the car?"

"Yeah. It'll be here in four—"

She jabbed a syringe into his neck, pushed the plunger, and then backed out of arm's reach. Mitch clapped his hand over the spot as he turned around. His heavy brow furrowed as he stared at her.

"What did you do?"

Her eyes narrowed. "Call it a preemptive strike. You've been sneaking around making secret plans and doing goodness-knows-what. I don't trust you not to mess up the Resistance's plan."

He rose from the sofa and took an unsteady step toward her, then sank to his knees and fell facedown on the carpet.

Seamus stared in horrified fascination. "What did you do to him?"

She untied the boy's hands. "Intramuscular diazepam. Should knock him out for at least a few hours. I'm not sure we can get him back on the sofa. Just tie him up where he is." She knelt and, with the tweezers, pulled out the earpiece that connected him to Kevin. "Better tie his feet too. I have some therapy bands and a jump rope in the hall closet. I'm sorry to leave you with him, but I've really got to go."

5:32 PM
Quadrant DC-005

Tommy led his family, Eduardo, and Careen to the conference room where he and Atari had met to plan Careen's rescue with Jezz a few weeks before.

His father laid a hand on his arm. "How have you been?"

"Fine, I guess, but in the dark. Atari hasn't let us watch the news for a week. Danni was here yesterday, and according to her, it's pretty bad out there. Dad, what's really going on?"

"The protests and rioting have definitely eclipsed the food riots. The OCSD has used Careen's disappearance to convince people that an activated Link is the only thing that can truly protect them. The whole country seems divided on the issue. There are plenty of adults who don't want their children Linked, while others are demanding Links for themselves."

"I thought the Resistance had things under control! Once Madalyn's arrested, though—"

His father shook his head. "Garrick's case against Madalyn is anything but ironclad. He's got enough evidence to bring charges against her for Stratford's murder, but the evidence is mostly circumstantial."

Eduardo chimed in. "At best, the scandal could be enough to remove her from the director's post."

Tom nodded. "She's wiggled out of plenty of scandals, including the most recent one with the contraband coin, so nothing is certain at the moment. We didn't want to say anything in front of Jaycee, but Mitch's behavior has been erratic. He seems to have cut emotional ties with the girl and doesn't communicate with us anymore either. David and Grace fled BG-098. They believe he'll make sure Trina confronts Madalyn at the State of the Union, but he's not trustworthy. We came here to make sure the State of the Union address runs smoothly."

Tommy's nerves got the better of him, and he laughed.

His parents looked at him like he was the one who was crazy. "What's the matter?"

"Dad, we're just as worried about Atari. He's been acting stranger and stranger since you left. I mean, you saw him just now. He doesn't seem to be sleeping or eating much, and he's quit taking care of himself. Danni was here and told us he's been ducking Mitch's calls. She was supposed to help us get in touch with Mitch, but she left."

"That may have been all for the best, if you believe David's assessment that Mitch has gone, how did he put it? Oh, yes, 'plumb crazy.'"

"Atari's been acting paranoid. He hid in Command Central when he heard the elevator. We heard him arguing on the phone a couple of times."

"With whom?"

"We're pretty sure it was both Mitch and Madalyn. He won't say what's going on. Danni thinks Atari wants to activate the Link, but he won't do it as long as Careen's here, because it would give away the location of his safe house."

Lara seemed taken aback. "Surely Atari wouldn't give control of the Link to Madalyn."

Careen spoke up. "We think he's counting on Madalyn being arrested. Then once she's out of the picture, he'll activate the Link and run it himself. He's been really unpredictable." She glanced at Tommy, and he shook his head as a signal not to say anything about Atari's attack on her.

Tommy added, "He and Mitch have been arguing about the Link ever since I got here."

Tom looked concerned. "Should we delay our meeting with President Wright and Garrick?"

"If you all stick around watching him, he's sure to be suspicious. I get the feeling he's going to try activate it after Madalyn's arrest at the State of the Union. You have to go. We can handle him for a few more hours."

Lara shook her head. "What if he tries to hurt you?"

Tommy pulled the gun out of his waistband and tilted his head toward Careen. "We both know how to use it. Besides, Atari's more of a punching bag than a fighter." He grinned. "Careen broke his nose last week."

His mom looked like she wanted to laugh and scold at the same time. "Really?"

"Yeah. Even Dad socked him when he was here last time."

Lara shot Tom an are-you-serious glance, and he shrugged.

Eduardo nodded. "All right. As soon as the State of the Union address is over, we'll bring Garrick back with us and help you deal with Atari."

They filed out of the room and up the stairs to the lobby, where Atari was waiting on the black leather sofa. As they approached, he looked away with catlike disinterest. Tom spoke first.

"This is an impressive facility you have here, Atari. I don't think I had time to appreciate it on my first visit."

Lara chimed in. "We're grateful to you for hosting Tommy and Careen."

Tom continued. "We have a pending appointment, but before we go, could we get a look at what you've done with the video Mitch and Trina sent up?"

"Of course." Atari swept into Command Central, and they all followed. He pulled one of the keyboards within reach and bought up a file on the large center screen.

They watched in silence as it played.

"Remarkable." Lara nodded. "I'd never have guessed that footage was shot in the bunker. How clever of you to make it look so convincing. And have you sent this along to Kevin?"

"Yes, of course. I like to think my skills are put to good use for the Resistance." Atari popped a chip drive out of one of the machines and handed it to her. "A souvenir of your trip to the capital, milady."

"Thank you." She put it in her coat pocket.

"Excellent. Well, we're heading out to meet with Garrick."

"Right on. Let me see you to the elevator." In the lobby, Atari reached inside his shirt for the elevator key and inserted it to summon the car.

Chapter 27

Trina hurried out of her apartment just as the black town car pulled up. The last time she'd gotten into a car with a stranger, she and Kevin had ended up at Resistance headquarters. This time, the driver was taking her back into the belly of the beast.

As they drew near the Capitol building, Trina stared through the tinted windows at the groups of protesters outside in the chilly, overcast evening. Lights winked from Links on many of their wrists. They held signs with slogans like LINKED FOR SECURITY and LINKS LIGHT THE WAY splashed across them. Others raised their bare left wrists and carried signs with CXD, LIBERTY, and PRIVACY on them. Even as she watched, a fight broke out. Someone crossed the open space to bash another protester over the head with a PEACE–LOVE–LINKS sign. The crowd pushed and shoved, roiling like a stirred-up anthill.

They passed the scene, turned the corner, and pulled into a restricted area where a lone figure was waiting for them. Hoyt Garrick opened the door. "Come this way. I've cut the security forces to the bone so we could sneak you in unnoticed. We'll get you into position in a few minutes." She followed him, the chilly breeze whipping her skirt and coat around her knees. Inside, her heels clicked on the marble floor as he escorted her through a metal door, down a long corridor, and into a room with a conference table. A grid of eight television monitors mounted on the wall showed the House of Representatives chamber from several different angles.

She'd be meeting her greatest enemy there, in a place where many historic things had happened. She hoped when it was over history would be on her side.

"Trina!" Lara Bailey got up from the conference table to greet her, and they embraced. Tom and Eduardo also came to shake her hand.

She looked around. "Where's Kevin? I had something I wanted to talk to him about."

"He'll be arriving shortly, but he's bringing Madalyn to make sure she gets the pertinent information." Lara squeezed her arm. "We saw the completed video. You were quite convincing. We've got no way of knowing exactly how she'll react, though we expect her to be so focused on you that she makes herself vulnerable. You've got to be ready for anything."

Trina felt like nothing could stop her now. "Don't worry. I've been waiting a long time for this moment. I'm going to give Madalyn her birthday present and get what I came for."

7:08 PM
Quadrant DC-005

Atari headed back to Command Central as soon as the elevator door slid closed, and Tommy's scalp prickled at the look he gave Careen as he shut the door. He hoped Atari didn't have another bamboo shoot for his blow darts. *Just don't turn your back on him.* Now that his parents and Eduardo were gone, he wished he'd asked at least one of them to stay behind to increase the numbers against Atari in their favor. He took Careen's hand and tried to sound upbeat. "Now we just have to wait it out. It's going to be okay."

Careen looked around. "Wait. Where's Jaycee?"

"I don't know."

"She said she needed to talk to me about something. I completely forgot!" She motioned for him to wait out of sight and then opened the door to Command Central and asked Atari if he'd seen Jaycee.

"She's in the solarium. There's a lovely view of the capital from up there." His voice sounded normal, and she responded as though she had no concerns at all.

"Yes, there is. It's my favorite place here. Okay, thanks!"

Tommy started to follow her, but she shook her head. "I'm not sure what's bothering her, but why don't you give us a few minutes alone for some girl talk? We'll meet you back here."

The stairwell door had barely closed behind her when Atari hurried out of Command Central. He looked around and glanced at his watch. "Where did she go?"

"You told her to go to the solarium."

"Oh yeah, right." He motioned to Tommy. "Can I show you something?" Tommy shrugged and followed him inside. Atari stood in the center of the room and stared at the white Pong ball ricocheting around the television screens. The oniony odor of Atari's sweat reminded him of a middle-school locker room. His eyes watered. *Jeez, how long has it been since he's showered?*

Atari was silent for so long that Tommy wondered if he'd forgotten anyone else was there. Then he spoke. "Madalyn is a rat who exists in the maze I designed for her. It's full of roadblocks and red herrings. It was hard to predict what she'd do. That made it fun." He looked over his shoulder at Tommy. "There aren't many people who challenge me." He picked up the Rubik's Cube on the shelf above his desk and began twisting the faces without seeming to look at it. "But it's not because she has a superior intellect. She's certainly not my equal. Not even close. Her self-centeredness and her ignorance are what make her unpredictable." He tossed the solved puzzle onto a pile of papers on the desk.

"She knows almost nothing about her pet project. She was shocked when the clasp on her Link locked and she couldn't take it off again. Duh. I mean, how else could you guarantee people would wear it? I figured she'd freak out and give up the program right then and there, since full disclosure and transparency would be bad for her image. The Link doesn't discriminate or differentiate between people. It simply identifies. Yet she still believes she's above it all.

"When she had me Link Careen, I realized she wasn't going to scrap the program. So I did the only thing I could. I got ready to launch it."

Tommy's heart pounded. "So, wait. You're okay with condemning millions of people to a lifetime of being monitored and watched?"

"Information is power, Brainless, but it's also freedom. People will have access to all the information and the freedom that comes with it."

"Doesn't sound like anyone will be free."

"Take away the secrecy and surveillance will become an ordinary part of every Linked person's life. They'll learn to self-censor. They'll invent sneaky little ways to gain some privacy. I wonder what your life will be like with Careen. You know, if you remain an unLinked person."

"That's none of your business, is it?"

Atari's look was pitying. "It will all be my business. You'll be on the outside looking in on *my* relationship with Careen. You may think you share everything with her, but I'll know things about her that you won't. I won't have to wonder whether her pulse races when you touch her ... or not."

Atari snatched his tablet off the desk and shook it in Tommy's face. "Everyone wants something. Trouble is, they all want something *different*. They want Links for their kids. They want Links for themselves. Others want no Links at all. Mitch says 'the Link must fail!' I could delete the software program and leave the OCSD high and dry. But then all the people who want the protection of the Link will be *so devastated*. But will they learn anything? No. They'll still believe they want a life that's one hundred percent secure. It's better if they get a dose of reality.

"The Link technology exists, and we can't call it back. We can only go forward. Mitch was wrong. Letting the Link fail won't solve the problem, just as neither will activating it."

Where are Careen and Jaycee, anyway? "So you don't side with either Mitch or Madalyn?"

"Hah! Everyone knows Madalyn would run the Link into the ground. I've decided to take credit for my creation. After all, it's my magnum opus. That means my most important work."

"Hell, if that's your conclusion, I'll destroy it for you." Tommy pulled the gun and aimed at the main computer, but Atari blocked it with his body, the barrel of the gun no more than a foot from his chest.

"No! Shooting the computer won't do any good."

"Says you. Get out of the way, or I'll shoot you too."

Atari smirked. "Would you?" When Tommy didn't back down, he raised his hands. "Fine. You're responsible for whatever happens next, and you have no idea what you're doing. You can't brute force your way out of this, Hercules." He sized Tommy up. "Or maybe you'll find that you can."

He turned and assumed a spread-eagle position on the wall. Tommy dropped the gun halfway and glanced around for zip ties or an extension cord or anything he could use to subdue him. He was unprepared when Atari lunged for the nearest weapon and, with a perfect golf swing, smashed the marble base of his chess club trophy against Tommy's right leg. Pain like a jolt of electricity radiated from his scarred calf to the base of his skull, and tears welled up in his eyes. Before he could regain his senses, Atari drew the trophy back and drove it like a battering ram into Tommy's knee. He howled in pain as the leg crumpled beneath him. As he fell, the gun skittered out of sight beneath the desk. He saw Atari raise the trophy and swing again, and everything went black.

Chapter 28

Kevin double-checked that the video loaded on his phone was ready to play and then gave himself an extra spritz of cologne. He'd been playing double agent for almost a month, but tonight he was perspiring like he had opening-night jitters. If the plan worked, it would be Madalyn's swan song as director of the OCSD.

He turned up his collar and lined up the ends of his tie, but his hands were shaking and the resulting Half Windsor knot looked sloppy. He undid it and began again.

When he was satisfied, he stuck his head out into the reception area, motioned for Nicole to come into his office, and closed the door behind her.

"All the party plans in order?"

"Oh, yes, everything's ready. I was just about to head over to the Capitol."

"You don't need to do that. Actually, I was wondering how much of it you can send back or cancel."

"Why? Aren't we having the director's surprise party?"

"Not exactly. But she needs to think we are, so I didn't want to say anything until the last minute. You don't have to go to the Capitol. And this place is a ghost town. If you have plans, go."

"If you don't need me, I think I'll see what food can be donated and then go home. I don't know if I'll be able to find an appropriate place for the ice sculptures." She sighed. "I really liked the ice sculptures."

He felt bad that she'd been excited about the party, and that she'd planned the nonevent with such care. "On second thought, don't get rid of the champagne fountain, okay? We might want to ring in 2035 when all this is over."

"All right. Kevin?"

"Yes?"

"Happy New Year."

He followed her out of his office and headed for the lobby. It was showtime.

7:45 PM

Madalyn had initiated the five-million-dollar wire transfer before her hair and makeup person arrived, and she'd been so nervous she'd badgered the woman to tears. But the end result was stunning. Her navy dress was perfect. All she wanted for her birthday was Careen.

Should she wait in her office until Atari delivered the girl? It would be more dignified, but the longer she waited, the more anxious she became, and her dignity eroded. She didn't want anyone to know she'd found out what Kevin and Nicole were up to the other day, but with the prospect of getting Careen back dangled in front of her, she found she couldn't care less about the surprise party. She checked the time on her phone and headed for the lobby. Kevin was already there and hurried toward her.

"Come on! Let's go!"

She couldn't go until Careen was in custody. "So soon? I mean, don't we still have a few minutes?"

"No! Didn't Garrick get ahold of you?"

Kevin's phone pinged with an incoming text. He looked at it and swore. "We don't have time to discuss the details now. We have to get over there before it's too late." He took her by the arm and hustled her out to their waiting town car.

As soon as they were settled, she asked, "What in the world is going on?"

"The real terrorist was inside the OCSD building all along. I still can't believe it. The chemical weapons attack was an inside job."

"What? There was never any real chemical weapons threat. Stratford made it up, remember? You reminded me just the other day."

Kevin shook his head. "Turns out that's not true. Garrick turned up evidence that Stratford and Trina were working together from the beginning. She knew everything. When she demanded too much power, Stratford shut her up." He added, "There really is a poison, and Phase Three really is the antidote. Somehow, Trina's got them both."

"She was working with Stratford? Why didn't I ... so she really was a terrorist?"

"Looks like it. She fooled me too. Garrick's got intel that she's returned to the capital, and he has the QM out looking for her."

"But where? How?"

The car pulled up to the Capitol. When the driver had helped Madalyn out, Kevin took her by the arm again and hustled her inside. When they were in the hall outside the House of Representatives chamber, he checked his phone and swore again.

"We're too late."

"I thought we'd ordered increased security!"

"She got past it somehow. This is the live stream from the State of the Union address."

Madalyn grabbed the phone out of his hand and watched in horror. Trina Jacobs, looking dignified and professional, just as she had when she worked at the OCSD, stood in the center of the room and addressed the House and the Senate.

"The chemical weapons threat you heard so much about last fall was real, and Lowell Stratford's plan was farther-reaching than anyone realized. Once he'd used CSD to bring everyone under his control, he planned to unleash the chemical weapons anywhere in the world that he believed posed a threat to our security. That, combined with a civilian army that was on a heavy dose of CSD, would have put our country firmly in control as the world's greatest superpower."

There was a murmur of assent from the members of Congress.

"Obviously, the man was insane. And as it turns out, we've got some people in the room who agree with him! I'm here to tell you that the days of complacency, complicity, and corruption are over. In a few minutes, the president will giving his final State of the Union address—but not all of you will be alive to hear how it ends.

"Some of you think it's a fine idea to poison people. But how does it feel to know that the same toxins you'd unleash on other humans have been piped in through the ventilation system here? We have three minutes until the poison will be released."

Everyone started yelling and jumped up from their seats.

Madalyn clutched at her throat as she watched Trina on the screen. *How long can I hold my breath?* If she turned and ran, could she get away in time?

"Wait!" Trina's magnified voice boomed over the crowd. "You can't get away in time. Your only hope is one of these." She held up a little amber bottle.

"You stood by and let Lowell Stratford do whatever he wanted. Search your soul and be honest with yourself—if you can. Did you accidently fail the people you were elected to serve? Or did you knowingly lord your power over everyone? Did you refuse to abide by the rules and laws that apply to everyone else? Did you have plenty to eat during the food riots? Did you push to have humans drugged and microchipped so they could be controlled and kept under constant surveillance?"

Madalyn stood frozen in the hallway as Trina glanced at her watch. "Okay. I could go on and on, but obviously I gotta wrap this up. The Resistance has been watching you, and you're either on our Naughty or Nice list. There's a bottle taped to the underside of your chair. If you're on the Nice list, the antidote will save you. But if you've been too naughty, you have a placebo dose."

The members of the legislative branch of the federal government abandoned all dignity as they overturned their chairs, jostled, and crawled over one another to claim the bottles.

Trina craned her neck and grinned as she watched them scramble. "Everyone drink up! We've got about fifteen seconds left."

Madalyn went cold with horror. She'd sold the formula for the poison to that terrorist and passed it off as CSD. She had a vague sense that all this was related. She'd be responsible for what happened to the people in the next room, not some terrorist's minions! She shoved Kevin's phone back into his hand and burst through the double doors.

"Wait! Stop! It's poison!"

Chapter 29

Careen dashed up the stairs and burst through the door of the rooftop solarium, calling for Jaycee, but there was no reply. Night had fallen, and the huge space was cast in shadow. Could the girl be refusing to answer, sulking because she'd been left out of the meeting?

She checked every corner, hoping she'd simply curled up and fallen asleep on one of the chaises, but she was nowhere to be found.

Careen ran back down the stairs to check the library and then the gym. She was driven to speed by her mounting concern and was panting when she arrived at the basement.

Someone had been there since she and Tommy had taken target practice. The locker that Tommy said had contained Atari's bomb-making supplies was open and empty.

Her heart pounded as she headed up the last flight of stairs. As she rounded the turn at the landing, Atari's voice rang out.

"Oh, there you are."

He stood several steps above her, clutching a trophy.

"Where is she? Where's Jaycee?"

"Don't know. Don't care. She told me she forgot something in the car. That was the last time I saw her."

"Then why did you tell me she was in the solarium?"

"My bad. Come on. We'll go find her together."

She followed him up the stairs. "Where's Tommy?"

He turned around and lunged for her. She wobbled on the top step, and his hand closed around her left wrist. "He doesn't figure into things anymore."

He held her arm up as he dragged her into the lobby. "Why, your heart's going like a little bunny rabbit's!" The rank smell of him filled her nostrils and conjured the memory of the QM interrogator who'd laughed and taunted as he'd nearly strangled her. She drew gasping, panicky breaths. Atari's face was just inches away. "What's the matter? Don't you still believe the Link will protect you? Madalyn's looking forward to seeing you again." He laughed as the light on her Link flashed even faster.

Her panic turned to anger as she realized she wasn't powerless this time. She wrenched her arm free and he fell against the sofa. He made a grab for the tablet lying there as she pulled the .22 out of her waistband and leveled it at him.

"You're just postponing the inevitable." He advanced on her, holding the tablet where she could see it. "Put it down, sweetheart, and come with me now, or I'll activate the Link."

She stood her ground. "I'm not going anywhere with you."

"Of course you are. You have to. It's part of the game."

She glanced around the lobby.

"There's no one to help you." Atari's lips curled back around his feral smile. "I think this is what Eduardo would call a Mexican standoff, and it's just about to end." He held his finger poised over the Activate button on the screen.

The door to Command Central opened. They both looked, and Careen cried out in horror. Tommy, hair matted with blood, sagged against the frame.

"Don't!"

Atari's finger touched the screen just as Careen pulled the trigger.

8:40 PM
Quadrant DC-001

Finding the OCSD building had taken Jaycee longer than she'd anticipated. It should have been easy, since it towered over all the nearby structures. Instead, she'd been confused by the traffic and the one-way streets. City driving was more difficult than driving on the country roads at home.

She parked the van with the OCSD logo on the side panel at the back of the employee parking lot, and chewed her lip as she looked out at the imposing building before her. It was something like a portal to hell, if her father was to be believed. Now that she was here, she had doubts about her plan.

She gave herself a mental shake. *I can do this. Tommy and Careen and Wes all snuck into this building before. It can't be that hard.* As long as no one looked at the name or the photo on the ID badge clipped to her coveralls, she'd be just fine.

She glanced at herself in the rearview mirror and adjusted the knit cap, pulling it low over her eyes. None of her fiery red hair peeked out. *Stop stalling. Just go.* Whatever danger she faced now would be worth it if she could cripple the OCSD and destroy their ability to use the Link.

She swung the duffel bag onto her shoulder as she headed across the lot, swiped the ID card at the employee entrance, and the guard on duty at the security stand waved her through. Thick carpeting muffled her footsteps, and she tried not to stare as she crossed the expansive lobby. She wished she had time to climb the curving staircase to see what everything looked like from the balcony above the lobby. *I might be one of the last people to ever visit here. It's an awfully pretty place, maybe the prettiest I've ever seen, but what they do here is bad. They've done bad things to Careen and Wes, and now to me. I'll be the one who puts an end to it.*

She found the elevator and studied the directory before she pushed one of the buttons. The director's suite was the perfect place to begin the end of the OCSD. But when she peeked around the corner, she saw a woman at a desk in the outer office. She looked nice, even though she obviously worked there, and Jaycee was struck by a pang of conscience. But then she felt her resolve strengthen.

If I give a shout and let people escape, it won't fix the problem. She headed back to the elevator.

8:38 PM

Madalyn skidded to an undignified halt in the center of House of Representatives chamber. It looked nothing like the scene she'd witnessed on Kevin's phone. The room was in perfect order, each member of Congress in their seat, though a few of the representatives jumped to their feet and applauded when she came in. She looked around in confusion. "Where is she? Where's Trina Jacobs? There's no surprise party.... " The applause stopped, and everyone sat, as confused as she.

"I'm right here."

Trina made her way through the rows of seats until she faced Madalyn across the open floor. Madalyn looked around wildly. "Bailiff! Arrest this woman at once!" No one moved.

Trina took another step to close the distance between them. "Don't you have something you'd like to confess?"

"I could ask you the same thing."

Trina grinned like she was having the time of her life. "Why don't you go first?"

Madalyn, cornered, cried, "I don't want a surprise party. I'm not turning forty! I'm only going to be thirty-six!"

Someone in the seats guffawed.

Trina turned and pointed to acknowledge the man who had laughed. "Okay, Madalyn. Let's run with that. Tell us more."

"I lied about my age and falsified my records so I could go straight to law school."

Some of her audience burst into incredulous laughter, but angry murmurings rose above it. Madalyn's face flamed. "What? I didn't need college. Professor Tom Bailey thought he was teaching me a lesson when he had me kicked out of law school. But I found that academic credentials and honesty don't matter in the real world. Isn't this proof? I'm the director of the OCSD, and I'm only thirty-five."

Trina advanced on her, flashing the amber bottle she held in her hand. Madalyn tried to dodge, but Trina caught her by the arm. "Relax. It's the same formula you gave me." Then she spoke to the room. "That certainly explains a few things, but it's not the confession I had in mind. What else will we find out about you when the Link is activated?"

Madalyn tossed her head and tried to pull free. "I don't know what you're talking about. You're the wanted criminal."

"Who killed Lowell Stratford?"

"You did! Everyone knows that. It happened on live television!"

"Not everyone believes it's true." Hoyt Garrick moved to the center of the floor. "Where did you get the poison?"

Madalyn looked at Trina as though expecting her to answer. When Trina remained silent, Madalyn pointed a shaking finger at her. "Trina made it."

Trina laughed. "I would have destroyed that experimental batch of antidote if Stratford hadn't locked me up. You found it in the refrigerator in my lab and used it to poison Lowell, didn't you?"

"I didn't mean to poison *him!*" Madalyn bit her lip, and Trina gripped her arm harder.

"Who then?"

Madalyn's glance flicked to where President Christopher Wright stood at the podium.

Garrick stepped forward and reached for Madalyn's other arm, but Trina gave him the antidote bottle and then signaled for him to wait.

"Madalyn has something to say to me and to Careen Catecher. Don't you, Madalyn?"

Madalyn looked around for some means of escape. Kevin stood in front of the nearest door, arms folded, grinning from ear to ear. She tried to wrench free again, but Trina hung on, slapped her across the face, and shook her by the shoulders.

"I want an apology in front of God and everyone. Now!"

Madalyn tossed back her tumbled hair. Her chest heaved with unvented fury and humiliation. Garrick unscrewed the lid on the antidote bottle, but Trina shook her head.

"It doesn't count if she's dosed."

"Fine!" Madalyn spat out the word. "I'm sorry. Okay?"

Garrick took over and fastened on handcuffs. "Madalyn Davies, you're under arrest for the murder of Lowell Stratford and the attempted assassination of the president of the United States, and for high treason for aiding a suspected terrorist organization. You have the right to remain silent ... oh, wait. Criminals don't have Miranda Rights anymore, do they? I'm looking forward to hearing the details of your confession."

A smattering of applause echoed through the chamber as he led her toward the door.

Relief showed on President Wright's face as he called the room to order. "Members of Congress, I realize it's unusual to ask you to respond on such short notice, but in light of recent events, I ask you to attend to this matter immediately, as it's within my capacity to recommend measures that I deem necessary and expedient.

"Now, about that vote to reduce the power of the Office of Civilian Safety and Defense.... "

Chapter 30

The gun blast that echoed in the lobby was louder than any of Atari's video games. Careen stared down at the red stain blossoming on Atari's shirt.

Tommy limped toward her, and she could hardly hear her own words as she shouted, "Is he dead?"

Atari groaned and clutched at his shoulder. "I *totally* did not see that coming!"

Tommy looked down at him. "Nope. Not dead."

"Are you all right?" Careen asked Tommy, the gun still pointed at Atari.

"More or less. He smashed my knee pretty good."

"Your knee? What about your head? You're bleeding an awful lot."

Atari groaned. "*I'm* bleeding an awful lot, you stupid girl!" He tried to sit up and fell back, clutching his shoulder. "Help me!"

She shook her head. "Where's Jaycee?"

"She told me she forgot something in the car. I put her on the elevator, and that was the last I saw of her."

"You let her leave?"

"No. Maybe? Ow! Jeez, it hurts so much I can't even think."

"Where would she have gone?" Tommy shouted to Careen.

"Stop yelling, both of you! We can track her." Atari winced as he raised his arm to tap his left wrist. "She's in the club."

"Oh, shit. She's Linked?" Tommy turned to Careen. "No wonder she wanted to talk to you." He looked down at Atari. "How much time do we have before the QM starts hunting people down?"

"I don't know. It's not like anyone said, 'On your mark, get set, go!' The QM has had a training sim running on their hand scanners for about a week. Now it will switch over, and at some point, they'll realize it."

Careen handed Tommy the gun and dashed down the hall, returning a few moments later with the getaway bag they'd packed and two heavy winter coats. "The disguises could help for a while."

"My gun's under the desk in Command Central. Can you please get it?" She hurried off again, and Tommy kept the .22 pointed at Atari as he reached for the man's throat. Atari cowered and tried to fight him off, but Tommy's fingers closed on the chain around Atari's neck and liberated the elevator key with a single tug.

Careen reappeared, took shelter outside the open doorway, and opened fire on the computer equipment in Command Central. Sparks flew as she emptied the magazine. Atari covered his head with his good arm and writhed on the floor.

When she was finished, Tommy shook his head. "Overkill much?" he shouted.

She grinned. "I know you've got plenty more bullets."

He limped over to the elevator and inserted the key. It whirred as the car ascended.

Atari reached out to Careen. "Don't leave me here! I'll die alone."

She stayed out of his reach. "How did Jaycee get Linked?"

He let his hand fall and clutched his shoulder. "No idea. And to be honest, it's not my biggest concern at the moment."

Tommy pulled the emergency stopper to hold the elevator and grabbed their getaway bag. "Come on!" When Careen didn't move, Tommy gave her a pointed look. "He probably won't die. It's just a flesh wound. But so what if he does?"

Atari groaned. "How would you know? You're not a doctor."

Tommy ignored him. "We can come back for him later." Then he looked down again. "Just keep pressure on it."

"What if you don't come back?" His fingers came away red with fresh blood. "I'm still bleeding! You have to get me to a hospital."

"After you show us how to use the program to find Jaycee."

"All right, all right!"

Tommy put the tablet in his coat pocket, and he and Careen got Atari to his feet, into the elevator, and across the underground garage to one of the marked OCSD vans. Careen sat in the second-row seat and busied herself twisting her hair into a ponytail and pulling on the light brown wig.

"Are you all right to drive?" she asked.

"Yeah, I think so. It doesn't hurt much anymore." Tommy handed the tablet to her, and she addressed Atari as Tommy started the engine.

"How does it work?"

"You can do a search by name or ID number."

Careen typed clumsily as the van lumbered up the ramp. "I have a Carraway, Josephine."

Tommy asked, "Is that her real name?"

"I guess."

Atari groaned from the passenger seat. "Now choose Locate."

Careen touched the button on the screen, and a map of the United States appeared. The view zoomed in to a single flashing red dot among many. *It really does work in seconds.* "It says she's at the OCSD building." She locked eyes with Tommy in the rearview and then poked Atari on the back of his wounded shoulder.

"Dammit, that hurts! What's the matter with you?"

She was unrepentant. "Why is this thing telling us to go to the OCSD? Is this part of the game?"

"You're the one who's using it, not me. It's telling you that because that's where she is."

"Why would she go there?"

Tommy braked to a stop inside the automatic gate. "Do you think she's been arrested?"

"How am I supposed to know?" Atari said.

"For all we know, you could have set her up." He looked over his shoulder at Careen. "It's up to you whether we go or not. It's New Year's Eve, so the building's probably nearly empty. Madalyn's got to be at the Capitol for the State of the Union by now. If no one at the OCSD building realizes the Link is live, they might not be watching the scanners. But you're the one with the most to lose."

She pushed down her own panic. "If they've caught Jaycee, she'll be tortured just like I was. We have to try to get her out of there."

"Okay. I'm in." He guided the van onto the road.

They rode in tense silence down the empty streets as Careen read the navigation directions on the tablet. "We're two minutes out."

Atari stirred. "What time is it?"

"Almost nine."

"Here. If you must." Atari opened the glove box and pulled out an OCSD ID badge. "All access backstage pass." Tommy parked the van in the lot and reached for the ID. "No, not here. Park in the back. Get as far away from the building as possible so ... they don't notice me."

"I don't want to have to run all the way across the lot on our way back." Tommy cut the engine, and Careen slid open the side door, but Atari made no move to get out.

"I can't. I feel faint."

"Fine. Then just wait here. Remember to keep pressure on it." Tommy dabbed at the blood on his face before putting on his wig and glasses. He and Careen headed for the employee entrance.

8:51 PM
Quadrant DC-001

Garrick led Madalyn out of the chamber and into the West Hall. One of the security staff met them there, clutching a walkie-talkie. "Sir, the number of protesters on the grounds has doubled in the last hour. We're working on clearing a secure way out for you. If you could hold here for a few minutes?"

Garrick had taken Madalyn out of the chamber, partly to remove her influence or fear of her wrath, but also to signal to Congress that she was done for, no matter how they voted. But that didn't mean he wasn't dying to find out what would happen next.

He looked over his shoulder. "I wouldn't mind hanging around for the vote. We'll stay out of sight so no one feels pressured or influenced." Madalyn shot him an angry look, and he grinned in return.

The guard nodded and left through the double doors to the main hall.

As the applause in the chamber died down, Kevin caught Trina's eye and gave her a low-key thumbs-up. He strained to hear Mitch's voice in his ear. It was strange that he hadn't heard from him, after the way Mitch had micromanaged everything leading up to the moment Trina confronted Madalyn. Kevin intended to follow Garrick, and had threaded his way to the aisle when he changed his mind. If Mitch's earpiece had malfunctioned, he'd want a play-by-play of what happened inside the chamber. He returned to his seat and focused his attention on the representative who was speaking.

"We haven't had any time to discuss this. I object to having to make a decision on the spot."

Another who was seated a few rows away from him agreed. "We don't know what this will mean for our country. Downgrading the OCSD's power could open us up to a whole new set of problems."

There was a murmur of assent, in which Kevin heard the word *terrorism*, and he suppressed a sigh of frustration.

"There are programs in place that will be affected if we just cut the OCSD off at the knees like this."

"Think of all the OCSD employees who will lose their jobs."

"People could have starved to death under the Restrictions if President Wright hadn't stepped in during the food riots." *Finally, someone who gets it!* Kevin waited for someone else to agree.

"Shouldn't this require a full investigation before we make a decision?"

Senator Brandon Renald stood. "We have a plan ready that outlines how to move forward without the OCSD and the Restrictions. It's simple and straightforward enough that we can all take a minute and look it over. Please keep an open mind. Time is of the essence." He signaled to several pages at the back of the room, who then began distributing the report prepared by David Honerlaw and Grace Hughes.

An elderly senator seated two chairs away from Kevin pushed his copy of the report aside without reading it. "Madalyn Davies was the problem. Now that she'll be stepping down, there's no reason to discontinue the Cerberean Link program."

The vice president, as presiding officer, repeated his instructions to read the report, but the elderly senator didn't comply. Kevin glanced through his, and sat biting his nails until everyone was done and the vice president called the vote. The members of Congress lined up to use the electronic voting machines located at various points around the room, swiped their key card and then pressed Yay or Nay.

When the votes were tallied, the vice president announced, "Congress votes not to downgrade the powers of the Office of Civilian Safety and Defense."

Kevin made his way out of the chamber, feeling the weight of the stares. He emerged in the main hall just in time to see Garrick and Madalyn about fifty paces ahead of him. As they turned the corner, he heard what sounded like a heavy book being dropped flat on a wooden table, followed immediately by another. As he wondered who was dropping books and why, he saw Hoyt Garrick fall and lay, unmoving, on the carpeted floor.

Kevin's instinct took over, and he dove across the hall into a coatroom before he fully comprehended what had happened. He heard two men's voices getting closer as he crouched in the shadows.

"Shit! That was lucky. Talk about being in the right place at the right time."

"Sitting ducks, man."

The door opened, and then closed with a click. The two men must have gone inside. He heard another gunshot, and began to shake as he remembered Trina was still inside with the others. He had to get help.

He held his breath as he listened for sounds of others approaching but heard nothing. He waited another moment before gathering the courage to crawl to the doorway and peer out.

Garrick lay on the floor, glasses askew, with one arm thrown out to the side. Kevin scrambled to his feet and ran toward him. As he drew near, Madalyn Davies came into view around the corner, a few paces away, where she lay crumpled on her side, eyes open. Blood had turned her navy dress black around the bullet wound in her chest. Her Link wasn't flashing.

Fearful of another ambush, Kevin glanced around before kneeling between them and pressing two fingers to Garrick's neck. His own pulse was thudding so hard he couldn't tell if Garrick was alive or dead. Then the chief marshal's eyelids fluttered and he made a wheezing sound.

Kevin pulled out his phone and dialed 911. "Hang on. I'm getting help," he said to Garrick as he applied pressure to the wound on his chest. He realized with a jolt that he was going to have to keep a level head—and keep his head down. He was now acting director of the OCSD. He might well be the next target.

Chapter 31

Sheila Roth's smile trembled as she addressed the camera. "And so it seems there's a bit of a delay going into President Wright's final State of the Union address. If you've just joined us, the fugitive Trina Jacobs has brazenly attacked OCSD director Madalyn Davies in the House chamber, in front of the entire Congress, the president, and the vice president. Chief QM Hoyt Garrick has escorted Director Davies to safety. No word on whether or not Jacobs is in custody at this time. We'll take you back to the State of the Union when they're ready to begin."

Pete shook his head as he watched Sheila grasping to fill the on-air time by herself. He turned to the station manager. "That is the most ridiculous fictionalization I've heard from her yet! We should be broadcasting the debate and the vote!"

The manager shook his head. "I'm not sure if we should have let any of that go out."

"Hell, yes, we should! This is the beginning of something big. Don't deny what you just saw. Madalyn Davies was arrested for murdering Lowell Stratford! History is happening tonight." He pulled out his phone, texted one of the camera operators on the remote team, and told him to make sure he had all his gear in the truck.

The station manager grabbed his own phone and asked to speak to the floor manager. They both kept one eye on the monitor where Sheila, with nothing to read on the teleprompter, was back from a commercial break and obviously having someone feed her information over her earpiece.

"Oh ... all right. Yes, we're getting some new information now. It appears President Wright has called for a vote to ... oh my goodness! To downgrade the powers of the OCSD?" She turned her face away from the camera, but her microphone was still on. "Are you *sure*?" When she recovered her dignity, she folded her hands on the desk. "Well, regardless. Though that seems like the last thing that should be done at a time like.... I'm sure everything will be just fine. In just a moment I understand we'll ... oh, okay. Yes, we'll be taking you back to the Capitol, live, for the vote."

Pete clapped the station manager on the shoulder. "PeopleCam is the only news outlet available in this country. We can't ignore this or be like Sheila and try to cover it up. We should have every available reporter out there. Live feed, no censors. Let everyone in the country see what's going on." He headed for the door. "My suspension was complete BS, and I know you did it to appease Madalyn. I'm commandeering a mobile unit, and you're putting me on lead. I'll be in front of the Capitol and ready to go in twenty minutes."

Pete doubled back and stuck his head into the station manager's office. "And get Sheila off the air, for crying out loud! She's an embarrassment."

9:10 PM

Half an hour before, Trina had wanted to pinch herself to make sure she wasn't dreaming. She'd confronted Madalyn Davies, just as she'd imagined, and gotten a confession *and* an apology. Never mind that the apology was less than heartfelt. Madalyn had her limits.

When she realized Kevin was staying for the discussion and the vote, she sat too, though she couldn't wait to talk to him. When they'd been at Resistance headquarters together, they'd half-jokingly discussed doing this very thing to Madalyn, and a celebration was definitely in order. Suddenly she grinned. With Madalyn out of the picture, Kevin was the acting director. It really had worked!

She grew impatient as the discussion went on and on. *The OCSD is corrupt and evil. Fact. What else is there to talk about?* Evidently, the members of Congress thought there was plenty. She folded her arms on her chest and tried not to roll her eyes. She saw many of them give no more than a cursory glance to the report David and Grace had worked so hard to prepare.

When the vice president announced the vote to downgrade the OCSD's powers had failed, she wanted to scream. Kevin would be a much better director than Madalyn, but that wasn't the point. The Resistance had thrown all their efforts behind getting rid of the OCSD once and for all. Whoever succeeded Kevin someday could be every bit as power-hungry as Stratford and Madalyn had been.

When she saw Kevin hurry out of the chamber immediately after the vote she stood up to follow, but he was out of sight by the time she walked around the back of the chamber. As she headed for the door, two security guards in dark suits blocked her path.

"If you'll have a seat, ma'am."

"Oh, I'm not a congresswoman. I'm just on my way out."

"There's been a bit of a security issue in the hall. We need you to stay here."

She looked from one to the other. There was no way they were going to let her pass. She turned and took the nearest open seat.

The senator next to her leaned over and whispered, "Nice speech."

She couldn't help smiling. "Thanks."

His gaze was on the two security guards. "What did they say to you?" She started to turn around, but he shook his head. "Don't look."

"There was a security issue in the hall."

"They're not our security. Not QM or Special Forces, either."

The vice president stepped down from the podium and made way for the president, who looked out over the room, ready to begin his State of the Union address.

She murmured, "There are a bunch of stupid people in Congress, present company excluded. How can they actually think that getting rid of Madalyn will be enough? It wasn't enough when she got rid of Stratford."

He was looking over her shoulder again and shushed her. "We've got trouble."

This time Trina didn't try to be subtle when she looked around. Everyone was aware of the men in dark suits that rushed through the doors on all sides of the room.

A shot rang out. The senator shoved her sideways, and she toppled out of her chair and landed sprawling behind the desk. Screams mingled with the crash of chairs that tipped over as their occupants sought similar cover. Trina peeked between the desks at others who had made a run for the exits and now found themselves trapped in a logjam in the aisles. The scene looked so much like the video Atari had created to trick Madalyn that her brain refused to accept it as real.

A man's voice boomed out over the disorder and noise. "Ladies and gentlemen, if we could have all of you please return to your seats. Place your hands on the desks in front of you. Don't reach for your phones. We're going to reopen the discussion about the vote. But this time, we're going to talk and you're going to listen."

9:15 PM

Pete, his camera operator, and their producer had to talk their way through a security barricade to pull the mobile news unit close to the Capitol. When he stepped out of the van, Pete felt a rush of adrenaline, like he was headed into battle. And what a battle scene was what it was!

Protesters filled the plaza in front of the building, waving signs and chanting. Some of the Linked raised their left fists in solidarity and cheered. Others without Links waved signs and showed their bare lefts wrists as they shouted down the Linked.

Pete stood positioned himself so the protesters were visible in the background. "'If you don't want it printed, don't let it happen.' The student newspaper at my alma mater adopted that slogan back in the early part of this century. It's become increasingly clear that we in the media can't stop things from happening. But neither can we turn our back on the truth. I'm going to be here, bringing you live coverage of the disturbance at the Capitol, for as long as there's more story to tell. Here's what we know so far. Madalyn Davies confessed to killing Lowell Stratford with a dose of poison meant for President Wright, and has been placed under arrest. This should lead to Trina Jacobs and Careen Catecher being cleared of the charges against them. The president has called for a vote to downgrade the powers of the OCSD. How this will affect the pending activation of the Cerberean Link is yet to be determined. Stay tuned to PeopleCam for continuing coverage as the events unfold."

Pete's producer was listening on his headset. "You're clear. They say they're going back to the feed from the House chamber." He paused and listened again. "Really? We didn't see anyone go into the building. We'll try and find out what's going on." He turned to Pete. "The studio received video of armed gunmen invading the House chamber. Then they lost contact."

9:25 PM

As soon as the paramedics loaded Garrick into an ambulance, Kevin's driver took him back to the OCSD. It was the safest place they could think of to go; security was on duty there around the clock.

He'd barely made it through the doors when an alarm went off. Two guards from the security stand ran past him. "What's going on?" Kevin shouted after them..

"Security breach at the visitor's entrance. Stay here, sir."

Seconds later they were back, dragging a young man and woman with them.

The young man struggled to free himself as he shouted across the lobby. "Kevin! It's us! We need your help!"

The guard, in an attempt to silence the young man, struck him and knocked his glasses off.

Kevin did a double-take. "Release them immediately!"

"No can do, sir. They used an ID that was flagged as stolen."

"It's all right. They're with me." The guard still looked as though he might refuse. Kevin shouted above the alarm, "Madalyn Davies is dead! I'm the director. I'm in charge now. Do it."

The guards looked at each other and let go of Tommy and Careen, and Kevin took a few steps closer so he wouldn't have to shout. "What are you doing here?"

Tommy swore. "Did you say Madalyn's dead? What happened?"

Careen nudged him. "First things first. Jaycee's in here some-where. Was she arrested?"

"Not that I know of. I just came from the—"

"What the hell?" One of the guards drew his weapon, and Kevin turned to see Atari, his face bruised and his clothes bloodstained, staggering across the lobby. He wavered on his feet as he pointed at Tommy and Careen, and Kevin had to strain to hear him over the alarm.

"Careen Catecher and Tommy Bailey kidnapped me and shot me. The Resistance has seized control of the Link. There's a bomb in the ... " His eyes rolled up in his head. No one made a move to catch him, and he collapsed to the floor.

Tommy and Careen both started shouting at once.

Kevin couldn't understand what they were saying, so he bellowed at the guard. "Call an ambulance! Turn off that alarm and lock this place down. That's an order!"

Tommy shook his head. "No! No! Don't lock it down. Evacuate! We didn't set a bomb, but what if Atari did?" He turned to Careen. "Oh my gosh! That's why he was gone for hours the other day."

"And why the explosives locker at the safe house is empty."

Tommy slapped his forehead. "Create a diversion and set off an explosion. Why didn't I see it? He does this every time. We've got to hurry and find Jaycee. She doesn't know!"

Kevin could hear the approaching ambulance's siren. "I'll send guards after her."

"No! She'll panic if she sees guards, but she probably won't hide from us." Careen pushed the button to summon the elevator and pulled a tablet out of her coat pocket. "We can find her faster using her Link. This thing has an indoor search function. You hurry and clear the building."

Kevin wanted to make sure he hadn't missed anything. "Jaycee's Linked. Madalyn's dead. Garrick's been shot. Everyone in the House chamber has been taken hostage. And Mitch is missing."

As the elevator door slid closed, Tommy called after him, "You guys really know how to celebrate New Year's Eve in the capital!"

Kevin pulled out his phone as he ran up the grand staircase.

Chapter 32

Tommy watched Careen's face as she studied the tablet. "You're doing a great job with the computer. I thought you didn't use them."

"I said I don't like to. I didn't say I couldn't."

The elevator doors slid open, and he checked to make sure the coast was clear before he let her follow Jaycee's signal into the basement of the OCSD.

She whispered, "I'd hoped I'd never have to come back here."

He nodded. "I know. I say that every time."

Careen consulted the tablet and pointed to the right. As he rounded the corner, a thin figure in coveralls stood outside what he recognized as Kevin's old office. "Jaycee!"

The girl whirled around and thrust out her chin as they hurried toward her. "What are you doing here? You're wasting your time if you're here to try to stop me."

Careen's tone was soothing. "Whatever Atari told you—"

"This is the only way I can make things right."

"—it isn't true. Come with us. Right now."

Careen handed Tommy the tablet and reached out.

Jaycee pushed her hands away and swiped the ID card she carried to unlock the door. She started inside, and as they looked past her, the backpack she carried slid to the floor with a thump.

Blocks of plastic explosive were piled high on the desk and the copy machine that occupied the tiny space. Tommy spied the timer and watched the countdown pass five minutes and thirty seconds.

"There's already a bomb? I saw Kevin's old office and thought it would be a good place to plant one ..." Jaycee's words were lost as the building's security alarm began to bleat again. They all covered their ears, and Jaycee wailed, "This place is a maze. We'll never get out in time!" She dashed over and jabbed the elevator button, but the light didn't come on. "Why isn't it working?"

"There's another way out!" Tommy led the way down the corridor. Careen grabbed Jaycee by the arm and followed at his heels. He swiped his ID card at the entrance to the secure ward, and they sprinted down the long hall, through the dungeon-like room, and up the concrete stairs, bursting out into the cold night air that flowed through the adjacent concrete parking garage.

Their footsteps echoed off the walls as they ran. They were about halfway to an exit when a shockwave threatened to knock Tommy off his feet. The girls staggered, and as the whole structure trembled, an ominous rumble rose behind them. Tommy ignored the throbbing pain in his leg and ran for all he was worth, but the girls were faster, and the distance between them increased.

The rumble became a roar, and he knew without looking that the concrete was collapsing behind him. Each painted line that marked the parking spaces became a yard line on a football field. *First and ten won't cut it. I have to go for the touchdown.*

Careen was first to vault the half wall. She pulled Jaycee over and then hesitated as if to wait for him.

"Go, go, go!" He waved her on as the cloud of dust rolled up, swallowing him and obscuring his view of his goal.

A chunk of falling concrete grazed his shoulder. He struggled to recover his balance and didn't even see the car in his way until he fell against it. There was nowhere left to go. He covered his head and huddled beside it as the rubble rained down around him.

9:18 PM

Tom, Lara, and Eduardo had watched Trina confront Madalyn on the closed circuit television from a conference room in the Capitol building. Eduardo had cheered when Trina slapped Madalyn, but Tom came to life when Garrick led Madalyn out of the room.

"Finally, this is the moment to have a reasoned discussion and begin to make changes." He squeezed Lara's hand.

As the discussion strayed away from downgrading the OCSD's powers, Tom grew agitated. "Someone call the vote! Do it before they have time to talk themselves out of it. How can they consider leaving the OCSD in power? Renald needs to take control. Oh—there he goes." When the vice president announced the results, Tom slumped in his chair and covered his face with his hands.

Lara gripped his arm. "Wait, what's happening now? Is it another of Atari's videos?"

Armed men in suits swarmed the chamber. They sat in silence, watching the scene unfold until they lost the signal. Within minutes, the president and vice president burst through the door with their security detail and locked themselves inside.

Tom stood. "What happened, sir?"

President Wright seemed dazed. "It was ... I think it was a coup. They had the halls blocked off. We couldn't get to the Emergency Operations Center. You double-crossed me!"

"No, sir! I can assure you it wasn't us."

"Then who?"

Tom was afraid he knew the answer to the question. He turned to Lara. "How quickly can you get ahold of Mitch?"

Eduardo handed her his phone, but the vice president spoke up. "You can't get a signal out of here with that. Use that line." He pointed to a desk phone.

Lara looked up Mitch's number in Eduardo's contacts. "I don't know if he'll pick up if he doesn't recognize the number. If he does, I can put it on speaker," she said as she dialed.

Tom shot her a warning glance. "Maybe it's better if you try to talk to him privately first."

She glanced at all the men in the room. "Maybe you're right. If he has anything to do with what happened in the chamber, I'll find out."

Tom nodded.

Lara didn't recognize the young, scared voice that answered on the third ring.

"May I please speak to—"

"Umm ... he can't come to the phone right now."

"Who is this?"

"Quadrant Marshal Seamus Owens, ma'am. Badge number 8861276."

"I see." All eyes were on her. "Can you apprise me of your situation, please, Marshal Owens?"

Tom frowned. "What's going on?"

She shot him a give-me-a-minute look and held a finger to her lips.

"Umm, I'm guarding a prisoner. Sort of. He took me hostage back in BG-098, and now ... umm, we've kind of switched places. Except he's not a hostage. Just detained."

"Why?"

"I'm not sure if I can tell you. I think it might be classified."

"Oh, in that case, you can certainly tell me. I'm here with the president of the United States."

"Seriously?"

"Yes. I'm serious." She pushed a button on the phone. "I just put you on speaker."

His voice quavered. "Is the president listening?"

President Wright answered, "Yes, indeed I am. Please go ahead."

"Well, sir, Mr. Carraway says he's starting a revolution."

Lara shot Tom a worried glance. "Who took him prisoner?"

"That was Dr. Jacobs. And me."

"I see. May we speak to him about the situation?"

"Dr. Jacobs gave him a shot of diaza-something. He's still pretty loopy, but you can try."

Mitch's voice came over the speaker. "Happy New Year! How's the revolution going?"

Lara kept her voice calm. "Mitch, we're a little surprised about the revolution. You didn't include us in the plan."

"No, I didn't, because I didn't want you all working against me. This is my gift to our great nation. Intellectuals may dream about revolution, but they don't have the stomach to carry one out. That takes a man of action. The American Revolution took seven years to fight. I've been planning this one for about sixteen, and nothing's going to stop it now."

Tom asked, "Can you tell us who invaded the Capitol building?"

"I hired a private security team to do some work for me." He snickered. "Private security is just a fancy term for mercenaries."

Tom shot a glance at the president. "Mitch, call it off. End it before anyone else is killed."

"What are you now, Wright's lap dog?"

"No, but—"

"I had to do it this way. The OCSD keeps people in line by exploiting their fears. How else was I going to get through to anyone except by threatening them and making them afraid?" His laugh was harsh. "I guess I should've given orders for my men to go in before the vote and apply a little pressure. Would've saved time."

There was a boom in the background. Lara felt the tremor in the soles of her feet.

Mitch asked, "What was that?"

9:23 PM

Kevin was panting by the time he reached the second-floor atrium. He covered his ear with his free hand to shut out the bleating alarm as he shouted into the phone. "Send a hostage negotiation team and all available units to the Capitol building. Unknown forces have taken over. They shot Madalyn Davies and Chief Garrick and they're holding ... Who am I? I'm Kevin McGraw, the acting director of the OCSD. Just do it!"

He shouldered through the double doors without breaking stride, and they slammed back against the walls. To his relief, Nicole was hurrying toward him. He shouted over the alarm. "Is anyone else still here?"

She pointed behind her. "I saw Jack Fischer heading back to his office right before the alarm went off. I think everyone else is gone. What's happening?"

"It's a credible bomb threat. Don't panic, just get out of the building and as far away as you can." Then he took off in the opposite direction, and as he rounded the corner, he saw the head of Analysis and Integration carrying a three-foot stack of file folders.

"Jack! Are you crazy? There's a bomb. We have to get out of here!"

"I can't leave the files behind. I loaded up my pockets with chip drives. If the building blows, I'll lose all the pending investigations."

This was no time to argue. Kevin grabbed half the stack. "Come on! The elevators are shut down. This way!"

They rushed down the curved staircase, through the empty lobby, and out the nearest door. Kevin saw Nicole, a few of the custodial staff, and the security guards headed into the parking lot. There was no sign of Tommy, Careen, or Jaycee.

His ears felt as though they were stuffed with cotton, and the bleating alarm inside the building was muffled and far away. They took shelter behind an OCSD van and crouched with the stacks of files. Jack panted beside him, and as they waited seconds that seemed like minutes, Kevin wondered if maybe it had been some kind of trick. He stood up to peer at the building through the van's windows just in time to witness the fireball that burst up from the lower regions of the building. The glass blew out of every window, and smoke, dust, and debris rose as the building crumbled. The force of the blast rocked the van, and papers from the Analysis and Integration files they'd worked so hard to save spun up into the air and were carried away on the wind as the dust cloud settled over the parking lot.

Chapter 33

The rumbling stopped. The dust cloud blotted out the night sky and glittered in the light from the streetlamps. Jaycee knelt on the gritty, cold lawn and raised her arm to breathe into the crook of her elbow. Beside her, Careen sat up, coughing.

"Are you all right?"

"Yeah."

Jaycee looked around. "Where's Tommy? Did you see him come out?" Huge chunks of concrete and other debris blocked their exit point.

Careen took in the scene and cried out in horror. She scrambled to her feet, screaming his name as she ran toward the collapse. Jaycee dashed after her. "Stop it! Do you want someone to hear you?"

Careen sobbed as she ran the length of the garage and back, searching for a way inside. "No! I can't go through this again. I can't lose him this way." She struggled through the rubble and tugged at a piece of concrete until Jaycee grabbed her around the waist and pulled her away.

"Wait! The rest of it could fall. Don't rush in there until we know it's stable."

"We can't wait. What if he's hurt? What if he's dead?"

"If I was dead I wouldn't want you risking your life for me." Tommy's voice sounded far away.

Careen buried her face in her hands for a moment and then waded back through the rubble to lay her forehead against the concrete that separated them. The gesture was so tender and intimate that Jaycee looked away. Careen's voice was gentle. "Are you all right?"

"Yeah. I don't think I'm hurt much. I'm just bruised—and stuck."

Jaycee called back, "We'll get you out." She scanned the scene, looking for an opening in the concrete big enough to crawl through. Beside her, Careen gave a little shriek and grabbed her arm.

"What? Do you see him?"

"No." She began sobbing and laughing at the same time. "The security guards know who I am. My Link will show them where to find us."

"Then we have to hurry." Jaycee called inside to Tommy. "Can you tell us where you are?"

"I almost made it to the wall. I'm beside a black car and a concrete pillar. I have room to breathe, but I can't stand up all the way."

"Do you feel a draft? Is there cold air blowing on you?" She wished she had a light brighter than her Link to shine inside the garage.

"Yeah. I can feel it coming from under the car."

"Okay." She turned to Careen. "Let's get him out."

She nodded and brushed a tear off her cheek. "What should we do?"

"I wish I had a flashlight."

Tommy spoke up. "The tablet's in my coat pocket. Hang on a second."

The glow of the screen pierced the darkness.

"I see it!" They peered inside, and Jaycee said, "He can't be too far away. Shine it around, Tommy. Do you see any openings? Any rubble you can move?"

The glow grew stronger. "There! You're pointing it right at us now."

He replied, "The car's between us."

"Okay." Jaycee chewed her lip for a moment. "Is it crushed?"

"Umm ... no. The window on my side is broken, though."

Jaycee motioned to Careen to follow her. "Tommy, we'll get to you as fast as we can. First we have to make the passageway bigger." They began shifting smaller pieces of debris out of the way.

Careen seemed calmer as soon as she had something to do, and together they worked quickly. After a time, Careen broke the silence. "When I first saw you at the safe house, you said you wanted to talk about something?"

Jaycee nodded. "Wes was in love with you, you know."

Careen seemed confused. "I liked Wes once I got to know him better, but I didn't have romantic feelings for him. Tommy's the one I care about."

"I know. I care about Tommy too. I care about him so much that I hoped . . . well, I hoped you'd choose Wes."

"Oh. Is that what you wanted to talk to me about?"

"Actually, no, it's not." She dragged another chunk of concrete away by the rebar sticking out of it.

"Okay." Careen tried again. "So you're Linked?"

"Oh, that doesn't even compare to what I've got on my mind."

"Like what?"

"It's about our fathers. I guess Tommy's father too."

"I don't understand. Did they know each other?"

"No. At least I don't think so." She turned to Careen, tears in her eyes. "I'm afraid you're going to hate me when you know the truth."

"Why?"

"Because my daddy was responsible for some terrorist attacks that later got blamed on Mr. Bailey. But the worst part"—her chin trembled—"is that he set up the explosion that killed your dad. I'm so sorry for what he did. I hate that he's a murderer."

Tears welled up in Careen's eyes, and she was silent for a moment. "And you think that will change the way I feel about you now?"

Jaycee sniffled and nodded.

"You don't have to atone for anything. You're not responsible for what Mitch or anyone else has done." She hugged the girl. "You're the closest thing to a sister I've ever had. My mom's dead, and now the only family I have left is you and the Baileys. I don't want to lose anyone else I love. For any reason."

Jaycee swiped at the tear that ran down her dusty cheek. "I swear I've cried more in the last month than I have in my whole life."

Tommy's voice came out of the darkness. "So . . . how's it going out there?"

His words broke the tension, and Jaycee said, "You heard every word, didn't you?"

"Sorry, but it's not like I can leave and give you privacy."

"Yeah, I know. We're coming." She climbed over the low wall and Careen followed her. Together they moved a loose chunk of concrete to expose a larger hole. "It's sort of like when we go caving at home. Only, this is probably more dangerous. There's always more than one way out of a cave."

Tommy asked, "Jaycee? What's the ID number on your Link?"

She read it to him. "What are you doing?"

"The Link program is still open. I've been trying to shut the whole thing down. No luck yet, but I want to try something. Okay, Careen, check yours."

She held her Link next to Jaycee's. "Hey! Our numbers match."

"Excellent!"

"So now we're both Jaycee?"

"The computer thinks so. Atari made it awfully easy to edit the profiles. Since Jaycee's not a fugitive, I'll leave it this way."

Jaycee bit her lip and didn't say anything about her run-in with Marshal Nelson in OP-439. She crawled into the opening and motioned for Careen to follow.

The passage got wider after a few feet, and they had enough room to stand as they approached the black car. The door was locked.

"Slide me your gun under the car."

"Too dangerous. A bullet could ricochet."

"I know that! I'm not going to shoot it. I need it to break the glass."

Careen reached into her waistband. "We can use mine."

The 9 mm skidded to a stop by Jaycee's feet, and she picked it up and took out the magazine. "We can use 'em both. Hit there, near the bottom corner. Tempered glass shatters into pebbles when you break it."

They both struck the glass several times before it broke. Jaycee used the sleeve of her coveralls to brush away the bits of glass before she reached inside and unlocked the door. Once inside, she could see there was no room to open the door on the other side. "It's going to be a tight squeeze to get you out. Cover your head."

It was easier to shatter the already-cracked window, and when the opening was clear, she stuck her head through and he grinned up at her. She took the tablet and handed it back to Careen. "Stand up and we'll pull you through."

Together, they helped Tommy worm his way through the window and across the front seat. When he emerged from the car, Careen used the tablet to light their way out. When he'd squeezed past the last slab of concrete into the open, he breathed a sigh of relief and pulled them both into a hug.

"Jaycee, you were amazing. How did you know what to do?"

She reveled in both the praise and the feel of his arms around her. "Wes taught me. He was really good at caving. The rescue stuff is from his QM training."

"Speaking of the QM—" Tommy pointed at the tablet. "Let's find out what's going on before we end up walking into more trouble."

Jaycee handed it to him. "Looks like the battery's low."

He frowned at the screen. "There it is again. The Link program lets me make changes, but it keeps asking for a password. I wonder what it's for."

Jaycee said, "Maybe the right password will let us shut it down."

Careen snorted. "The last thing Atari wants to do is shut it down. We're nothing more than chess pieces to him."

Tommy opened another tab and pulled up PeopleNet. They gathered around the screen as he scrolled through the news feed. "Whoa! Check it out. That was some explosion. I wonder if Kevin's all right?"

Careen asked, "What about Atari?"

"I'm not wasting any time worrying about him." He looked around. "We'll never find the van in this mess. Let's walk to the Capitol. Pete's there with a PeopleCam crew, and that gives me an idea."

9:42 PM

Trina sat silently among the 535 members of Congress as the guard who'd called them back to their seats stood at the podium. "I have a message. Hope this will clear up a few things.

" 'You, members of Congress, elected representatives of the people, are responsible for this coup. You've brought this on yourselves after years of knuckling under to the oppressive rule of the OCSD while you pretended you cared about what happened to the American people.

"The only things you cared about were your own power and comfort. You cared about getting elected and reelected. You cared about lining your pockets by doing favors for each other.

"You stood by and let the OCSD strip the people's civil liberties, and you didn't care. Most of the Restrictions didn't apply to you, or if they did, you found ways around them. You were still allowed to have a car. You had plenty to eat and sent your kids to great schools and into careers. You counted yourself lucky to be among the elite. You made rules that you claim are to protect our nation's children, while your own relatives remain exempt from participating.

"Meanwhile, the de facto leader of this administration—and you all know I'm talking about Madalyn Davies—sold the CSD formulas to a terrorist organization. Or so she thought. She was so anxious to make money off her failed program that she didn't even bother to check out the group. So she ended up selling them to me, one of the leaders of the Resistance.

"You might wonder how she could be stupid enough to sell the formulas to the Resistance? She had no qualms about selling them to terrorists who might use them against us. I know y'all think the Resistance is full of terrorists, but I imagine we'll have to agree to disagree about that.

"Now don't give yourself airs about being smarter than Madalyn Davies. Last month you passed a bill into law that had a whole bunch of stuff tacked on. So much, I bet you didn't read it closely. You didn't think much about how you were spending other people's money. How do I know? I know because you voted to appropriate funds for private security officers who would protect the American people. Look around and wave at one of the gentlemen holding you at gunpoint. Your vote appropriated taxpayer funds for this coup. Seems like you finally took a step in the right direction. Now you're the ones who are under someone else's boot heel. How does it feel? Sincerely, The Resistance.'"

Trina heard two people murmuring behind her. The first sounded surprised. "I didn't vote for this."

The reply was even more disconcerting. "I don't think I did, but I can't be sure. Who has time to look closely at everything we vote on?"

A rumbling boom caught Trina's attention, and she looked around to see if anyone else had heard it.

Senator Renald whispered, "You're Resistance, right? Did you know all this was going to happen?"

"No. I had my suspicions that one of the guys was going rogue, but I didn't expect a coup. Or an explosion. This was supposed to be civilized." She leaned closer. "I shot him up with diazepam. If these guys try to contact him, they won't be able to get a coherent response for at least another couple of hours."

"Nice work. That gives us some time to get organized. Excuse me. I'm going to say hello to an old friend." Senator Renald stood up and edged past Trina. He put his hands on his head as he approached one of the guards standing at the nearest entrance to the West Hall. Trina couldn't hear what they said, but after a moment Renald pointed at the one who had read the message.

The guard left and spoke to the leader, who then followed him up the aisle. There was a murmur from the seats as he passed, and when he joined Renald, he shook his hand warmly.

"We've been waiting for instructions. Haven't been able to get ahold of him since this afternoon."

"Then cut him out of the deal. Work with me, and maybe we can negotiate your way out of this." Renald looked around the room. "You turned off the cameras, so none of this is being broadcast, right? No one's allowed to use a phone. This is as much privacy as we'll ever have. The public saw Trina confront Madalyn, the debate, and the vote before you cut off contact. If we can get everyone in the room on the same page and present a united front, maybe all of us can walk away from this."

Chapter 34

Nicole, covered in dust from the blast, clutched her tablet and hurried after Kevin while he ordered one of the guards to check everyone present in the parking lot against the day's sign-in log, and sent another to direct the emergency vehicles that rumbled onto the scene.

As soon as there was a lull, he turned to her, worry creasing his forehead. "There are at least three people in the building who are unaccounted for. I can't believe this is happening again."

She tried to be reassuring. "You couldn't know someone was going to set off a bomb."

It's more than just the bomb. Madalyn's dead. Garrick's been shot. I think everyone in Congress has been taken hostage. Can you get the president on the phone? I'm not sure if he's still in the House chamber or if he made it to the Emergency Operations Center. Why don't I know the protocol to reach him?" He put out a hand to halt an approaching quadrant marshal and pointed toward a group of people massing at the edge of the parking lot. "Report to the guard with the walkie-talkie for search and rescue duty."

The marshal towered over him. "You're under arrest."

Nicole looked up from her tablet in surprise. Kevin didn't seem to have heard what the marshal said and responded automatically, "Because I'm in charge now. I'm the acting director of the OCSD."

Nicole shuddered as Art Severson emerged from the crowd and addressed Kevin, eyes narrowed. "You're not in charge anymore. You're a Resistance sympathizer. You helped stage a coup and got the director murdered. I'm taking over, and Marshal Nelson is taking you to jail."

Nelson reached for his arm, but Kevin pulled away. "In case you haven't noticed, we're in the middle of a crisis. I'm needed here."

Severson sneered. "The guards say they had Tommy Bailey and Careen Catecher in custody, but you insisted they be released because *they were with you.* You helped those kids set the bomb, didn't you?"

"Absolutely not. I had no idea there was a bomb until ten minutes before it went off."

"Yeah, right."

Nelson twisted Kevin's arm behind his back, and Nicole ran after them as the marshal dragged him away from the scene. "Kevin! I'll make that call!"

She halted beside Jack Fisher, who had been sitting inside one of the OCSD vans trying to organize the remnants of his files. As they watched Nelson manhandle Kevin into a transport van, Nicole felt a fighting spirit rise within her. "That Severson guy will be a worse director than Madalyn. We can't stand by and let him take over."

Jack shook his head. "Now that they know Kevin's Resistance—"

She raised her chin. "We need him back more than ever." She pulled out her phone and dialed. "I have Kevin McGraw on the line for the president, please."

10:25 PM

Tommy turned up his coat collar against the cold rain that had begun to fall. The tablet's battery was dead, and he put it back in his pocket as he, Careen, and Jaycee picked their way through the debris from the blast. When they got to the road, Jaycee paused to straighten Careen's wig. "There. That was bugging me."

The sirens grew louder as they headed toward the Capitol, and people jostled them as they hurried past, some moving in the same direction and others hurrying away. When they had to pause on a corner to let three armored vehicles rumble past, Tommy pushed both girls behind him to block them from the quadrant marshals' view, though he knew that wouldn't hide them from the marshals' scanners. But none of the marshals who passed appeared to be using them.

He avoided the patrol cars that were parked near the plaza in front of the Capitol, and as they came in view of the scene, Jaycee gasped and grabbed his hand. Thousands of people milled about in the darkness, many of them carrying signs. Links blinked like fireflies in a forest as people raised their clenched left fists and chanted. He wasn't prepared for the sensory overload after spending weeks in virtual isolation at the safe house, and he could only imagine how overwhelming it must seem to her. He craned his neck as he scanned the crowd for the PeopleCam van. It was going to be harder than he'd thought to find Pete Sheridan.

Jaycee's voice quavered. "How do we know who's friendly?"

"No idea." He gave her hand a reassuring squeeze and reached for Careen's. "Let's stick together so we don't get separated." He spotted the satellite on top of the mobile news unit and led the way into the crowd.

They were deep in a group of people holding pro-Link signs when the crowd surged around him, squeezing him and nearly lifting him off his feet. He tried to pull the girls closer, but Jaycee's hand slipped from his grasp. She cried out in terror as she was sucked into the roiling sea of bodies, and he dragged Careen with him as he forged a path after Jaycee. He lost sight of her for a moment, and then spotted her rust-colored hair and elbowed his way toward her.

The crowd changed direction, but there was no place to go. The tightly packed bodies crushed the air from his lungs. Careen was pressed against him, her face turned toward the sky as she struggled to breathe. People fell and were lost beneath the surface, and Tommy prayed he and Careen would be able to stay on their feet and that he wouldn't have to step on anyone.

Small artillery fire whistled as it passed overhead and landed with an explosion that shook the ground and made his ears ring. People screamed all around him, and he would have fallen if the crowd hadn't been holding him up. A volley of shots rang out in reply. Just when he was starting to believe he and Careen would suffocate, the pressure gave way. He sucked in a deep breath before looking around for Jaycee.

Marshals in riot gear worked their way through the crowd and headed for the Capitol steps. Someone began shooting out of the building, and when the marshals returned fire, some of the protesters who were caught in the middle fell.

On the lawn, a group of about thirty adults held up their wrists, Links flashing, as they ran screaming toward a squad of marshals. Outnumbered and panicked, the marshals attacked the terrified civilians with their batons and beat them to the ground. Someone sprayed pepper spray and touched off another stampede, in which many people, temporarily blinded, fell and were trampled. Tommy's eyes watered as the irritant spread on the wind, and tears streamed down Careen's cheeks as she watched marshals load dozens of people into transport vans. Not all of them were cowed, though. Tommy couldn't help admiring an older woman who kept kicking open a van's back door whenever the marshals tried to close it.

Careen swiped at the rain that ran in rivulets down her dirty face as she shouted, "How are we ever going to find Jaycee?"

Her wig was crooked again, and he tugged it back into place. "I don't know, but I'm not sticking around out here if I can help it. We're too vulnerable. Let's keep moving. Maybe we'll see her."

Tommy kept firm hold of Careen's hand as they hurried through the thinning crowd. He could feel his heart pounding in time with the *chop-chop-chop* of the helicopters that had swooped in and now wheeled overhead. Machine gun tracer bullets streaked across the sky like shooting stars, and the remaining protesters scattered in all directions. The PeopleCam truck was in sight, engine running. They dodged the fleeing people and dashed up to it. Tommy put both hands on the hood to keep the driver from leaving.

Inside, he saw Pete Sheridan do a double take, and then he opened the side door and hollered, "Get in!"

They scrambled into the back, where Jaycee, soaked and muddy and with a fresh gash on her forehead, sat in the director's chair at the instrument panel.

Careen threw her arms around the girl. "Are you okay?"

"Yeah. I just went along for the ride, and the crowd spit me out pretty close to the van. They got some good video." She pointed at one of the screens. "Wanna see? I've watched it twice."

Tommy noticed Pete staring at him, and the older man shook his head as if to clear the cobwebs.

"I'm sorry. For a minute I thought … you look a lot like my son."

"You look familiar to me too." He lowered his voice. "Do you know who we are?"

He smiled at Careen. "I do recognize this young lady. Your wig is crooked."

Careen rolled her eyes and pulled it off.

Tommy held out the tablet. "I got this from Atari. It controls the Link, but the battery's dead. Can we charge it?"

"Sure." Pete took it and plugged it in.

"We want to show you this too." He fished the chip drive out of his pocket. "You've been great about helping the Resistance get messages out, and I've got an idea how to use it."

10:30 PM

The president's security detail barricaded the conference room door and took up positions, guns drawn, to listen for any disturbance in the hall. Everyone else had taken shelter on the far side of the room, where they huddled out of sight below the long table.

Tom hunched next to President Wright. "Will they be able to evacuate you someplace safer, sir?"

"At present, it doesn't look like it. I lose command authority if we're pinned down here without access to secure communications. That may be what the Resistance intended to do all along." He looked at Tom with raised eyebrows.

Tom hastened to protest. "Mr. President, the Resistance has been working to overthrow Madalyn Davies ever since she assumed the role of director, but on my life, I swear we never considered an all-out coup."

"And do you deny that the Resistance was responsible for the bomb at the OCSD building?"

"I had no prior knowledge of the bombing at the OCSD building. Kevin McGraw is our point man at the OCSD. You've met him. He's as committed as we are to affecting change without violence—and without attempting something as foolish as a forced regime change. The main faction of the Resistance is not your enemy. We support you and your administration. Mitch Carraway chose a different path; he's no longer allied with us."

Tom heard Lara murmur to Eduardo. "We were supposed to go help Tommy and Careen with Atari. I wonder if they're all right. Is there any way to get in touch with them?"

Everyone jumped when the landline phone rang. An aide crawled over to answer it. "Sir? It's Kevin McGraw on the line for you."

The president took the receiver. "Yes?" He listened for a moment. "Wait. Who is this?... He's been arrested? Do you know what's going on inside the House chamber?"

He hung up. "It appears there's more than one coup in progress."

Chapter 35

Pete listened to Tommy's plan. "Sure, we can do that, but you'd be crazy to try to broadcast out here in the open where someone's likely to recognize you."

"Can we do everything from in here?"

"It'll be a bit of a squeeze, but these are desperate times."

Pete sat in the swivel chair in front of the control panel in the mobile news unit, microphone in hand, while the cameraman adjusted his lens from where he sat in the front passenger seat. The producer counted him down, and Tommy, Careen, and Jaycee pressed against the walls to stay out of frame. "Skirmishes continue here in the capital quadrant at this hour as unidentified forces occupy the Capitol building, where they are holding Congress hostage. We have word that the president and vice president may have been removed from the House chamber. It is not known whether Madalyn Davies is still inside. Just a half hour ago, an explosion of suspicious origin destroyed the OCSD building.

"And who is to blame? Is it the Resistance that now controls and terrorizes our country? I must warn you: the following footage is disturbing, and contains graphic images."

The video, apparently recorded by a street camera, showed a woman running down a dark city sidewalk. When two marshals intercepted her at a corner, she struggled in their grip. One of them lost his hold on her, but the other shoved her against a wall, pinning her there while his partner zip-tied her hands behind her back. She tried to pull free, but the marshal slammed her against the wall one more time before flinging her to her knees. A fourth figure stepped out of the shadows, gun in hand. The marshals stood aside as a blond young man fired point-blank into the back of the woman's head.

"The woman in the video has been identified as Careen Catecher, murdered by Tommy Bailey, son of Resistance leader Tom Bailey. Tommy just happens to be here with me now." Tommy, minus his wig, moved into frame with Pete and they shook hands.

"Tommy, thanks for dropping by. So what can you tell us about that video?"

"It's one hundred percent fake, and I want to set the record straight about a few things." He reached out of frame, pulled Careen to his side, and put a protective arm around her. "Obviously Careen's still alive. I didn't shoot her. I love her and I'd never do anything to hurt her." He smiled down at her.

"So what does the video mean?" Pete was an expert at leading the viewing audience to the preferred conclusion.

"One of our Resistance operatives created that video to prove how easy it is to be manipulated by what we see. The Link can be manipulated too."

"Is the Resistance really a terrorist organization, as the OCSD would have us believe?"

"When Careen was accused of being a terrorist, I was ticked. She wasn't a terrorist any more than I was. But since then I've realized that the only way to be true to my country is to fight the oppression we face at the hands of the OCSD. If that makes me a terrorist, then I guess I am one."

Careen spoke up. "The OCSD makes decisions and imposes Restrictions that are supposed to protect us, when instead they strip us of our freedoms and leave us powerless. Our elected leaders don't represent our best interests, because they're afraid to defy the OCSD."

Pete asked, "Are you afraid of the OCSD, Careen? You were once their spokesperson. They say you were kidnapped by the Resistance."

"Of course I'm afraid of the OCSD, but I'm done lying for them. It's horrible to be accused of something you didn't do, and I don't want that to happen to anyone else. But it will. Every one of you could be like me, falsely accused of a crime. It doesn't matter if you haven't done anything wrong. A surveillance program like the Link in the wrong hands—well, in anyone's hands—is an invasion of our privacy that makes us vulnerable, rather than keeping us safe."

Tommy gave her a reassuring squeeze. "All our lives we've heard the OCSD say, "it's a small price to pay for our safety." It's easy to agree with that until you're the one who's accused of something you didn't do. So to prove how easily this can happen, we've hijacked the Link. Everyone with a Link will now show up on the scanners as Careen Catecher, a wanted fugitive, and according to the law, may be arrested and charged with her crimes."

"What do you say to people who call the Link a solution to our security issues?"

"Linking people makes them different and divides us instead of bringing us together. The OCSD keeps trying to isolate us so we don't feel the strength in our numbers. The people who run the OCSD fear us. They don't want us to speak out against them. They know they can't keep us safe, but they need our compliance—and our tax money—to survive. They need us a lot more than we need them."

10:45 PM

As Trina ascended to the podium, she prayed for strength to touch the hearts of the people around her and hoped her passion would equal that of the country preachers she remembered from her childhood. "I worked for the OCSD on the development team for the Counteractive System of Defense drug, CSD."

She saw puzzled looks on many of the faces in the crowd. One representative asked, "So if you developed the antidote, how can you expect us to believe the Office of Civilian Safety and Defense hasn't done anything to prevent terrorist attacks?"

She hid her exasperation. "I worked for them for three months before I caught on that the antidote was never meant to protect anyone. Stratford had always intended to use it for mind control."

"Preposterous. No one was controlling my mind."

"Probably not, sir, because you were receiving a placebo dose reserved for government officials. When I realized what Stratford was up to, I called him out, and he gave me an extra-large dose of the drug and locked me up to get me out of the way. As soon as I was able, I began to fight against the OCSD, and I haven't stopped. Why do you persist in believing they do good?"

A congresswoman raised her hand to be recognized. "I have always supported the OCSD. I have to continue to do so, because my constituents favor a strong antiterrorism stance."

"But the OCSD doesn't do anything to stop terrorism. They pander to people's fears!"

Several people in the room spoke at once.

"You're out of order, Dr. Jacobs. You're no better than a terrorist yourself. You're in the Resistance."

"The OCSD hasn't harmed us."

"How will we stay safe without it?"

Renald stepped up to the podium beside Trina. "Please, everyone. Our captors are willing to let every one of you walk out of here unscathed. All you have to do is vote to get rid of the OCSD."

The clamor rose again, and a man in the front row shouted, "If we go along with this we'll just be giving in to terrorists. We have no real say. We're literally being forced to comply at the point of a gun."

Trina retorted, "How is that different from people who are being Linked? You didn't have any problem with that. You only protest when it's you on the wrong end of the gun."

Movement at the back of the room caught Trina's eye. One of the guards ushered a man carrying a large stack of papers into the room.

"Jack?" Trina hardly recognized her coworker under the caked-on dirt and dust.

"Hey, Trina." He shifted the stack of papers he carried. "Thought you might want some stats on the OCSD's effectiveness. It won't take me long to sum up the terrorist attacks the OCSD has prevented since its inception in 2019."

"Sure, that would be helpful." She and Renald stood aside.

"Good evening, everyone. I'm Jack Fischer, head of Analysis and Integration at the OCSD. It's my job to track suspected terrorists using intel provided by both government and private sources. I've been in this department since the OCSD was formed, and in that time, the number of terrorist attacks foiled by the OCSD has been exactly zero."

The congresswoman with the strong antiterrorism stance spoke up. "What about all the attacks that led up to the forming of the OCSD?"

"I have Lowell Stratford's files, and I've been over them many times. All but three were staged by the OCSD—some to elicit fear, others to demonstrate their ability to stop attacks before they happened."

She persisted. "What about the other three?"

"Those were carried out by the same man who orchestrated this coup."

An angry buzz of conversation rose from the members of Congress.

Jack called for attention again. "Before we get too self-righteous, I also happen to have the Resistance's dossiers of crimes committed by members of Congress."

Renald leaned in to the microphone. "None of us wants this to escalate. We have the president's okay to call it a draw, call the vote, and let everyone walk out of here. Jack has agreed to head up a task force that will investigate and, if warranted, file charges against any person who was here tonight."

The leader of the guards spoke up. "Let's get this show on the road. No electronic voting. Call the roll."

11:00 PM

Tommy picked up the newly charged tablet. "I wonder if there's a way to delete a profile from the Link registry."

Careen looked over his shoulder. "Can you delete everyone?"

"Maybe." He tried to access the list, but a popup appeared. He frowned. "It won't let me into the registry without a password now."

Jaycee looked down at her Link. "Hey, just so you know, it says I'm me again."

Tommy tried to access the field he'd used to change the ID numbers and was met with the same password request. "Okay, this is not good. It makes Careen too vulnerable. We need the password. Any guesses?"

Careen shrugged. "You know Atari best."

"Let's start with his video game obsession." She watched while he typed in *Pac-Man*. Incorrect. *Pong*. Incorrect. *Asteroids*. Then a message appeared: "Too many failed login attempts. Try again in 30 minutes."

Tommy swore. "Pete, is there anyone at PeopleCam who can hack this thing? Careen's vulnerable until we can get back in and scramble the ID numbers again."

"Maybe. Should I call and make sure the coast is clear before we head in?"

"Yeah, although now that the girls' Links are live, there's no place to hide."

Pete grabbed his phone. Before he could connect the call, everyone cringed at the sound of machine gun fire nearby.

Jaycee spoke up. "Anyplace where they're not shooting at us would be nice."

Careen was silent as they rode to the PeopleCam building. Tommy put his arm around her. "Are you all right?"

She nodded. She'd never expected to return to the place where she'd been held captive and tortured. When they arrived, the producer and cameraman dropped them off and headed back out to get more footage of the riots. Careen kept a tight grip on Tommy's hand as they and Jaycee followed Pete through the back entrance to the PeopleCam building.

Pete looked back at them as they headed up the stairs. "I wonder if Atari was able to pierce the Shield. That was supposed to happen, wasn't it? I've got censored video and news reports of protests and people trying to escape being Linked, stuff the OCSD would never let PeopleCam broadcast. It's been running on a loop for a couple of weeks. I hoped the Shield would be compromised, and somehow people here, and maybe even in other countries, would be able to see it."

Careen began to tremble as Pete led them down a cinderblock hallway behind the studios. She glanced around, expecting at any moment to meet a security guard who would lock her in a room; or worse, take her to be interrogated.

Pete knocked on a door with Engineering Department on the plate. An elderly man whose scalp shone pink under his flyaway white hair was seated at a workbench, working on the insides of a playback machine. "Tommy, this is Chester, the chief engineer. If anyone can help you, it's him." Jaycee followed Tommy inside, but Careen balked, and Pete remained in the hall with her.

"My son was about his age." Pete fished in his wallet, pulled out a photo of a blond young man, and showed it to her.

She gasped and tears welled up in her eyes. "I knew him … just for a moment."

"He'd stopped taking CSD, and we argued about it on the phone. Next thing I knew, the QM came to me and said he had succumbed to the poison."

"Tommy and I had stopped taking CSD, but the QM picked up Tommy and dosed him with Phase Two. That dose was awful. It was like he was in a trance, and when he left the house and headed for combat training, I ran after him. When I lost sight of Tommy, I got scared and hid, and I saw your son running away from the QM. They beat him and left him lying on the ground. I was with him when he died."

"Did he say anything?"

She nodded and wiped her nose. "Something about death not being the worst thing that could happen."

Pete drew a shuddering breath and patted her on the shoulder. "Thank you for sharing that with me."

Her eyes were filled with tears, but she smiled. "Even though I'm Linked, I'm going to keep fighting and not give up. I have to do more than just tell the truth, because so far the truth hasn't been powerful enough to change anything. Why do people believe the lies?"

"They're too frightened to look for the truth. If you tell people to be afraid all the time, eventually they start to believe they need to be." He looked at the group in the control booth. "Let me show you something." He led the way down the hall to Edit Bay 10. "I imagine the world will be surprised to hear from us. I hope, over time, people will learn from what has happened here."

Careen pointed at one of the monitors. "Look! That's in OP-439, where I went to school."

He pushed a button to unmute the sound. "It must have just happened."

"This is Jeremy Howard, reporting live from inside the history building at the university in OP-439. Student activists who have been rounded up and Linked because of their so-called criminal activity are barricaded inside one of the lecture halls with a number of their classmates, who are the children and grandchildren of high-ranking government officials.

"Have the activists taken hostages? The answer is no. Here's the twist in the story: I've been told that all of these individuals have been involved in CXD from its inception, and have all been arrested since the Linking began. Those related to government officials, however, are exempt from being Linked, and have not been penalized. They stand in solidarity with their classmates who have been flagged as dissidents, and are sending a message to the country's lawmakers calling for the complete disbandment of the Link program."

Pete tapped another monitor. "Looks like the guys make it back and got the rest of the story over at the Capitol."

They watched in silence as people streamed out of the building. The helicopters shined spotlights down on the scene. The producer who had been with them earlier took on Pete's role and held out a microphone. "Can you tell us what's going on?"

"Yes. I'm Senator Brandon Renald. The coup is over. Congress just voted unanimously to eliminate the OCSD. A task force will be assembled to oversee the transition. We feel confident that we've made the right decision as we head into 2035. Oh, and the State of the Union address has been postponed. Happy New Year."

A man spoke behind them. "I told you she was here."

Careen whirled around. Art Severson and Sheila Roth stood in the open doorway. He pointed a gun at Careen as he pocketed a QM handheld scanner.

Sheila seemed intent on fueling the drama. "Pete, how dare you associate with a murderer! And after what that girl tried to do to me!"

Pete ignored her and stepped between Careen and the gun. Severson attempted to wave him out of the tiny room. "Get out here. Hands on your heads."

With Pete blocking Severson's view of her, Careen slowly reached back for the gun in her waistband.

Pete shifted position as he pointed to the monitor, and she froze, her fingertips just brushing the gun's grip. "Look what's happening! The coup is over. Congress has voted to downgrade the authority of the OCSD. Citizens are calling for the elimination of the Link. You missed your chance. Leave this young woman alone."

"Do you really think a Congressional vote will be enough to get rid of the OCSD? Now get out here!"

Careen pulled the .22 free, but Pete surprised her with his own plan of action, lunging at Severson before she had time to aim. Sheila ducked out of the way as the two men grappled over Severson's gun. A single shot rang out, and Pete slumped to the floor.

"Oh no!" Careen fell to her knees beside him, dropping the gun to press both hands against the blood that spurted from his neck. Atari had hardly bled at all compared to this, and within seconds Pete was fading. His lips moved and she leaned closer.

"Don't give up. Death is not ... the worst evil. Keep fighting." Then he was still.

She choked back the bile that rose in her throat. Pete's blood had splattered her clothing, and now it dripped from her hands. Severson reached in and hauled her up by the elbow, making her step over the body, and then shoved his gun into Sheila's hand. "Take her into the studio."

Chapter 36

"So it didn't used to require a password?" Chester peered at the tablet and then looked over his glasses at Tommy, who shook his head. Jaycee stared around the dusty office, which doubled as a workshop and was crammed with all manner of audio and video equipment, some of it current and some looking beyond repair. Ancient reel-to-reel tape spilled out of a flat box, and hundreds of VHS tapes, something Tommy had never seen in person, were stacked on metal shelves.

"I could go in and make changes to the data until about half an hour ago, when it locked itself down," Tommy said.

"Easiest way to take care of that is to wipe the contents. Gives you a fresh start."

"But won't that eliminate the only way to control the Link? We need to get back to that particular program, the sooner the better."

The engineer glanced around before he spoke. "I do have some software that might open it. I have it because sometimes we share tablets, phones, and other station equipment. Sheila can never remember passwords, and, God help us all, she'd try to change them and then mess everything up. I had to get special approval, you understand, and I'm required to file a report with the OCSD every time I use it to unlock a device."

"I'd appreciate it if you'd give it a try." Tommy handed over the tablet, wondering if there was some trick to the password in case the tablet was stolen or compromised.

Chester rolled across the floor in his chair, grabbed a patch cord, and then rolled back to connect the tablet to one of his computers. As soon as he started the diagnostic, the tablet emitted a loud, annoying alarm.

The engineer winced as he disconnected the tablet, and when it fell silent he shook his head. "This thing's got extra protection and a paranoid owner, it seems. I won't be able to get past it. Sorry." He handed it back to Tommy.

Jaycee asked, "Couldn't Atari help us?"

Tommy realized he had no idea where Atari was and no faith that he would be willing to help if they could locate him. "He wouldn't help us. He'd gloat about being the smartest one in the room. He likes to put people in mazes and watch them fight their way out." Tommy closed the cover. "At least no one else has control of it either."

Someone spoke behind him. "That's about to change."

Jaycee yelped in fear and Tommy turned around. The quadrant marshal who stood in the doorway looked familiar. *Nelson. He's Wes's old partner.*

"Get out here." He motioned with his gun. As they filed out, he shook his head at Chester. "Just the kids. We don't want to hurt you." He grabbed Jaycee by the arm and held his gun to her head as he spoke to Tommy. "Tie him in his chair."

When Tommy was finished, Nelson patted him down and took his gun. "Give me that tablet. Hands on your head. Let's go." He shoved Jaycee ahead of Tommy and held his gun at Tommy's back as they headed down the hall.

Somewhere nearby, a single shot was fired. "Stop!" Nelson halted them and glanced around. Before long, Tommy heard rapid footsteps approaching and lowered his hands to be ready for whatever.

Severson, his shirt and pant legs splattered with blood, rounded the corner and ran toward them. He grabbed Jaycee by the hair and forced her to come with him. Tommy felt Nelson's gun at his back, warning him not to interfere, but he shouted in protest as he and Nelson followed them down the hall.

"Take it easy. She hasn't done anything to you!"

Severson ignored Tommy and spoke to Jaycee. "Imagine how delighted I was to find you and Careen together, and then to learn that you girls were with Tommy Bailey. Looks like I'll be taking over the OCSD *and* settling all my old scores before the year's over."

Jaycee struggled to free herself. "If you hurt Careen, I'll kill you!"

"Shut up." Severson opened the door to a utility closet and sent her sprawling inside. Nelson shoved Tommy in after her.

Tommy heard the click of the lock, but he rattled the doorknob anyway. When it refused to yield, he pounded on the door in frustration and called Severson a few choice names.

Jaycee whispered, "Did he shoot Careen?"

"I don't know." He threw himself against the door, but it held fast.

Jaycee found the light switch, and began to rummage around by the light of the single uncovered bulb. She handed him a crowbar. "I didn't know you knew him. Besides, it's not like he counts as my stepfather or anything."

He tried to force it into the space between the door and the frame. "Wait, what? He's your ... so Beth is your *mom*?"

"Yeah, although I just met her last week."

He tossed the crowbar on the floor in defeat. "Huh. I'm trying to picture your mom and Mitch ... wow. Weird. I always thought she could've done better than Severson."

"I know, right? Wish I'd bitten him, too, when he and that marshal Linked me."

Tommy raised his eyebrows. "You bit the marshal? Way to go! Severson's the one who sold out my parents and got us into this whole mess in the first place. The nicest thing I can say about him is that he's a power-hungry jerk. But he's got a reason to be pissed at me. A few months ago, I threw his keys and his cell phone in a lake and left him stranded in the middle of nowhere."

"We have to get out of here." She looked up. "Hey, there's a drop ceiling. Maybe we can...." She climbed up on the edge of the cast iron stationary tub and pushed at one of the ceiling panels.

"Here." Tommy grabbed a stepladder from the corner and set it beside her.

"I don't have to get far. Just up and over will do it." Her head and shoulders disappeared into the space. "Here goes."

He heard her land outside the door, and within seconds he was free. He grabbed the crowbar and followed as she ran down the hall.

Severson strode into the soundstage, the tablet under his arm and Nelson at his heels. "Sheila, give us a spotlight."

She hurried over to the panel on the wall and flipped about ten different switches until she turned on one of the overhead spots. As she turned off the rest of the lights, Careen fought to control the panic that gripped her as memories of being interrogated and abused nearly overwhelmed her.

Severson nodded to Careen. "I believe you remember how this works."

She shook her head and folded her arms on her chest to control her trembling. "I don't have anything to say to you. Where are Tommy and Jaycee?"

"It's over, Careen. You can't continue to reject the OCSD's authority."

She felt braver in the shadows. "The OCSD is nothing but rubble."

"That sounds symbolic, and actually it's all for the best. Madalyn's tenure was short-lived and fraught with scandal and mismanagement. It's time to move forward and think of the future. Under my direction, the OCSD will rise from the ashes, and the Link will proceed as planned."

"You can't make me advocate for the Link."

"I wasn't going to suggest it. Everyone knows you're a liar." He smiled. "No more subterfuge or tricks. Together we'll show people what happens to those who defy me." He nodded to Nelson, who twisted Careen's arm behind her back and forced her into the circle of light.

Severson joined him in the shadows and held out the tablet to Careen. "Open the program."

"I can't. I don't know the password."

Severson tsk-tsked. "Surely you don't expect me to believe that when just hours ago you were on television bragging about being able to manipulate the Link."

"We were able to for a while, but now we can't!"

"Lies."

Nelson slapped her across the face so hard it knocked her to the floor. She dabbed at the blood that trickled from her nose, which smeared with Pete Sheridan's that had dried on the back of her hand.

"Get up."

She took her time getting to her feet.

"Tell me the password."

She looked him in the eyes. "*Resistance.*"

He typed it in. "That's incorrect."

"Try *disobey.*"

He looked at her askance before he entered it and then swore. "That's not it either. Tell me the truth."

"The truth is, you only get three tries at a time before it locks you out." She held up her arms, poised to ward off the blow that was sure to follow, when Tommy's voice came out of the darkness.

"Leave her alone!" He dashed into view and swung a crowbar at Nelson like it was a baseball bat. Nelson sidestepped him, and when Tommy rounded on him again, Nelson deflected the blow, wrenched the crowbar from his hand, and twisted Tommy's arm behind his back. He wrapped his other arm around Tommy's neck and seemed to enjoy holding him there for Careen to see.

A moment later, Jaycee came forward. Sheila Roth had a gun to her head.

"Ah, your would-be rescuers vanquished." Art extended the tablet to Tommy, and Nelson relaxed his hold and took a step back. "Give me the password, tough guy. I'm looking forward to Linking you and keeping a close eye on you in the future."

As everyone stared at him, Tommy's brain seemed to stall out. He couldn't think of a single thing Atari might have chosen for the password. He looked at both of the girls and realized he was going to fail them. He decided to keep talking until he came up with a better idea. "The program's running. The Link is working."

"You miss the point. Without the password, I lack the ability to truly control it," Severson said, eyeing Tommy without emotion. "Stratford was too lenient with your parents. He could have quashed their little rebellion months ago. I won't make the same mistake. Give me the password, or we'll kill Careen."

Sheila spoke up. "You'd better listen to him, Tommy. He killed Pete."

Tommy stared down at the tablet, fighting the urge to snap it in two. *Atari always acted like I wasn't smart enough and said the only way I could solve a problem was through brute force.* Nelson moved into position behind Careen, and she stood trembling, waiting for the kill shot, the light on her Link flashing as though it knew it would soon be stilled. He'd promised to protect her. Now he couldn't even look her in the eye.

"Let her go. Kill me instead." *I'm already in hell. Wait...*

Severson sneered. "Oh, so noble, but too easy. And it doesn't solve my problem."

I might as well be a character in one of Atari's games. His heart leaped at the idea. *I have to get past Cerberus. It's the only way out of hell.* Suddenly he knew. He typed in *Hercules*, and immediately the screen lit up with fireworks. *Initiating Hercules. Join network.* Tommy touched the prompt, and images spilled forth so fast he couldn't look at any single one. Something called Google appeared. Several progress bars sprang up on the screen, and he saw *Banned Books Database* and *Banned Films Database* among them.

Severson grabbed the tablet away from him. "What did you do?"

The studio door burst open, and in rushed a squad of soldiers in bulletproof vests, weapons drawn. Nelson dropped his gun and put his hands on his head. Sheila tossed her gun away like she wasn't really part of what had just happened and tried to scurry out, but one of the soldiers stopped her before she was halfway across the room. Severson raised his hands, and Tommy did too, just to be safe, but dropped them when he saw his parents, Eduardo, Kevin, and Trina hurrying in.

He was at Careen's side in an instant, swept her into his arms, and kissed her like there was no one else in the room. It was the kind of kiss that held the promise of the future, and it wasn't even close to over when Jaycee interrupted by throwing her arms around both of them. Tears were streaming down Careen's cheeks, but she laughed as the three of them clung to each other in the spotlight.

"You did it! Hercules got past Cerberus! Look." Jaycee held out her arm. The ID number on her Link was gone, and in its place was *Hercules Network*. She grinned. "I love mythology."

The soldiers handcuffed Severson, Nelson, and Sheila and were leading them out when Lara stopped them. "Do you mind? I just need a moment. There's one little thing ..."

The soldier nodded, and she slapped Severson across the face. Some of the soldiers burst out laughing, and as she stood aside to let them pass, someone spoke from the doorway behind her.

"Aw, come on, Lara. You can do better than that."

Mitch Carraway stepped into the room and dealt a smashing blow to Severson's jaw. He staggered and fell to his knees. The soldiers hauled him up and guided him out.

"Daddy!" Jaycee pushed through the crowd and ran into her father's arms. There was a moment of uncomfortable silence, and Mitch addressed the squad leader over Jaycee's head.

"I figured I should turn myself in. I just wanted to say goodbye to my girl first. Getting to pay my respects to Severson was an added bonus." He held her at arm's length. "Everything's going to be okay. Understand?"

Jaycee nodded.

"I raised a fighter. I'm proud of you."

Tommy watched as one of the soldiers took Mitch by the arm and led him out past a teenaged boy who'd followed Mitch into the studio. "Who's that?"

Jaycee gasped. "Seamus?" She grinned as she hurried toward him. "I think he's with me," she said over her shoulder.

"Tommy?" A voice came over the intercom. "The computers in the control booth went nuts with downloads. We can access all the search engines and news agencies that have been blocked."

Tommy looked around. "Chester? Is that you?"

"Yeah! Rolled down here from my office. Recorded most of what just happened and sent it out with the rest of Pete's video archive. I always said I could run a control booth with one hand tied behind my back. Speaking of which, can you send someone in here to cut me loose?"

Everyone but the Resistance had cleared out when his dad came over and pulled Tommy into a hug. "Good work, son." Tears welled up in Tommy's eyes, and he held the embrace until he got control of his emotions. When they pulled apart, he was surprised to see his dad looking a little misty, too. Tom coughed. "I can't wait to hear all about what happened this evening and piece the whole story together. Do you think we should move this gathering back to the safe house?"

Tommy grinned. "Sounds great to me. We have everything we need there—food, hot showers, extra clothes."

"The perfect place to begin anew." His dad clapped him on the shoulder. "They've got cars waiting for us downstairs."

"Dad?"

"Yes?"

"Earlier, Atari said the Link meant freedom. I thought he was nuts, and I tried to stop him from activating it, but now I think he was planning to break the Link all along. Why didn't he just say so?" He gazed at Careen, who was smiling as she talked to Trina. "It's going to be awhile before I understand everything that's happened."

His dad followed his gaze. "Just take it one thing at a time. If there's something you really want, don't ever give up."

"That's the plan." He strode over to Careen and led her out of the studio and down the stairs.

"What? I was talking to Trina."

"Plenty of time for that. We're all going back to the safe house in a bit." They crossed the lobby and ran out through the main doors into the crisp night air, their frosty breath mingling with the falling snow that glistened in the streetlights. Careen threw her arms wide and spun around, laughing as the snowflakes swirled around her and settled in her hair.

Her kiss warmed him to his very core, and he smiled down at her. "Happy New Year, Careen."

SIX WEEKS LATER

5:47 PM
Washington, DC

Tommy put the top bun on his loaded burger and passed the ketchup to Jaycee. "Atari's on a tropical island bragging to some girl in a bikini about his gunshot wound."

Jaycee turned up her nose at the suggestion. "I bet they'll find his body when they clear away the rubble of the OCSD building."

No one had seen Atari since New Year's Eve. A recently completed forensic audit of the OCSD's accounts revealed a five-million-dollar wire transfer sent just hours before Madalyn Davies's death. The fact that Atari and the money were both missing seemed like too big a coincidence to Tommy.

"No chance. He's still alive. He knew about the bomb."

"But what if he didn't get away in time? You said he fainted right in the middle of the lobby!"

"He was faking. I mean fake-fainting ... or whatever." They laughed, but then he sobered. "I think, in the end, he wanted to see if we could outsmart him."

"Good thing we did." She looked around the safe house kitchen. "It's weird living here in his place. I wonder if he'll come back someday."

They heard the elevator door slide open, and Tommy leaned on his stool, craning his neck so he could see into the lobby. He smiled as he called out, "You're just in time for dinner. We were starting to wonder what had happened to you."

Careen strode into the kitchen and dropped her messenger bag and car keys on the counter. "Great. I'm starving." She fixed a plate and took a seat next to Tommy. "I thought that informational meeting was never going to end."

"I know Mom asked you to, but you don't have to apply for a seat on the Council."

"If I'm chosen, I'll serve, and I'm honored that Lara asked me. I keep thinking of all the children who'll have to wear a Link their whole lives. If we don't establish rules to protect them now, they could be exploited. The Council needs to exist until the last Linked child dies of old age."

"That could be a hundred years from now."

"I know." She took a bite of her burger. "And the danger isn't just from people like Atari. There are people who still want the Link to be used for its intended purpose."

"You used to be one of them."

"That's why I have to be on the Council. I understand both sides of the issue, and I'm one of those directly affected. The adults who wanted Links for themselves are talking about creating a registry of the Linked. They want to make us eligible for special privileges and in exchange, be allowed to use us for some kind of testing. That sounds ominous, and I don't like it. The generation of kids who were forcibly Linked deserve a normal life."

Jaycee glanced down at her wrist. "I don't like the thought of being on anybody's list."

Tommy mopped up the last of his ketchup with some fries. "Mom, Kevin, Renald, and Garrick will make sure nothing bad happens. I thought you wanted to go back to college in the fall, Careen. With me. You know we'll ace the undergraduate seminar Dad's teaching, since we've basically lived it already."

"I do! I can do both. The Council isn't a full-time job. All our problems aren't solved just because the OCSD is gone, even though it's so much better already. Everyone's getting used to the Restrictions being lifted. I like driving. I like being able to come and go whenever I choose. People like Jaycee and me shouldn't feel like victims or some kind of marginalized group."

"Linked people aren't marginalized. If anything, they've got special powers. Come on over here," he said, and pulled her onto his lap. "My Internet reception has been weak ever since you and your Hercules signal left for the Council meeting."

She giggled. "See? You're part of the problem, exploiting me for your own gain." He kissed her before she could get back on her soapbox.

Jaycee rolled her eyes. "My signal and I have been here the whole time." She slapped Tommy on the back of the head playfully as she carried her plate to the dishwasher. "But I can take a hint."

ACKNOWLEDGEMENTS

Susan Hughes of myindependenteditor.com, my editor and friend, who has been part of this project from the beginning. I appreciate her input on the storyline and how she tracks down wayward commas and patiently puts them in the right places.

My sister, Kim Stone, who took it in stride when I texted to ask, "What do you have in your medical bag that would incapacitate someone?"

Sadie, Sam, Sarah, and Bruce, personal trainers at Fit 180 in Dallas who guided me through reps and sets while letting me hash out the storyline for *Revolt* during my gym time.

My niece, Alex Pearson, gave invaluable assistance as a beta reader before the book went to formatting.

ABOUT THE AUTHOR

Once upon a time, Tracy Lawson was a little girl with a big imagination who wanted to write books when she grew up. Her interests in dance, theater, and other forms of make-believe led to a career in the performing arts, where "work" means she gets to do things like tap dance, choreograph musicals, and weave stories.

Her greatest adventures in musical theatre included creating disco choreography for forty middle schoolers on roller skates in *Xanadu*, building cast members' endurance during an extremely aerobic jump rope number in *Legally Blonde*, and wrangling a cast of amazingly enthusiastic teenaged tap dancers in *Crazy For You*. This past season, she had the pleasure of adding productions of *Footloose* and *Lion King, Jr.* to her resume. She can also spin plates on sticks while she tap dances. Just ask her. She'll be happy to demonstrate!

Though teaching dance and choreographing shows was a great outlet for her creativity and boundless energy, Tracy never lost her desire to write. Faced with her only child leaving for college and her husband's simultaneous cross-country job relocation, it seemed she'd found the perfect time to switch her focus. But fear not— she has maintained her ties to educational theatre by returning to choreograph shows each year at Bexley City Schools in Columbus, Ohio, so she can continue to nurture students and share her passion for putting on a great show.

Tracy, who is married with one grown daughter and two spoiled cats, splits her time between Dallas, Texas and Columbus, Ohio.

To learn more about Tracy and all her books, visit http://tracylawsonbooks.com

For the inside scoop on Tommy, Careen, and the Resistance Series, visit http://counteractbook.com

OTHER BOOKS BY THE AUTHOR

Counteract: Book One of the Resistance Series (2014) is the story of a guy, a girl, the terrorist attack that brings them together, and their race to expose a conspiracy that could destroy their country from within. What Tommy Bailey and Careen Catecher learn about the true nature of the terrorist threat spurs them to take action, and their decisions lead them to run afoul of local law enforcement, team up with an underground resistance group, and ultimately take their quest for the truth to the highest reaches of the United States government.

Finalist in the 2015 International Wishing Shelf Book Awards

Resist: Book Two of the Resistance Series (2015). Tommy and Careen are no longer naïve teenagers who believe the Office of Civilian Safety and Defense's antidote can protect them from a terrorist's chemical weapons. After accidentally discovering the antidote's real purpose, they join the fight to undermine the OCSD's bid for total control of the population.

Being part of the Resistance brings with it a whole new set of challenges. Not everyone working for change proves trustworthy, and plans to spark a revolution go awry with consequences far beyond anything they bargained for. Tommy and Careen's differing viewpoints threaten to drive a wedge between them, and their budding relationship is tested as their destinies move toward an inevitable confrontation with the forces that terrorize the nation.

Silver Award in the 2016 International Wishing Shelf Book Award

Best YA Fiction for 2016 in the Texas Association of Authors Book Awards

Ignite: Book Three of the Resistance Series (2016). Nationwide food shortages have sparked civil unrest, and the Office of Civilian Safety and Defense's hold on the people is slipping. The Resistance's efforts to hasten the OCSD's demise have resulted in disaster, with Tommy Bailey and Careen Catecher taking the blame for the ill-fated mission in Tommy's home quadrant, OP-439.

Both teens struggle to survive the circumstances that force them into the national spotlight—and this time, they're on opposite sides. On the run and exiled from his fellow Resistance members in BG-098, Tommy makes his way to a Resistance safe house in the capital.

The OCSD is preparing to monitor all under-eighteens with the Cerberean Link, a device that protects them against hunger and sickness and can even locate them if they're lost. Tommy's now living in close quarters with Atari, an operative who has been assigned to sabotage the Link. But does Atari plan to use it for his own purposes?

Through it all, Tommy refuses to believe Careen's loyalties have shifted away form the Resistance, and he's willing to assume any risk to reconnect with her. Will they be able to trust each other when it matters most?

Fips, Bots, Doggeries, and More: Explorations of Henry Rogers' 1838 Journal of Travel from Southwestern Ohio to New York City (2012) is based on a journal written by Lawson's great-great-great grandfather, who kept a daily account of his family's fifty-five-day journey by horse and wagon. He notes in the journal that he endeavors to record everything he finds interesting, and the journal is a treasure trove of information about the social and political environment of the times, emerging technology, agriculture and topography, sites of interest, and his family's health and comfort.

After receiving the journal as a Christmas gift, Lawson conducted research to lend context to the journal, and ultimately made most of the same trip herself by automobile, with her young daughter in tow. They kept their own journal, and the book compares and shares information about both trips, taken over a century and a half apart.

Winner Best Nonfiction History for 2012 in the Ohio Professional Writers Association Book Awards

Pride of the Valley: Sifting through the History of the Mount Healthy Mill (2017). After she finished writing *Fips, Bots, Dogeries, and More*, Lawson was curious about what happened after her ancestors returned home from their 1838 journey to New York. Their working vacation was partly to visit relatives, and partly to observe mills and determine how best to add grist milling to their sawmill business.

She happily dug into the research, and even picked up a co-author along the way, in historic millwright Steve Hagaman. Though their efforts to locate business ledgers or miller's journals came to naught, they found clues in land and census records, a poem, and a stereoscope image from the 1860s. It might not sound like much, but it was enough to go on, and those clues directed them to other long-forgotten information both enhances and challenges accepted accounts of the mill's history.

Pride of the Valley tells the story of the beginning, life, and eventual demise of the Mount Healthy Mill, which operated on the banks of the West Fork of Mill Creek in Springfield Township, Ohio for over one hundred and thirty years. But the story is only half-told without also getting to know the families who owned the mill and discovering how their lives were interwoven with pivotal events in our country's history.